*magic is in your
blood & soul!*

THE LAST
RHEE WITCH

BY JENNA LEE-YUN

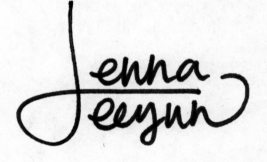

𝕯𝖎𝖘𝖓𝖊𝖞 • HYPERION
Los Angeles   New York

First Edition, May 2024
10 9 8 7 6 5 4 3 2 1
FAC-004510-24081
Printed in the United States of America

This book is set in ITC Slimbach Std/Adobe Systems
Designed by Zareen Johnson
Stock image: cat 484089916/Shutterstock

Library of Congress Control Number: 2023943538
ISBN 978-1-368-09907-3

Reinforced binding
Visit www.DisneyBooks.com

SUSTAINABLE FORESTRY INITIATIVE

Certified Sourcing

www.forests.org
SFI-01681

Logo Applies to Text Stock Only

To my sister, Seung,
for believing in me and this book 100%

ONE

WELCOME TO CAMP FOSTER

Standing in the parking lot at Camp Foster, Ronnie Miller reminded herself that ghosts did *not* exist. She was ninety-nine percent sure, which was as certain as a person could be. One percent was set aside for just-in-case and you-never-know. Because there should be a percent likelihood for everything. Even the impossible.

Like that gleaming white figure hovering in the treetops . . . a hundred feet in the air . . . with a streak of crimson running down the front. Ronnie was ninety-nine percent certain it was the morning mist messing with her vision. And after staring at nothing but mountains and forests on the long drive to Central Washington, you're bound to start seeing things—eighty-five percent positive.

Squeezing her eyes shut, Ronnie gave them a good rub. When she opened them again, there was no white ghost. No red streak. Only gray mist. She sagged with relief. If she started seeing things that weren't there, her dad would worry. And by the look on her dad's face as he stepped out of the SUV, he was already plenty worried.

"Are you sure you're up for this?" The crease between his brows deepened as he glanced around the parking lot filling up with other kids and their parents. "I mean, with everything that's going on?"

By *everything*, he meant the way Ronnie had been rhyming when she spoke. It began a few months ago on her twelfth birthday. At first, he thought it was clever. But then he realized she couldn't control it, especially when she was upset.

Like when he broke their birthday-dinner tradition of cooking their favorite foods together at home. Not only had he insisted on going to a restaurant for Ronnie's birthday this year, he'd also invited Kristie-with-a-K. Apparently, she'd been *dying* to meet Ronnie. Ronnie, on the other hand, had never heard of Kristie—with a K or otherwise. At least eighty percent of Ronnie's sentences that night were in rhyme.

It must have freaked Kristie out, because Ronnie never saw her again. She could live with that. But it freaked her dad out, too, which troubled Ronnie. He worried it had something to do with Ronnie losing her mom at a young age. Or her having a single dad. Or being Korean. Or not being Korean enough because her Korean dad was adopted by white parents. And like with any problem he couldn't fix with modern medicine, he either ignored it or got rid of it.

First came the new rule of speaking only Korean or Konglish (a mix of Korean and English words) at home. Ronnie was about as fluent in Korean as a three-year-old and her dad wasn't much better, so there was a lot of bad miming and awkward misunderstandings. And Ronnie always felt a little embarrassed speaking Korean because she was sure she had an American accent. It wasn't long before Ronnie was rhyming more than ever.

When that failed, her dad had brought up summer camp.

"It'll give you a chance to try something new!" he'd said two weeks ago at the medical center he worked at.

Ronnie's back was to him as she organized the books on his office shelf. She could hear the forced, over-the-top smile in his voice, but Ronnie knew what was really going on: He was getting rid of the problem. He was getting rid of *her*.

"But I like the things I do now," she'd protested as she squeezed *Digestive Health* into its place to the right of *Clinical Gastroenterology*.

"You'll get to do all sorts of *kid* things—normal things—like swimming and kayaking. I hear there's a ropes course. And campfires with s'mores."

Ronnie waited for the punch line. Although she was a really good swimmer, her dad made her take swim lessons every summer because drowning was "one of the top five causes of death for people aged one to fourteen years." He kept her off ladders because "the second leading cause of unintentional injury deaths worldwide" was falling. Not to mention the seasonal fire drills—*at home*. Her dad was famously risk-averse. So this talk of water sports, heights, and playing with fire *had* to be a joke.

"Maybe you'll even make new friends!" he added, which was not even a little bit funny.

Ronnie spun around to face him. "I already have friends, Dad."

He crossed his arms. "Besides Jack. Who, by the way, is also going to be at camp."

Ronnie mirrored his crossed arms, annoyed that her dad would use Jack to get rid of her. Then she was doubly annoyed that Jack had suddenly become the kind of kid that did stuff like go to summer camp and try new things and make new friends. Her stomach began to twist into a knot, but she smiled against it—big and radiant and aimed straight at her dad. "I have you!" she said cheerfully. "And Julie on Monday through Wednesday, Edgar on Thursday and Friday, and Patty on call!"

Her dad's smile fell. He dropped his arms, letting them hang at his sides. "They're front-desk staff, Ronnie. And I *am* your friend, but I'm also your dad. And as your dad, I say hanging out in a waiting room is no way for a kid to spend her summer."

"But I *like* our routines." The book in her hand was suddenly very heavy. "I thought you liked me coming to work with you."

"Of course I do. But a new routine might be in order. We can consider clubs when school starts up again." He saw Ronnie's grimace and tried again. "What about sports?"

"Why not just send me away to boarding school?" she said under her breath.

Her dad didn't seem to hear her. He dragged a hand down his face and started mumbling to himself. "I don't know. A new routine might not be enough. Maybe what we need is a fresh start. A new city—with a strong Korean community. Or maybe a mother figure—"

Move? Stepmom? The last thing she needed was another Korean adult shaking their head at her for not being able to speak Korean better. That only made her want to never speak it at all. The knot in Ronnie's stomach pulled tighter and tighter until she blurted out, "I want to go to summer camp!"

And that had been that.

▲ ▲ ▲

"It's only two weeks, Dad," she said now. "I'll be okay." *I just have to watch the words that I say.* The rhyme crashed into the back of her teeth and her stomach somersaulted.

Two weeks.

It wasn't long enough for her dad to move them across the country or get married, but it might be long enough for Ronnie to get rid of her impulsive rhyming so her dad would stop trying to get rid of her. Plus, she and Jack could still do most of the things they usually did at home during the summer. Yes. She could definitely survive summer camp for two measly weeks—ninety-nine percent positive.

Two weeks away from home to stop her dad from turning their lives upside down.

Two weeks to fix it all and return everything to normal.

"Wait." Her dad pulled a duffel bag from the car. "*Two* weeks? I only signed up for one week, six days, and nineteen hours. We're going to have to rethink this whole summer camp business."

Ronnie rolled her eyes extra hard to mask a smile. He hadn't cracked a proper dad joke since her rhyming began. Hope fluttered in her chest. This was going to work.

"It was *your* suggestion—I just agreed! Came without question and followed your lead!" She bit down on her tongue fourteen words too late. The grin on her dad's face slipped at the rhyme, making Ronnie want to kick herself. *Move on quickly. Make him forget. Distract from the rhyme before he's upset.*

"You should go check me in." She slung her backpack over her shoulder. "I bet there's a line. And don't worry about me. I'll be just—" *Fine,* she almost said. She'd caught herself *just* in time. "Looking for Jack!"

Ronnie and Jack Park had been neighbors and best friends for almost their entire lives. Their dads were best friends, which made them practically family. And being best friends with practically-family had the added bonus of sticking-together-no-matter-what. Like when Jack's parents got a divorce two summers ago. Ronnie and her dad spent a lot of time with Jack and his dad, helping them figure out the single-parent lifestyle. And when Ronnie's grandfather—her dad's dad—died last summer, Jack and his dad came over all the time to distract Ronnie and her dad from being sad.

Ronnie rushed off to a grassy lawn in front of a cluster of squat camp buildings to her right. People were gathered around a fabric banner pulled tight between two trees. It read WELCOME TO CAMP FOSTER in colorful hand-painted block letters.

Meanwhile, her dad headed left toward a sprawling

mansion sitting under the shadow of the last cloud in the sky. A stone sign with RHEE ESTATES engraved in elegant script stood before the gloomy gray structure. A strange feeling washed over her, like she'd stood in that very spot and seen that very structure before.

But this was her first time here. She would definitely remember a place like this. With its black-curtained windows and pointy-witch-hat rooftops, the manor belonged in a ghost story set in October—not at a summer camp in July.

Ronnie gave an involuntary shudder that shook her from head to toe. It must have worked to loosen a memory because she realized where she'd seen it before: the camp pamphlet. The main office was located inside.

"Hello there!"

Ronnie jumped about a mile high before whirling around. She was ninety percent sure no one was nearby a moment ago. Now an Afro-Asian woman with a warm brown complexion and curly auburn hair cut just above her chin stood before her. She peered expectantly at Ronnie over a clipboard with wide amber eyes. And at her feet, a black cat lazily licked its paw, as though he'd grown bored waiting.

"I'm Ms. Akemi," the woman said, tapping her name tag. "The camp nurse."

"Um. I'm Veronica Miller, but I go by Ronnie." She gestured at the cat, who had paused its bath to saunter over to her. "Is he yours?"

Ms. Akemi's brows shot up at the sight of the cat rubbing up against Ronnie's leg. "Boojuk is no one's, really. He's been around longer than this camp has." She leaned in close to stage-whisper, "Some say Boo's a familiar spying on campers."

Gooseflesh tingled along Ronnie's arms, but she shook it off. "A *familiar*? Like a witch's magical pet?" Witches and their familiars were about as probable as ghosts: one percent.

Ms. Akemi nodded, her curls bouncing. "He's not always so friendly."

As if to demonstrate, Boo stiffened and lowered into a crouch, his gold eyes fixed on a point near the manor. There, a boy and his dad stood in the shadow of its towering walls. Boo released a long, slow hiss before darting toward them.

"If you love 'em, let 'em go." Ms. Akemi shrugged. "Although that one may not come back to you. He really can be quite prickly." She nodded toward the manor. "I take it your guardian is signing you in at the main office?"

Ronnie was nodding when her gaze snagged on a flicker of white between the pitched rooftops where the surrounding forest was visible. Small at first, the white shape grew—either expanding or drawing closer. She got the sinking feeling it was both. A chill scraped up her spine.

It was back.

The voices around her grew distant, and Ronnie's vision tunneled around the haunting figure she had been ninety-nine percent sure was impossible. It lurched through the trees, bare feet dragging lifelessly behind. Terror seized Ronnie's lungs. She couldn't breathe, couldn't scream.

It jerked forward. Again and again. Closer and closer. And ninety-nine percent certainty dropped to eighty-nine.

Luckily, the figure didn't move beyond the tree line, and an entire manor stood between them. But Ronnie could see now that this impossible thing was a woman in a white nightgown. Her long, stringy black hair went down past her waist. Her face was pale, with bottomless pits for eyes and lips the same color as the red trailing down her center.

She stared unblinking at Ronnie, who stared back, frozen in fear and seventy-nine percent disbelief. Then the woman reached out and beckoned with a hand as gaunt and pale as death.

TWO
FRECKLES

Ronnie stumbled back, seeing nothing but the eerie woman and hearing only the blood rushing in her ears. The heel of her foot hit a stack of stones hidden in the tall grass. They came crashing down, bringing Ronnie back to her surroundings. She bent down to restack the half-dozen flat beige stones and spotted even more stone towers scattered all over the grounds. It was a strange place to stack stones.

"Ronnie?" Ms. Akemi's voice broke through Ronnie's thoughts. "Are you all right?"

Ronnie straightened. "I knocked over some stones by accident. What are they doing in the middle of the grass?"

"Ah yes. They're all around the manor and the buildings around the courtyard." Ms. Akemi nodded as if that answered it.

Ronnie was about to ask *what* they were doing everywhere when the nurse thrust a plastic name tag into Ronnie's line of sight. She nearly stumbled again. It was a deep and glossy red. Red, like the eerie woman's center. Red, like blood.

"Your name tag." Ms. Akemi motioned for Ronnie to pin

it to her shirt. "The color indicates your cabin assignment—red is Sparrow's Nest."

As Ronnie accepted the name tag, her gaze drifted back up to the rooftops. But the woman in white was gone.

"Well then," Ms. Akemi said with a wink. "I'm located in the manor, so feel free to knock on my door if you ever need anything. An ice pack, antiseptic, a tonic, a brew . . ." Ms. Akemi trailed off as she walked away. Ronnie frowned at the word *brew*. She was probably hearing things. Just like she was probably seeing things.

Rhee Manor looked so different from a moment ago. The mist had all but burned off, and the single, stubborn cloud was gone, leaving behind a clear blue sky. It looked even less foreboding when her dad stepped out of the manor, waving both arms at her with a huge grin on his face. Suddenly the idea of a maybe-ghost in the forest was ridiculous. She would have laughed at herself if a shrill whistle hadn't sliced through the chatter of the crowd, making her jump.

"You okay, kid?" Her dad approached and placed two steadying hands on her shoulders. "You look like you saw a ghost."

Ronnie laughed a little too loud. "I'm fine. It's that whistle—" The whistle sounded again, and Ronnie flinched.

A Korean woman with glossy black hair in a tidy bun and a thick curtain of bangs above her brows stood next to the Camp Foster welcome sign. She had a penetrating gaze and a whistle poised in front of her pointed chin. She blew into her whistle twice more before pulling her mouth up into a smile that was all teeth. She scanned the crowd with

11

her frosty gaze, looking very much like someone who'd have a familiar.

The woman's eyes narrowed as though she had heard Ronnie's thoughts. Ducking her head, Ronnie tucked herself into her dad's side.

"Can I have your attention, please?" the woman called out. "My name is Hana Shin—campers will call me Ms. Hana—and I am the director here at Camp Foster, where we foster positive physical, mental, and emotional growth. Thank you, parents and guardians, for allowing your children to partake in what will undoubtedly become some of the best experiences of their lives. I look forward to getting to know each and every one of them throughout our time together."

Ms. Hana paused to make eye contact with those in the crowd like she was trying to make some personal connection. But somehow, it felt like a threat. Judging by the look on Ronnie's dad's face, he felt the exact same way.

"Parents with registration queries, please see Ms. Pavani at the front desk. If you would like to speak with the camp nurse, you'll find Ms. Akemi at the nurse's station. If you have any other questions or concerns, please see me or any of the staff in the Camp Foster logo shirts and we'll be more than happy to help you." She gestured to a few people wearing the shirts, who waved at the group.

"For those not requiring assistance," Ms. Hana continued, "I will ask you to say your good-byes now. Your children have a very full day of orientation ahead and are expected to be seated in the courtyard in the next ten minutes. Punctuality is one of the core values upheld at Camp

Foster, and 'my mother wouldn't stop hugging me' isn't going to excuse anyone from a tardy mark."

Many of the parents laughed. Ms. Hana did not.

"Yikes," Ronnie's dad said under his breath. "I better get out of here before you get in trouble with the camp dictator—I mean *director*." He gave her a firm salute while she tried to suppress a giggle. "Just one more hug."

Ronnie groaned as she walked into her dad's arms. Though she wouldn't admit it, she kind of wished she could stay inside the hug for the next two weeks. "You said one more, like, five hugs ago. At this rate, you won't make it back home, you know." She winced as her dad's arms went rigid around her with the rhyme.

Wriggling away, she pasted a huge smile on her face. "I'm excited—that's all."

"Listen, Ronnie—" He stopped short and shook his head as if to clear it. Then, reaching into his pocket, he pulled out a tube of sunscreen. "I'm going to get some on those cheeks."

She hated having it done for her and had already put some on thirty minutes ago—like you're supposed to. But she held still, grimacing against the stickiness, wishing he'd point out her freckles that had returned for the summer. She waited, hope tightening her chest, for him to make the same old comment about how she looked so much like her mom. How freckles weren't too common among Koreans and that's how he knew she was her mom's kid. It was one of the few things he remembered about her mom. Or maybe it was one of the few things he wanted to remember.

Then he'd make some joke about how he knew Ronnie

was the kid of a gastroenterologist—a gut doctor—by the way she ate and pooped like clockwork. But for the first summer in years, he didn't seem to notice the freckles. And he still hadn't reminded her it's okay to poop in public bathrooms. Everything was off.

The impulse to rhyme pressed on her tongue, and Ronnie bit down on it so fast and hard she tasted blood. She had to figure out how to stop the rhyming—and fast—before she ended up biting her tongue clean off.

THREE

"CAMP FRIEND"

The courtyard was boxed in by cabins and lined with tall evergreen trees. At one end stood a platform stage facing rows of log benches. Ronnie frowned. The edge seats near the center rows were her favorite spots, but those were already taken.

She was surveying the remaining options when she spotted Jack. He was talking animatedly to a boy with honey-blond hair swept tidily to one side, a Sinbi comic open between them. Jack never left home without at least one issue of the Korean-lore-based comics. They sat at the far end of a bench—just behind the middle section. Not bad. It was close enough to the stage to hear the speaker, but far away enough to get away with whispering to each other.

Adjusting her backpack, Ronnie made her way across the dry, flattened grass toward the boys, when a prick in the side of her neck stopped her in her tracks. She swiftly slapped a hand over the spot, but it was too late. A small bump had already formed where the mosquito had bitten.

"*Bug* spray," a voice called out from behind. "*That's* what I forgot."

Ronnie spun around and came face-to-chin with a tall

girl who looked even taller because of the Afro puff on top of her head. She had a soft tawny complexion and brown eyes that glimmered bronze at the edges. She looked about the same age as Ronnie, but that was where the similarities ended. This girl wasn't wearing shorts and a tee like Ronnie and everyone else. She was in a *dress*. At summer *camp*. And her backpack was *teeny*. There was no way she could have fit bug spray—or much of anything—inside. How did this girl survive? Ronnie couldn't imagine being without a single item inside her normal-sized backpack. It went with her everywhere.

The girl cocked her head to peer at Ronnie's neck. "I think it got you."

Ronnie showed the girl her palm with the flattened mosquito and a smear of her own bright red blood. "I got it back."

"I did *not* need to see that." The girl adjusted her small, useless backpack. "I'm Olivia. I'm from Seattle. How about you?"

"I'm Ronnie." She rubbed her palm on her shorts. "I'm from West Seattle. It's my first time here."

Olivia's face brightened. "Me too! My parents put me on the waiting list months ago!"

"Waiting list?" Ronnie and her dad had only heard of the camp a couple weeks ago, and signing up was a breeze.

"Yeah, but looks like we both made it in!" Olivia's cheeks dimpled with a grin. "Which is perfect because I was planning on finding another newbie to cling on to for dear life." She raised her brows expectantly at Ronnie. "Now we both have a friend!"

"Well"—Ronnie looked over at Jack, who finally met her

eye—"my friend Jack is here, too." It felt wrong to call Jack a *friend* when Olivia had just used the word to describe herself even though she was just a step up from a stranger. At most, Olivia could become a "camp friend." But there was no way anyone Ronnie met at a one-week-six-days-nineteen-hours-long camp had the staying power to become an actual *friend* friend.

"Great," Olivia said, already on the move. "Let's go!"

As Ronnie neared Jack with dress-wearing, tiny-backpack-carrying Olivia in tow, his eyebrows climbed up higher and higher on his forehead. Ronnie shot him a "beats me" shrug, and Jack smirked in response.

"Did you see the manor?" he asked as soon as Ronnie was within earshot.

She nodded. "It's almost as good as Pennywise's lair in *It*."

Jack pushed back the strands of golden-brown hair that were always in his eyes. "It's even better, because it's on a campground surrounded by a creepy forest." He spoke so animatedly that his hair fell back over his forehead, landing in that perfectly mussed way.

His soft curls were from his mom, who had curly blond hair, and the fullness of the strands was from his dad, who was Korean, like Ronnie. Or at least this was what Jack had memorized to say whenever people got excited about his hair, which was often.

Ronnie's hair was thick and straight, and always stayed put. She kept it long enough to tie back easily and short enough so it didn't get in the way. She was glad for it, and even gladder no one ever asked her where she got it from.

Ronnie turned to the boy next to Jack, who had been silently spinning a pen between his fingers. She offered a friendly smile. "Hey, I'm Ronnie. So, do you think Rhee Manor is haunted?"

"No." The boy's reply was sharp as he caught his pen midspin and stuffed it into the side pocket of his backpack. He frowned at her as if she was as much of a pest as the mosquitoes. As if she didn't belong there with him and Jack.

Ronnie was ready to glare right back, but she was momentarily struck by his strange eyes. They were hazel with bright green specks in just the left eye, like a shimmering gemstone.

Catching herself staring, Ronnie shoved Olivia in front of her. "Jack, this is Olivia!"

Olivia beamed at both boys. "Hi! I'm Olivia Reynolds!"

"Hey," Jack said. "Nice *backpack*." He smiled, but the gleam in his eyes was enough for Ronnie to know it wasn't a compliment.

Olivia's smile broadened. "Thanks! It goes perfect with my shoes." She kicked up one foot to show off the tassel on the zipper pull of her open-toed boots. It was identical to the tassel on the drawstring of her mini backpack.

"But does it go perfect with summer camp?" Jack said sarcastically.

Olivia's smile fell, her lips forming a thin line. "This is just my orientation outfit. It's not like I'm planning to wear this to the ropes course or something."

"What's an *orientation outfit*?" Jack asked, baffled. Ronnie tried to shoot him a "shut it" look, but he was too busy scrunching his nose at Olivia.

"It's a first impression. Take Ronnie's outfit, for example." Olivia turned to study Ronnie's denim shorts and boxy white graphic T-shirt. "It says, 'I'm nice but not overly friendly. No nonsense but prepared for anything.'"

Ronnie glanced down at her clothes. "You got all *that* from this?"

Olivia turned to Jack. After a quick survey of his wrinkled blue T-shirt and faded gray army-fatigue-patterned shorts, she nodded to herself, her mouth pinched into a grim expression. "You fit in everywhere you go. You're confident to a fault. And a little careless, TBH."

Ronnie's mouth fell open in awe. "How did you do that?"

"Hey!" Jack jumped up to his feet in protest. He tugged at his shirt and shorts, which only underscored how rumpled they were in the first place.

"What about me?" Pen-Spinning Boy stood up. He wasn't as tall as Jack or Olivia, but he had an athletic build. "I'm Sam. Sam Gilmore." His voice was gentle as he drew Olivia's attention. Ronnie looked at him in surprise, and it hit her that Sam and his father were the ones Boo had hissed at earlier. It had seemed strange at the time, but now Ronnie was willing to bet the cat simply had good instincts.

Olivia tapped a finger to her lip as she took in Sam's outfit. He wore a simple T-shirt with a small logo of a local clothing company over a pair of green basketball shorts. "You're quiet but thoughtful. Easy to like and get along with."

Sam grinned at Olivia, but when he caught Ronnie's eyes, his smile soured. Olivia may have been right about Jack, but she was way off about Sam. He'd been treating Ronnie coldly from the moment they met.

But as the courtyard began to fill up, more kids passed by Ronnie's seat, and every other kid seemed to not only *know* Sam, but *like* him as well. To Ronnie's growing disbelief, they patted his back or shared a fist bump—always with a cheerful greeting. And Sam seemed to have plenty of smiles for them, just as he had for Jack and Olivia.

When Sam wasn't looking, Ronnie elbowed Jack and made a face, looking pointedly at Sam. He shrugged, the corners of his lips pulling up as he shot a glance at Olivia. Ronnie pursed her lips and widened her eyes at him as threateningly as possible. They hadn't said a single word, but they understood each other perfectly. It was agreed. They might not need camp friends, but they didn't need enemies, either. Ronnie huffed anyway. She'd give Sam another chance, but that didn't mean she couldn't hope he'd go find someone other than Jack to be camp friends with.

Ms. Hana stepped up onto the stage and raised her fingers in a peace sign. Others in camp logo shirts mimicked the action and soon many of the kids in the audience were holding up peace signs, too.

"Thank you!" Ms. Hana gave everyone that same big, cold smile. Ronnie turned her head toward Jack as he did the same. Both of their faces were twisted into their best terrifying grins. Ronnie giggled into her hand.

Ms. Hana gave a speech about the camp and the rules before introducing the staff—all but the surprise guest speaker who was scheduled to arrive in a couple days. Then she introduced the camp counselors—juniors and seniors in high school—before splitting everyone up into small groups for camp tours.

Ronnie pulled Jack to a group led by a senior named Robbie who had black hair with a closely shaved fade and deep ebony skin. Olivia and Sam fell into step with them.

"To our right are the swimming pools—my favorite place here." Robbie led the group past a building with large windows. Everyone peered into the sparkling blue pools lined with roped buoys. "I teach a swim class, and we have amazing facilities here." He slowed but didn't stop, walking backward to speak to the group while keeping them moving along.

Every summer, Ronnie and Jack got season passes to the local pool and spent hours every week in the water. She was about to nudge Jack, but he wasn't paying attention. He was hunched over another Sinbi comic with Sam. This was beginning to feel like Saturday Korean School all over again.

Last year, Ronnie and Jack enrolled in classes to get in touch with their Korean heritage and learn the language. But Jack's parents, who lived in Seoul for a couple of years before he was born, spoke Korean fluently, so Jack already knew a bunch of Korean. So while Ronnie was stuck in the beginner class with five-year-olds, Jack got to be in class with kids his age.

Ronnie quit Korean School after a month. And while she learned next to nothing in the way of the language, she did learn a handful of curse words and more than she ever wanted to know about creepy Korean lore, like Korean goblins. All the older kids were into dokkaebi fandom and Jack became obsessed. He vowed to convince Ronnie dokkaebi existed, and she let him try. This worked out perfectly because Jack got to talk about dokkaebi as much as he wanted, and Ronnie got to hang out with her best friend without having to pretend to buy into any of it.

But all of that changed during the first year of middle school. They were no longer in the same classes all day, and Jack started taking interest in activities Ronnie didn't care for. Even if her dad would have let her, she knew too well the dangers of things like wrestling and paintballing.

She had hoped going to summer camp with Jack would get their best friendship back on track, but all he seemed to care about now was geeking out over Sinbi comics with Sam. Ronnie groaned. She did *not* need another problem this summer.

"I can't wait to go swimming." Olivia appeared beside her and linked arms. "I brought the perfect suit! It's a one-piece with these super-sophisticated side cutouts. Is yours a one-piece or two?"

"My swimsuit?" Ronnie squinted up at Olivia, who nodded eagerly. "It's two pieces, I guess. A tank top and a swim short."

Olivia blinked. "A swim short?"

"Yeah, they're like regular shorts but, like, for water. I sometimes wear them even when I'm not swimming."

Olivia covered her mouth to muffle her laughter. "OMG. You're so funny!"

Jack looked up and shot Ronnie a puzzled look. "What's so funny about that? I'm wearing my swim shorts right now."

This made Olivia laugh even harder. Forgetting about Sam and the Sinbi issue, Jack shared a look of bewilderment with Ronnie. She smiled to herself at their identical reactions and wordless communication. Now *that* was best friend behavior. Suddenly Olivia the camp-friend-clinging-on-for-dear-life seemed like the perfect antidote to Sam the camp-frenemy-Ronnie-couldn't-shake.

Robbie took the group around the courtyard, pointing out the cabins, showers, and buildings for classes and large group meetings. Then he guided them through a narrow passageway that opened to a large grass field stretching out in all directions up to the tree line. To the far left was a sparkling lake, with an oversized inflatable slide and water trampoline secured to the dock. Straight ahead, a sprawling wooden ropes course straddled the borderline where the field met the forest.

Robbie gestured behind the group and to the left. "From here, you get a little peek of the gardens at the back of Rhee Manor. It's private, along with the upper levels of the manor, which are roped off for private use by the current owners. But the ground floor is open to the public."

Ronnie waited for the others to look back at the manor before chancing a glance over her shoulder, only sixty-five percent positive she wouldn't see a ghostly woman floating above the trees. But whatever hesitancy she had felt disappeared at the sight of colorful treetops poking out above the thick green privacy hedges. The sun was shining. The sky was clear. And it wasn't long before the memory of the haunting figure who summoned her into the dark woods faded from Ronnie's mind. Soon it was nothing more than a wisp.

Like a fleeting, vanishing ghost.

FOUR

THE HAUNTING OF CAMP FOSTER

T he night was clear and dry, but the din of a building rainstorm filled the Pit—a cozy clearing set up with rows of log benches to one side of a firepit and a raised platform to the other. Ronnie sat next to Jack in the front row, tapping her lap with her fingertips.

Jack shot her an exasperated look. "You gotta use your whole hand to make it sound real!" He demonstrated, adding to the sound of raindrops with each pat. Then, picking up the passing wave, he switched to snapping fingers that mimicked rain showers followed by clapping and stomping that simulated heavy rainfall and thunder. It had taken a few attempts to get the entire group synchronized, but once everyone had the hang of it, Ronnie had to admit the effect was kind of cool, like controlling a storm.

She followed along, picking up Jack's shifting actions to her left and passing them along to Olivia at her right. True to her word, Olivia had not left Ronnie's side all day. They were both assigned to Sparrow's Nest cabin, and when Olivia got stressed about being allotted only two drawers each, Ronnie offered up one of hers. It wasn't a big deal since her entire duffel bag fit into one. But Olivia was so grateful that she offered to share a bunk with Ronnie and let her choose top or bottom. Ronnie chose the coveted top bunk. This worked out for Olivia, who lined her shoes up under her bottom bunk. Maybe it was a camp thing, but since they'd become bunk mates, it felt natural to continue sticking together. And Ronnie had never met someone so determined to do just that.

Well, maybe besides Sam, who somehow managed to get assigned to Tanager's Nest, the same cabin as Jack. Sitting behind Jack, Sam shifted the rainstorm down from clapping his hands to snapping his fingers. He passed the motion on to Benji Guzman and Gigi Mura—both new friends of his. When Sam had introduced them to Olivia, Benji had smiled, showing off a mouthful of rainbow braces. Gigi, who was dressed in head-to-toe purple, glanced approvingly at Olivia's campfire outfit. But Sam didn't introduce Ronnie, so they all just stood there staring awkwardly at each other until Ronnie introduced herself. Jack brushed it off, saying Sam probably just forgot Ronnie's name, but that didn't explain why he still wouldn't look at her, much less talk to her.

Following Jack's lead, Ronnie shifted down to snapping fingers for rain showers, then lap patting for light rain, and finally, rubbing hands for wind. A few seconds later, the camp counselor leading the rain circle initiated the peace sign and the rain shower faded. Olivia nudged Ronnie with her shoulder, bright eyes gleaming over a wide grin. She mouthed, *That was awesome!*

When everyone but the chirping crickets fell silent, Ms. Hana rose from her seat. "Now that I have your full attention, I have an exciting announcement." She flashed her frigid grin, and several campers visibly flinched.

"Excited, like she's inviting us to her house made of candy with a kid-sized oven inside?" Jack quipped from the side of his mouth.

"Excited, like she prepared us each a hot bath in a tub that looks suspiciously like a cauldron?" Ronnie whispered back.

Jack opened his mouth, but Ms. Hana spoke first. "A scavenger hunt has been set up all around the campgrounds. Each clue will lead to one of eight different Camp Foster–themed pressed penny tokens. There are enough tokens for every camper here to collect all eight, and those who manage to do so will be allowed to carve their name into the climbing wall."

Excited whispers broke out among the campers until a few of the counselors started rubbing their hands together for the wind sound of the rain circle. It quickly caught on, and the whispering receded.

"In the meantime, how about the first clue?" Ms. Hana continued, and everyone leaned forward in their seats. "'I was the first to greet you, but you didn't greet me back. Perhaps I should have waved, but I had not any slack. I'm tied up at the moment, in the sun between two trees, relaxing in the heat or tense against the breeze.'"

Ronnie flinched at the rhyme even though it hadn't come from her. Next to her, Jack shifted awkwardly in his seat. They had an unspoken agreement to never speak of Ronnie's rhyming problem, but she knew it made him uncomfortable. Sometimes she wondered if that's why he wanted to go to camp this summer. Maybe Jack had wanted to get away. Ronnie's heart sank.

Meanwhile, all around her, panic filled the night air as campers tried—and failed—to recite the clue from memory. Ms. Hana raised a peace sign. "Not to worry. You may ask any of the counselors to repeat the clue for you as often as needed—during your *free time*," she added with a stern look. "And while I still have your attention, I'd like to take a moment to remind everyone of some rules."

Instantly bored, Jack shot a glance over his shoulder where Sinbi Issue #41, "Seven Shaman Spirits," was open on Sam's lap.

"This is why the front row is the worst," Jack grumbled under his breath. "I can't even pull out an issue."

Ronnie wanted to ask Jack when he'd started letting people borrow his comics. She wanted to remind him he'd read every issue, including "Seven Shaman Spirits," at *least* seven times. She wanted to point out that the front row was better than the second row because the front row was where she—his *best friend*—was sitting.

Instead, she muttered, "It's the best spot for roasting marshmallows." But in truth, it was Issue #41 she'd like to turn over the flames.

". . . don't forget the forest is off-limits," Ms. Hana was saying, "with the exception of supervised activities."

Ronnie nudged Jack with an elbow. "Did you know? About the forest?"

"What about it?" He was craning his neck to see the

comic, which showed an illustration of a shaman possessed by an aggressive spirit. She looked like a red Korean version of the Hulk.

Ronnie frowned. "It's off-limits."

Benji shifted at Ronnie's back. "That's because it's *haunted*," he whispered.

This triggered the memory of the woman in white that Ronnie was seventy-nine percent certain she'd imagined. She twisted around. "What do you mean, haunted?"

"The forest," Benji said in a low voice. "There's this really old camp ghost story."

"A ghost story?" Jack's eyes lit up, his curiosity kindled.

"Yeah. I guess someone swears each year to have seen the ghost."

Ronnie turned to Jack, prepared for the wide-eyed-open-mouthed expression he was probably aiming at her. But he was too busy shooting a look of awe at *Sam*. Bitterness stung the back of her throat. Sam shouldn't be Jack's go-to about all things supernatural just because he was into Sinbi comics.

"Oh man," Jack said to Sam. "I hope it's one of us who sees the ghost this year."

That's when it struck Ronnie that not even a believer like Jack had actually seen a ghost. It was one thing to believe in the supernatural; it was a completely different thing to experience it. One led to a fandom. The other, to a hospital. Ronnie grimaced against the sudden queasiness in her stomach.

"Ronnie," Olivia hissed, tapping a nervous rhythm onto

the side of Ronnie's leg. "Ms. Hana is shooting death rays at you guys."

Ronnie made the mistake of sneaking a glance at Ms. Hana. Her cold brown eyes trapped Ronnie's as she spoke. "Attention and respect for the rules are for *your* safety. Those who do not heed this warning will be held accountable for whatever danger befalls them."

Ronnie shrank back and wrenched her gaze away. Maybe it was the fire's glow in the darkening night or the searing glare of a terrifying camp director, but in that moment, a ghost haunting the camp seemed more than one percent possible. So when the counselors asked for a vote on favorite campfire activities, Ronnie raised her hand.

Willa, the counselor in Ronnie's cabin, smiled encouragingly. "Ronnie, let's hear it!"

"Well, I was wondering if you could tell us a ghost story. I heard there's one about this camp."

Every eye turned to Ronnie, but it was Jack's gaze that was making her squirm. She knew what he was thinking—that Ronnie had never been interested in anything with less than a fifty percent probability rate in her life. She wasn't a "what if" kind of person. She was a "what is" kind.

Willa rubbed her hands together. "Ooh . . . great idea, Ronnie. And what a perfect Camp Foster welcome for all you newbies." She let loose a devilish cackle, which started an impromptu sinister laughter competition.

"All right," Willa called out over the noise. "Settle down, everyone—that includes the counselors! It's time for a ghost story."

Willa took a seat on a stump facing the campers and cleared her throat. When all was quiet except the hiss and crackle of the campfire, she began.

"You've all seen Rhee Manor. Some of you have even been inside." Willa's voice, at first light and easy, turned dark and heavy. "But did you know that not one, not two, not even three, but *six* members of the Rhee family were killed? In fact, one murder took place right on these grounds. That's right. Camp Foster was built on the Rhee family estate after the last heir of the family fortune was murdered in the forest that looms around us."

The rustle of shifting bodies was harsh in the eerie quiet as kids peeked over their shoulders at the dark—and suddenly foreboding—woods.

"Although the Rhee family kept a low profile, they were well known for three things. One: Their entire wealth, including the estate, was handed down through their daughters. Two: Each heir was mysteriously killed, and their killers were never caught. And three"—Willa leaned in and dropped her voice—"the bodies of every murdered Rhee woman were found with a long red silk scarf wrapped loosely—and dare I say fashionably—around their necks. But there were no signs of physical injury, no clue as to how they died. And while those scarves are undeniably related to the murder or murderer, their purpose remains a mystery."

Ronnie's hand flew up to her mouth, and she jerked back, ramming into Benji's knees. She offered a quick apology over her shoulder.

"About seven years ago," Willa continued, "the body of the last Rhee daughter, Min-Young, was found in the forest with the same long red silk scarf. With no remaining heirs, the new owners of the estate decided the best use of the scene of a murder was a youth camp." This earned Willa a few snickers.

"But during the first Camp Foster summer, half the kids left early. Though reports blamed unfortunate food poisoning, several of the kids involved claimed Min-Young haunts the forest surrounding Camp Foster and demanded they leave. They say she wears a long white dress and that her stringy black hair"—Willa used her fingers to comb her shoulder-length red hair down over her eyes—"drapes over her face so you can just barely make out her coal-black eyes watching you from behind it."

Willa rose to her feet and ambled toward the fire. "But most importantly," she continued, her back to her audience, "they said the ghost wears a long scarf that's red as blood." She spun around and unzipped her jacket to reveal a strip of red beneath. With the light of the fire at her back, her hair and eyes were as dark as the picture she had painted. Screams rang out into the night.

Ronnie jumped back with a yelp, once again ramming into Benji's knees, which caused him to cry out as well.

"Whoa, what's up with you?" Jack whispered, a half smile on his face. "Thought you weren't into this stuff?"

"I'm not," she hissed. "Mosquito bit me." It wasn't a complete lie. She'd discovered four new bites on her legs that day.

Willa brushed her hair back from her face. The shirt beneath her jacket was red and, on second glance, bore white lettering.

31

Ronnie drew in a deep breath, working to slow her pulse. Willa had described exactly what she was seventy-nine percent positive was just a figment of her imagination. But now the figment had a story, a history, and a name. *Min-Young*. A shudder ran through her entire body.

This had to be Jack's influence—him and his Sinbi comics. It was probably a common ghost story he'd told her and she'd only half listened to. It was her imagination playing tricks on her. That *had* to be the explanation. Because ghosts didn't exist.

"And every year thereafter," Willa continued, "at least one camper claims to have seen the ghost hovering high among the treetops, seeking revenge upon the unwanted guests on her family's estate. That's each. And every. One. Of. You." Willa's voice, which had grown deep and ominous, softened to a whisper. "So heed the rules and stay away from the forest. For you are not wanted here."

FIVE

SANTA CLAUS AND VAMPIRES

On the way back to the cabins for lights-out, spirits were high with talk of the camp ghost and scavenger hunt. Waving flashlights cast darting spotlights and streaks of white in the pitch-black night. Gravel crunched loudly under feet concealed by the dark. Ronnie couldn't stop startling.

"Hey," Jack said, shining a light into her eyes. "You scared?"

Yes.

"Course not." Ronnie scoffed, shoving his flashlight away. "It's just a stupid story." She kicked a pine cone. It skittered off the path, the darkness swallowing it whole.

Olivia linked her arm through Ronnie's. "I don't believe in ghosts—only vampires—but hearing that story—" She shuddered. "Let's just say I'll be sleeping with my flashlight on tonight."

"Hold on." A beam of light slashed through the night as Jack threw his hands up. "You believe vampires are real, but not ghosts?"

"What's wrong with that?" Olivia asked.

Ronnie blew hair from her forehead. "Here we go," she muttered.

"Ghosts are spirits," Jack said. "They don't go by the rules of our world. But vampires? They're supposedly human *and* not human at the same time."

"Right," Sam added. "Vampires don't make much sense. It's as if someone mashed up ideas from random supernatural beings and slapped them on some good-looking pale guy."

"Vampires *are* hot," Olivia agreed, although that hadn't been Sam's point. "And witches are definitely real. I have a Wiccan cousin who practices witchcraft."

Jack snorted. "What, like *love* potions?"

"Oh, you just wait and see." Olivia's lips curled into a sinister smile. "I know a few useful spells myself."

"I quadruple-dare you to try!" Jack smirked, but Ronnie saw right through his act. He was extremely superstitious and would never take the threat of a curse lightly.

"If they can believe in ghosts," she said to Olivia, "then you can believe in vampires and witches."

Olivia shot Ronnie a grateful look. "Thank you, Ronnie," she stated in a loud voice, enunciating every syllable. "Finally, a voice of reason."

Ronnie nodded in agreement. She was a very reasonable person. "I mean, it's only fair."

Jack burst out laughing. "Since when, Ronnie? You never even believed in Santa Claus, and you *still* won't let it go that I did. I was eight!"

"You were *ten*!"

Olivia squeezed Ronnie's arm. "You never believed in

Santa? Like, ever?" Her face bore the kind of sadness only those who had believed in Santa Claus could feel.

"There are so many holes with Santa Claus!" Ronnie launched into her defense of disbelief. "I mean, what about all the good kids who don't get a thing they want because their parents can't afford it? And all the bad kids who are spoiled rotten! And someone, somewhere has to have seen Santa in the sky. How could you miss a flying sleigh piled high with gifts being pulled by *reindeer*? There's no mistaking that for an airplane."

Ronnie looked at Olivia.

Olivia looked at Ronnie.

"It's not like I believe in him *now*," Olivia said in a small voice.

"Not hot enough, I guess?" Jack snickered.

Olivia glanced sidelong at Jack. "You know what? I could be convinced to believe in a ghost if it haunted *you*."

"Gwishin," Jack said.

"What'd you call me?" Olivia snapped, pointing her flashlight at Jack's face.

He used an arm to shield his eyes. "Not *you*. What Willa described was a gwishin—a Korean ghost. Just like the last Rhee haunting this camp, gwishin wear white dresses and have long black hair hanging down over their faces."

"And isn't Rhee a Korean last name?" Olivia asked Ronnie, probably because Ronnie looked the most Korean. But she knew at best thirteen percent of what Jack knew about Korean things. She was glad it was too dark for anyone to notice her blush.

"Yeah, it is," Jack answered for her. "Plus, think about

how American ghosts are described. They're either trans-parent white sheets or they look completely normal because the person who sees them can see dead people."

Ronnie turned away. Even if she did believe in ghosts—which she didn't—she didn't want to be someone who saw them. She was already someone who randomly burst out into rhyme like an annoying preschool cartoon, and that was bad enough.

They were nearly at the courtyard when Ronnie finally dared to glance up at the trees again. There was no ghost or gwishin, real or imagined. Still, she couldn't shake the image of the woman in white gesturing toward the forest. The dress, the hair, the scarf—everything in the ghost story matched what Ronnie had seen.

But Min-Young didn't seem to want Ronnie to leave. She wanted Ronnie to come closer.

SIX
DOKKAEBI

The next morning, Ronnie piled her tray with pancakes and took a seat next to Olivia. Jack and Sam were already deep in conversation over Sinbi Issue #51.

Jack pointed at a page. "That poor sucker got Persuaded by a dokkaebi to believe river stones were actually gold," he said to Sam around a mouthful of pancakes and syrup. "Did you see his house? Stones *everywhere*. And he got so paranoid about his friends trying to steal the stones from him that he ended up all alone with nothing but rocks."

Sam tucked a wood-barrel pen into the side pocket of his backpack. It was that same pen he'd twirled on his fingers. The habit was annoying, but the pen was just plain *weird*. It looked like the kind that were sold in fancy boxes.

Sam looked up at Ronnie's arrival, and his expression darkened before he turned to Jack. "Not all dokkaebi are bad, you know."

"What's a doe-kay-bee?" Olivia asked, but Jack and Sam were too busy geeking out to answer.

Ronnie rolled her eyes at the boys and leaned in to loud-whisper over the dining-hall chatter. "Korean goblins that can brainwash people, move things with their minds, and see and hear things from miles away. Jack thinks they're real, but they're ninety-nine percent make-believe."

Jack shifted away from Ronnie, willfully ignoring her. "Sure, some can bring luck or fortune," he said to Sam. "But they don't give anything away for free."

Olivia scraped up the remnants clinging to the underside of her peeled yogurt lid. "Why not a hundred percent?"

"I don't like being wrong," Ronnie said with a shrug.

"Gotta know how to motivate one to give you gold instead of, like, the plague," Jack was saying.

Olivia pulled a face as she mixed granola and berries into her yogurt. "Isn't it a little too early in the morning to be talking about plagues and zombies?"

Uh-oh. Ronnie rolled her lips between her teeth to hold in the laughter bubbling up. Skewering a folded-up pancake on her fork, she sat back, ready to enjoy the show.

Jack's eyes bulged. "That is so offensive! Dokkaebi are Korean goblins with an actual purpose in life. Zombies are the undead with no thoughts or feelings other than a monstrous instinct to eat you or your brains. Totally different subgenres and fandoms. Both are great and deserve to be identified correctly." He paused briefly to suck in a breath. "And just to be clear, it is *never* too early to learn how to protect yourself from either."

Olivia froze, a spoon halfway to her open mouth. Slowly, she turned to face Ronnie, who waved her hand dismissively. It was classic Jack Park: supernatural geek at heart.

"Okay, then," Olivia said slowly, recovering from her shock. "What motivates dokkaebi?"

Sam opened his mouth to respond, but Ronnie jumped

up, almost knocking over her juice with her fork in her excitement. "Oh, oh, oh! I actually know this one! They trick people to believe their lies to become rich and famous, right?" She looked to Jack for approval, but Sam spoke first.

"Not *always*," he snapped. "Some just want to fit in with humans and not be found out to be goblins at all." He scratched at the back of his head like he was allergic to Ronnie and turned away to face Olivia instead.

"And they're really not far off from humans," he continued without a hint of his earlier irritation. "Dokkaebi spirits are literally created from lost human desires trapped in touchstones, which can be anything from the sword that impaled a loved one to the glasses of a treasure hunter who never found his buried gold. The dokkaebi's human form usually has something to do with that."

"Ah!" Olivia pointed her spoon into the air. "They're like ghosts with unfinished business."

Jack threw his head back, his hands over his face. "They aren't zombies! They aren't ghosts! They're *dokkaebi*!"

Olivia lifted a shoulder at Ronnie. "They seem pretty similar to me."

Ronnie tipped her head from side to side. "Zombies, ghosts, dokkaebi—they're all only one percent likely to exist."

Jack looked ready to implode, and Sam quickly jumped in. "It's more like this story about a dokkaebi who took the form of a fisherman in Alaska. They say his spirit came from a glass fish ornament belonging to a man who lost his wife at sea. Every excursion he captained returned with impossibly large catches."

Olivia sighed dreamily. "That's so tragically romantic. I wonder if the fisherman ever found his wife out there."

"If he had," Jack said, wrinkling his nose, "she'd have been bones and whatever else the fish didn't want to eat."

Olivia bristled. "Thanks for ruining it." She scooped up a tidy spoonful of yogurt. "All in all, they sound pretty harmless. Don't be a jerk and accuse anyone of being a dokkaebi, and you'll be all right. They might even lead you to a pot of gold at the end of a rainbow."

Jack sucked in a sharp breath. "They aren't leprechauns, either!"

"Whatever." Olivia swallowed the last of her yogurt and set down her spoon. "There's only about ten minutes before ropes course, and I still have to change."

"Oh yeah," Jack said with a sneer. "Better hurry if you want to get back into your *dress*."

Olivia rose stiffly to her feet. "Well, I'm not going to wear pajamas the whole day. I'm not a monster." She aimed a long, withering stare at Jack's crumpled T-shirt before snatching up her tray and marching away.

Ronnie reached over the table and punched Jack in the arm. "Why are you being a jerk?"

"Ow!" Jack cried out, rubbing the spot. "She's the one being a jerk!"

"You're the one who teased her—geez. Can't you just be nicer? Please?" A tingle ran down her arms—a weird reaction she sometimes had when she rhymed.

Jack and Sam both froze, and Ronnie winced. Although she expected this reaction from Jack, Sam had no reason to care. But by the look on his face, he was twenty-three percent shocked and seventy-seven percent aghast.

"What?" Ronnie snapped, glaring at the boys in challenge.

"Uh, nothing," Jack mumbled. Then he did a double take at the mosquito bite on Ronnie's neck. "Whoa. That grew." The bite had erupted overnight into a hot, red golf-ball-sized mutant.

Jack lurched back as if the bite bared teeth. "You should cover up that beast—suffocate it before it gets any ideas."

"It's only supposed to be in the *nineties* today. But sure, I'll just wrap a scarf around my neck," Ronnie grumbled. Again, Sam looked aghast. She didn't want to care what he thought about her, but she couldn't stop the heat from creeping up her cheeks. Propping her elbows on the table, she nonchalantly hid the mosquito bite behind her hand.

A counselor at the next table stood up and blew into his whistle. "Just a reminder. For those of you wanting to compete in the upcoming doubles kayak race, add your names on the sign-up sheet posted by the bathrooms no later than tomorrow at lights-out. Winners will get—*drum roll, please*—bragging rights!"

"Working up a sweat in this heat for *bragging rights*?" Ronnie was definitely not interested. Just thinking about rowing as fast as she could under the sun made her thirsty. She took a sip of her orange juice.

"I think it sounds fun," Jack said, turning to Sam.

Sam nodded and opened his mouth to reply, but Ronnie beat him to it. "Yeah, let's sign up, Jack." Juice dribbled down her chin.

Jack tossed his hair out of his eyes and aimed a disgusted expression at her. "I thought you said—"

"I love bragging!" she insisted, wiping her chin. "And I went kayaking with my dad a while ago and it was super fun." Ronnie hated braggarts, and she went kayaking with her dad when she was, like, nine. Once. Her dad had done most of the rowing while she squirmed in her too-tight life vest. Still, Ronnie was determined to be a part of Jack's next new hobby.

Jack shrugged. "Okay, then. But we better win!"

"I *love* winning." At least that wasn't a lie.

Another shrill whistle rang out. "One more thing," the counselor said before turning to look straight at Ronnie. "Ronnie, Ronnie, strong and able, get your elbows off the table!" His eyes danced with laughter as he gestured for others to join in the chant. "This is not a horse's stable, but a fancy dining table!"

Ronnie sat frozen, her eyes darting around the room as dozens of voices roared in unison. Everyone but her and Jack seemed to know the words. Still, the counselor grinned as he reached over and pushed her elbows off the table.

"Round the tables you must go, you must go, you must go! Round the tables you must go! You! Were! Naughty!"

The room fell silent. Everyone stared at Ronnie, their expressions expectant.

Sam cleared his throat and muttered to Jack, "She has to run around the dining hall now."

Ronnie blinked. "Why?"

Sam turned to Ronnie, a frown on his face like it pained him to look at her. "Because you had your elbows on the dining table. It's bad manners and a camp tradition to call people out for it."

Groaning, Ronnie got up to run the lap. As she jogged around the room, Jack and Sam talked animatedly. It was probably about another Sinbi comic or fandom—something Ronnie wasn't a part of. She was determined to fix that problem right away.

When she returned to the table, she made sure to keep her elbows off the surface and turned to Jack. "Did you know they have bikes we can use here? Should we ride around the grounds during free time today?" She grinned at him, ignoring the unpleasant look on Sam's face. He had been midsentence when Ronnie had interrupted.

"Huh?" Jack's brow furrowed beneath his flawlessly feathered bangs.

"Biking," Ronnie repeated. "Around camp. During free time."

Jack shook his head, already turning back to Sam. "You and Olivia go ahead without us. Sam and I are going to try to figure out the first scavenger hunt clue."

Ronnie frowned, slumping in her seat. When had it become Jack and Sam versus her and Olivia? Sam and Olivia were temporary "camp friends." Ronnie and Jack were *best* friends. Forever. And coming to camp was supposed to remind him of just that. But it felt like he was only forgetting her faster. Like *she* had been the temporary one.

Maybe this was just a rough patch, like she was going through with her dad. Now that she was at camp, he would relax without the daily reminder of her impulsive rhyming, and she'd have her old dad back. The one who cracked dad jokes and loved when she hung around his office during school breaks. The one who didn't bring home surprise Kristie-with-a-Ks and would never even *think* about moving away from Seattle. Ronnie would go back to normal, and so would he.

But it wasn't so easy with Jack. After all, there was more than one way to lose someone.

SEVEN

FREE FALL

Back at the cabin, Ronnie found Olivia dressed in head-to-toe athleisure. It looked like what Jack's mom wore when she was around—sleek black tennis shoes, black leggings with a floral stripe down the sides, a matching fitted tank top, and a baseball cap with her hair pulled through the back. Oh, and a mini mesh drawstring backpack, of course.

"You're dressed!"

Olivia smiled, all traces of annoyance gone. "I always feel better after a wardrobe change." She strolled toward the door, her spine straight and head held high. "I'm a firm believer in dressing for the part. Like in ballet recitals, it's not just the choreography and music, but also the costumes that tell the story and create the magic, you know?"

Ronnie threw on a clean T-shirt and jean shorts before hurrying to catch up to Olivia's longer strides. "Like the shoes for a sport—on the field or a court!" Ronnie cringed at the rhyme. It was still morning and she had already rhymed twice. Luckily, Olivia didn't seem to notice.

The ropes course was set up where the large grass field met the forest in the north end of the campgrounds. The area had several tall trees with metal rungs running up their trunks that looked like giant staples. The trees connected wonky-looking suspension bridges and nets with way-too-big holes hanging at various heights.

Ronnie's knees nearly gave out. She would definitely *not* be crossing any of those.

There was also a massive taut bungee cord reaching up into a tree high above the bridges, hooked into the ground with a *harness* attached to it. For *people* to strap into. People who were *not* Ronnie. The wood chips weren't going to protect anyone from anything other than a trip and fall at ground level. Even then, you're bound to walk away with knees full of splinters.

This was going to be torture.

Her spirits lifted when Jack approached. They shot right back down at the sight of Sam following close behind.

"Hello, Jack," Olivia said with a sniff.

Jack shifted on his feet and avoided Olivia's eyes. "Hey. Sorry you didn't have time to change."

Ronnie palmed her forehead. Jack, who lived in basketball shorts and T-shirts, was completely clueless about clothes. It wasn't his fault.

"Very funny." Olivia crossed her arms roughly.

Jack's brows pushed together. "I wasn't trying to be funny."

"Yeah, you were trying to be a jerk. Well, you don't have to try too hard."

"Hey!" Jack scowled through a sweep of shampoo-ad hair.

Ronnie groaned loudly and jumped in between them.

"No—don't fight! Jack is right. Fashion and clothes aren't things he knows! But you *both* need to stop! So can we let this drop?" She quickly added, "Please," to throw off the rhyme. Jack and Olivia were too busy glaring at one another to notice, but by the horrified look on Sam's face, he obviously had.

"*I* can," Olivia said stiffly. "If *he* can."

"Well, *I* can if *she* can," Jack shot back.

"Great, you both agree!" Ronnie lifted her hands in exaggerated jubilation. "That's good enough for me." Grinding her teeth in frustration to stop any more rhymes from slipping out, Ronnie stared straight ahead until Willa mercifully put up a peace sign to get everyone's attention.

"First-timers will join me at the low ropes course on the far right," Willa called out to the group. "We'll start outside the perimeter near that collection of stacked stones."

Ronnie was more than ready to follow Willa to a section of the course with low-hanging tires, evenly spaced tree stumps, and planks planted directly on the ground. Sure, the challenges looked like they were taken straight from a preschool playground, but at least Ronnie could say with confidence she was ninety-nine percent likely to survive it.

"Come on," Jack said. "I wanna go to the high course."

Ronnie shot him a look. "You're a ropes-course newbie. We both are."

"Me too!" Olivia sang out as if she was joining an elite club, not the baby group of ropes courses. "I hope I don't stink at it."

"I've done it a bunch and it's not hard," Sam chimed in. "You do ballet, so you should be a natural."

Jack wrinkled his nose. "What's ballet got to do with it? Does a tutu work like a parachute if you fall?" He laughed at his own terrible joke.

Olivia scowled at Jack. "Balance and coordination, obviously."

"Well, I've got both," Jack said to Ronnie. "And Sam's done the high ropes loads of times. Let's go."

Olivia grabbed Ronnie's elbow. "Ronnie, it's not just breaking rules—you could break your bones if you don't know what you're doing!"

Ronnie looked between Jack and Olivia. "I—I'm not sure the high ropes are even safe. I mean, when did they last test the harnesses anyway? And how many injuries and accidents have they had here? Do you even know how many people have died on ropes courses?"

Jack rolled his eyes. "I don't know."

"That's right! None of us do because they didn't tell us!"

"You sound just like your dad." Jack ran a hand through his hair and turned to Sam. "Come on, let's go."

"Jack!" Ronnie called after him, but he just waved and kept walking.

Olivia slipped her arm through Ronnie's, and they made their way to the low ropes course. "He could do with a good hex, maybe a sprained ankle—something to teach him a lesson."

Ronnie frowned. "I hope he *doesn't* get hurt. Jack's my best friend." She spoke each word slowly and carefully, making sure to avoid a rhyme. But it must have come across as angry because Olivia tensed at her side.

"I was just kidding," Olivia said, pulling away. "You can catch up to Jack if you want."

"No, that's not what I mean," Ronnie insisted. There was no way she was going on the high course. Her dad might have been the one to forbid risky activities, but Ronnie had never put up much of a fight. She liked knowing what she was getting herself into—even better if she was at least sixty percent certain she'd be good at it. But by the way her knees went weak at the sight of the zip line, her confidence was dipping down somewhere in the ten percent range.

"You know, he hasn't exactly been nice to me. Maybe that's hard for you to see since you only met me yesterday, and he's your best friend."

"Jack *is* my best friend," Ronnie agreed, "which is why I called him out for being a jerk earlier." She gave Olivia's arm a little nudge with her elbow.

"It must be nice to have a friend like that." Olivia's shoulders drooped.

"Oh," Ronnie said softly, her own shoulders lowering in sympathy. "You don't have a best friend at home?"

Olivia started toying with her name tag, staring at it like it was the most interesting thing in the world. "Well, my sisters are my best friends, but ballet's my life. It's all our lives, actually. My older sister's a prima ballerina in our company, and that's the goal for my little sister and me, too. But she's so busy I never see her anymore, and with all the competition at our company . . . it's been hard to make friends." She scratched at an invisible stain on the glossy red plastic. "My parents only let me come to camp this summer because I threatened to quit. I just got sick of missing out on so much other stuff. I needed a break."

"Oh," Ronnie said with a grimace. "You mean *kid* stuff with other kids, like swimming and roasting marshmallows. Things like that?" Things her dad suddenly thought Ronnie should be doing. Things she didn't care for because, unlike Olivia, Ronnie had a best friend. She was starting to understand why Olivia was so determined to be friends.

Olivia nodded, her face downcast. Ronnie wanted to say something reassuring or comforting, but she didn't know how to do that. Whenever she was sad, her dad would distract her, and she'd forget all about feeling bad. And when there were physical reminders of painful memories, he'd get rid of them to help her move on. He wanted her to forget, just like he did. Ronnie didn't realize this until she started remembering little things about her mom, like the way she styled her hair, her favorite restaurant, or their visits to the zoo. But when she asked her dad about it, he had no recollection of any of it, and there were no pictures to help jog his memory.

In the end, Ronnie just stood there awkwardly until Willa raised the peace sign.

"For the first challenge," Willa called out to the group, "everyone will pair up and take turns in a trust exercise where they'll free-fall backward into the arms of their partner. Like so."

Robbie joined Willa to demonstrate the free fall. First, Robbie caught Willa, which wasn't that impressive. It was when Willa prepared to catch Robbie (who was twice her height) that things got exciting.

Robbie folded his arms across his chest, closed his eyes, and fell back into Willa's waiting arms. She caught him with a grunt, earning her a smattering of exclamations and cheers.

"For some, this will be a simple thing to do," Willa said after helping Robbie back up to his feet. "But for others, it will be extremely difficult and even stressful. That's because it requires you to give up all control and place yourself in someone else's hands—literally."

Olivia turned to Ronnie and lifted a brow. "You ready for this?"

"Um . . ." Ronnie stalled.

"Don't worry, I'll catch you! You can trust me—one hundred percent!"

Ronnie winced. Not only because she didn't believe in one hundred percent, but also because it wasn't up to Olivia to decide how much Ronnie trusted anyone or anything. And lately, she couldn't even trust her own calculations.

Ronnie folded her arms across her chest, her heart pounding so hard it reverberated in her hands. Drawing in a deep breath, she squeezed her eyes shut and tipped backward.

With a yelp, she caught herself and stumbled upright. "Sorry! Let me try again."

Ronnie made three more attempts at free-falling. Each one ended with her catching herself before she lost control.

"Maybe I should go first," Olivia offered. Turning her back to Ronnie, she called out over her shoulder, "Can I trust you?"

"Yes!" Ronnie held out her arms and braced herself.

Olivia crossed her arms, locked her knees, and dropped back like a felled tree right into Ronnie's waiting arms. She made it look so easy.

"All right," Olivia said, catching her breath. "Your turn. You got this, and I got you!"

Ronnie slowly turned around. She clutched her shoulders. She locked her knees. She sucked in a deep breath. And then she let herself fall back—

And immediately caught herself. Her heart hammered in her chest. "Sorry, I can't do it. It really freaks me out!"

Olivia looked away. "Maybe if you were doing this with Jack, it wouldn't freak you out so much."

"Well—" Ronnie searched for the right words. "I don't know. Maybe. But only because I know him so well. I mean, I'm ninety-nine percent positive he'd be able to catch me—"

Olivia's head snapped back to Ronnie. "Are you saying I'm not strong enough, but Jack is? Like I'm all skin and bones because I'm a ballerina?"

Ronnie's eyes nearly popped out of her head. "What? No! I mean, he's had my back since kindergarten."

"You think I'd betray you?" Olivia's face fell. "I was joking about wanting Jack to get hurt. I'd never want anyone to get hurt—especially my friends."

Olivia was talking about *her*.

"I—I know," Ronnie stammered. Olivia considered Ronnie her friend—maybe her only friend. Kind of like Jack was Ronnie's only friend. "I don't think you're like that. It's just *me*. It's not easy for me to let go."

Olivia's face softened. "It's gonna take a little longer

before I hit that one hundred percent friendship mark with you, isn't it?"

"Exactly." Ronnie chewed on her lip. "But technically, I don't believe in one hundred percent."

Olivia threw her head back and groaned dramatically. "OMG—*ninety-nine* percent! Happy?"

Ronnie nodded, beaming with satisfaction. Olivia studied Ronnie for a moment before she broke out into a smile as well. "I have the weirdest friends."

She was talking about Ronnie again.

Ronnie laughed and linked arms with Olivia. Maybe having a camp friend wouldn't be so bad.

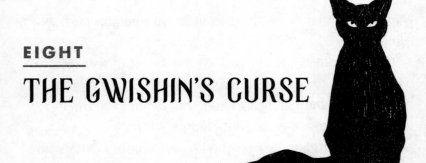

EIGHT

THE GWISHIN'S CURSE

Later that afternoon, Ronnie, Olivia, Jack, and Sam were toweling off at the lake after using the inflatable slide and trampoline, when Benji ran up to them. "Hey, guys, did you hear about Gigi?"

Ronnie squeezed water from her hair. "Gigi in Sparrow's Nest?"

"Yeah. Blond hair. Loves purple." Benji glanced from side to side before lowering his voice. "The Camp Foster Ghost is haunting her."

Ronnie stilled, watching for Jack's reaction.

"Why would the gwishin haunt Gigi?" Jack asked, his eyes narrowed.

A crease formed between Benji's brows. "What's a key-shin?"

"A *gwi*-shin is a Korean ghost."

Ronnie tossed her towel down and pulled on a T-shirt over her swim top. When she popped her head out of the shirt, she found everyone's eyes were on her, not Jack. They wanted to hear from the Korean girl. They expected her to say more, to *know* more. To be more Korean than Jack. To be way more Korean than she felt. And in moments like these, all Ronnie felt like was an imposter.

"Makes sense," Benji said when it was clear Ronnie wasn't going to say anything more. "Gigi says the ghost is drawn to her because she might be a distant relative."

Ronnie's brow furrowed. "Gigi's part Korean?"

"No, she's Italian. But I guess a cousin on her mom's side has a Korean stepmom."

Ronnie just stared at him.

Jack stared, too.

Benji shrugged. "It's what she said."

Ronnie raised her brows. "Did she say anything else about what she saw?"

"She said the ghost was wearing a white dress and slippers. Her black hair was really long, and her eyes were red, like her scarf." Benji shuddered. "The gwishin gave her a warning: Leave the grounds, or you'll all be cursed."

Slippers? Red eyes? Warnings? These weren't things Ronnie had seen or heard. It irritated her that Gigi was lying about seeing the gwishin when Ronnie actually had. It was Gigi who should be feeling like an imposter, not Ronnie.

"Wait, she'll curse us *all*?" Jack asked eagerly, as if Benji just told them the gwishin was passing out the latest Sinbi issue.

"What kind of curse?" Olivia asked, her voice pitched with worry.

"Not sure," Benji said. "But I think it's already started."

Ronnie smeared a thin coat of sunblock over her forehead,

trying not to scowl with annoyance. "What's happened?"

Benji met her gaze, and there was real fear in his light brown eyes. "Didn't you hear? Hitesh got food poisoning last night. He's still at the nurse's station."

Sam waved a hand. "Hitesh has an egg allergy."

"Yeah, I don't believe it," Ronnie said. She also couldn't believe she and Sam agreed on something.

Jack picked up Ronnie's towel and swatted her with it. "Of course *you're* going to say that. You just don't get this stuff." He turned to Sam. "This could be like Sinbi Issue—"

"Forty-nine," Sam finished for Jack. "Where they find the gwishin in the tower."

Irritation prickled Ronnie's neck. Hadn't Sam just denied the curse?

"Yeah!" Jack's face lit up with a fandom glow. "We need to get the details from Gigi herself."

The tension in her neck pressed on the back of her tongue. Ronnie recognized the impulse to rhyme and clenched her jaws against it.

"Shouldn't be hard," Benji said. "She's been talking about it all day."

Ronnie huffed, and that was all it took for the rhyme to slip right past her lips. "Well, not that I care, but the gwishin's feet are bare. And her eyes are black not red, so you're clearly being misled." She slammed a hand over her mouth.

"Whoa. Did all that just rhyme?" Benji quirked his upper lip, exposing a single bright red elastic along his braces. Everyone turned to stare at Ronnie.

"I . . . um . . ." Her heart was pounding, her face grew

hot, and it wasn't from the sun. If only she could disappear. Maybe she should run. Or say something—*anything*—to make them all forget, but even her thoughts were in rhyme, much to her regret.

Suddenly Jack shook his hair out, spraying the entire group with water droplets. Everyone jumped back, arms raised defensively and squealing at him to stop. Benji threw a towel at him, but Jack dodged it. He didn't need it. His hair settled salon-perfectly on his head.

"So who's going with me to find Gigi?" Jack grabbed his backpack off the ground and slung it over his shoulder.

Everyone followed Jack, and Ronnie sagged with relief. They seemed to have forgotten about her strange rhyming. Hoisting her backpack onto her shoulders, she lagged behind the group to avoid the risk of talking to anyone. But up ahead, Jack slowed his steps, waiting for her to catch up.

"Thanks for distracting them," she muttered. It was the closest they'd ever come to talking about Ronnie's rhyming problem.

He shrugged. "It's no big deal. Unlike your sudden interest in the gwishin." He looked at her curiously, like she'd grown a third eye.

"It's just that if Gigi's going to pretend to have seen the gwishin, she could at least get the facts straight."

Jack pointed a finger at her imaginary third eye, a huge grin stretching across his face. "You just used the words *facts* and *gwishin* in the same sentence! Are you finally ready to admit it's all real?"

Ronnie slapped his finger away, trying not to smile at the way his eyes lit up at the prospect of winning over her disbelief. This was the way things were *supposed* to be with Jack. He was supposed to want her to care. His greatest mission in life for the past few years had been to convince her the supernatural was super real.

Every Friday night, she and Jack watched the same scary shows over and over. He spent the entire time trying to convince her of the truth of the lore, to which she retorted with percent unlikelihood. Neither ever budged, and both were happy to repeat their arguments the following Friday. It was one of those things Ronnie had come to count on.

Like when they got placed into all different classes for the sixth grade, Friday nights were the one thing that stayed the same. Or when she was hospitalized for a week with Kawasaki disease, Jack brought the show and Hot Cheeto popcorn to her hospital room. And when Jack's mom moved out of their house, Ronnie took the movie and licorice to Jack's suddenly much-too-quiet house.

No matter the terrible, unexpected things life tossed their way, Friday nights were the one thing Ronnie could always rely on. Until this summer. Ronnie started rhyming, and Jack decided he'd rather go to camp instead of hanging out every day swimming or riding their bikes to the beach. That was two Friday-night movies he'd miss. He'd already missed a movie night two weeks ago when he decided to try night fishing.

"No one is seeing a ghost. Because they don't exist," Ronnie said. It was spoken without her usual zeal, but Jack didn't seem to notice the drop in her enthusiasm, probably because it was what he expected her to say.

"Says the nonbeliever," Jack retorted. "It'd be wasted on you." He snickered, as if the word was an insult. And for some reason, Ronnie was insulted.

She crossed her arms and locked eyes with Jack. "Would it? Or would appearing to me—a nonbeliever—be the ultimate proof they're real?"

He gave her a sidelong glance. "I can't believe you'd pretend you saw a gwishin just to one up Gigi."

Ronnie pouted. "You'd believe Gigi, but not me?"

Jack snorted. "It'd be easier to believe a dokkaebi Persuaded you to say you saw a gwishin than to believe you actually believed that you saw one."

Ronnie tipped her head to one side, trying to untangle what he'd just said. Jack seemed to have confused himself as well. He shook his head as if to clear it. "You know what I mean."

Planting her feet, she tugged at Jack's backpack to get him to stop. "Yeah. Basically, you wouldn't believe your own best friend!"

"My best friend would never see a gwishin." Jack raked a hand through his bangs. "But I guess people can change."

Ronnie's chest squeezed with panic. That was the last thing she wanted.

🌲🌲🌲

Apparently, it wasn't only people who changed, but also Gigi's ghost story. And it kept changing the more she talked about it. Which was nonstop.

At lunch the next day, half the camp had surrounded Gigi, who wore purple leggings with a purple-and-white-striped top. She fingered the purple hair ties around the ends of her fishtail braids, relishing the attention as her audience ate up every contradictory detail of her alleged ghost encounter. Even Jack and Sam were hanging on to her every word, trying to work out if Gigi's story lined up with the clues in one of the Sinbi issues.

"Her voice was like one long scream that shook the trees," Gigi said, making eye contact with her captive audience. Ronnie had to admit it: She was good. "It was so loud I covered my ears, but it didn't help. I was the only one who could hear it because the ghost chose *me*."

Ronnie stuffed a carrot into her mouth and crunched it as loud as possible.

"So I'm literally frozen in fear when I ask her what she wants from me, right?" Gigi waited a moment for people to nod or lean in. "She says, *All trespassers will suffer my wrath*."

Ronnie picked at her meat loaf. "I thought it was *Leave or be cursed*?"

"Same difference." Gigi shot Ronnie a glare that rivaled the gwishin's.

"What did the scarf look like?" a girl from Falcon's Nest asked in a hushed voice. "Was it bloody?"

Gigi furrowed her brow and pressed a hand dramatically to her throat. "From what I could tell, it looked like cashmere. I have a lavender one just like it—you know, with the fringes at the end? But the color was such a deep red it could have been soaked with blood and I wouldn't have noticed. I'll have to take a closer look next time I see it."

A boy from Rooster's Nest gaped at her. "You think she'll appear to you again?"

Gigi looked him square in the face. "Oh, I *know* so. There's this undeniable bond between us. It's like I'm a medium and she's trying to speak through me, you know?"

Falcon Girl gasped loudly. "You're *so brave*, Gigi."

Ronnie had had enough. "Seeing things isn't brave—it's a reason to find a shrink. But as you saw nothing, you'll be just fine, I think. Gigi," she quickly added to conceal the rhyme.

"You better watch your words," Gigi replied, her voice low, "or you'll be next. Ghosts don't take well to disbelievers."

Gigi acting like a ghost expert grated on Ronnie's nerves. "Is this what the gwishin told you? Was it before or after she warned you about Hitesh's egg allergy?"

Gigi shook her head, her blond braids slapping her shoulders like fish on a dock. "Laugh all you want, Veronica. But don't come crying to any of us when you're targeted."

Ronnie shot her a sarcastic smile. "It's really not that scary—I'll just stay away from dairy. There's also dust and pollen. They make my eyes all swollen."

Gigi wrinkled her nose. "What was *that*? Did you *rhyme*?" She burst into laughter. "Omigosh. You're so weird, Veronica!"

All the blood drained from Ronnie's face. Jumping up from her seat, she muttered something about the bathroom and ran off. Gigi's laughter followed her all the way across the dining hall.

Slamming the bathroom door shut, Ronnie pressed her back to it so no one else could enter. Everyone had heard her rhyme—including *Gigi*. It was so humiliating. Maybe running away wasn't the best move, but if she hadn't, there was a good chance she would have rhymed again. One thing she had learned about her rhyming was it got worse when she was upset. And Gigi upset her.

Ronnie drew in deep, calming breaths until her stomach stopped flipping and her heart stopped pounding. Then she peeled herself off the door and ran her hands under cold water, pressing her chilled fingers onto her hot cheeks.

She wasn't in any rush to return to the table, but she couldn't stay in the bathroom forever. And since disappearing into thin air or being swallowed up by a random sinkhole in the ground was only one percent likely, she braced herself to face Gigi again.

But when she pulled on the door handle, it didn't budge. She tried pushing. Then she pulled again.

It was locked. Only there wasn't a lock on the door. At least not that she could see from her side. Maybe the door was simply stuck. But no matter how hard Ronnie pushed and pulled, it wouldn't give. She even tried banging on the door and calling out, but there was no response. Giving up, she turned around to lean her back against the immovable door.

She didn't scare easily, but there was something about being trapped that made breathing difficult. The bathroom was large, with five stalls, but the space seemed to shrink by the second. She imagined the walls closing in and looked around her, desperate for an escape. She'd climb through the ventilation system if it meant she wouldn't be crushed to death.

Ronnie didn't realize she had started sweating until a cool breeze washed over her face. There was a window next to the sinks that was propped open, letting in the cool air. That was a *much* better option than the vents.

Climbing up onto the counter, she stuck her head out the window. She was ready to push her way out when she saw something that brought her to a crashing halt.

There in broad daylight—on the front lawn next to the Welcome to Camp Foster banner—was Min-Young, the gwishin.

NINE

THE SCAVENGER HUNT CLUE

onnie would have screamed had her throat not closed
tight like a fist. She would have turned away if her
entire body wasn't rooted to the spot in fear. But
the gwishin didn't seem to notice Ronnie. Her pitch-black
eyes were fixed on the nearby trees, her hands smoothing
down her long red scarf. Boo was at her feet, swatting at a
pile of stones in the grass. Every once in a while, his head
snapped up to the forest, his throat emitting a soft growl.

Ronnie followed Boo's gaze but saw nothing. Everything
was quiet and still except for the flapping banner agitated
by a breeze emanating from the gwishin. It circled her like
a dutiful pet.

The banner pulled taut against a particularly strong
gust, and the clue for the scavenger hunt rushed to mind.

*I was the first to greet you, but you didn't greet me back.
Perhaps I should have waved, but I had not any slack. I'm
tied up at the moment, in the sun between two trees, relaxing
in the heat or tense against the breeze.*

"That's it!" Ronnie cried out to herself. "That's the first
clue!" She slapped a hand over her mouth, but it was too late.
The gwishin's head swiveled on her neck in an unnaturally

slow and smooth motion that made all the blood drain from Ronnie's face. They locked eyes—Ronnie's bulging in terror and the gwishin's obsidian and unblinking. The skin that was visible past the clumps of long black hair was a ghastly yellow-gray—bloodless and lifeless. All except for her deep bloodred lips. Ronnie could swear the gwishin smiled, but in the way a monster smiles right before it sinks its teeth into you.

Ronnie tried to remind herself that gwishin don't exist. This was all a figment of her imagination brought on by the stress of being sent away by her dad, left behind by her best friend, and threatened with a stepmother, all while in a new and creepy place. She was sixty-nine percent certain. Ronnie pried her fingers from the windowsill and pressed the heels of her hands into her eyes, hoping to rub away the vision. But when she opened her eyes again, the gwishin was still there.

The wind shifted, and a gust rushed over Ronnie's face. She startled, but only a little, because as much as the breeze was unexpected, it was also warm and soft. And then Ronnie heard it—a faint voice she might have mistaken for the wind itself if it wasn't for the gwishin's mouth forming the spoken words, *"Beware the dokkaebi's scarf of silence."*

The gwishin flickered once like a glitch in a screen and reappeared a foot closer. She flickered a second time. Two feet closer. She flickered a third time—

"Ronnie?"

Ronnie fell back and cried out as her foot slipped on the wet countertop. She sucked in a sharp breath at the stabbing pain in her side as she hit the faucet before her butt landed in a sink.

"Ronnie, are you in there?" The voice came from outside the door.

"Olivia?" Ronnie launched herself out of the sink, wincing at the pain in her side. That was going to bruise.

"Did you lock this door?" Olivia called through the crack between the door and the frame. "Are you going number two?"

"No, I'm not pooping," Ronnie called back, pressing close to the door.

"OMG, Ronnie, I said *number two*!" Olivia rattled the door from the other side.

Ronnie tugged on the door from her side, though she knew it was useless. "The door's stuck. I was about to jump out the window."

"Let me go get someone—" Suddenly the door swung open, flinging Ronnie back as Olivia pitched forward. They fell to the ground, groaning.

Now sore on both sides, Ronnie gingerly climbed back onto her feet to check the door for some explanation.

"Do you see anything?" Olivia asked, rubbing her elbow, which she must have landed on.

Ronnie bit her lip, running a finger over the smooth doorframe with no lock in sight. "Nope."

Olivia's dark brown eyes grew wide with terror. "It's got to be the curse! This is exactly what Gigi said would happen."

Ronnie was about to argue when she realized this was the perfect distraction from her earlier rhyming flub.

Back at the table, Gigi's fans had dispersed. But the moment Ronnie began telling Jack about the creepy bathroom door incident, Benji appeared like a baby dolphin responding to his mother dolphin's whistle. If the whistle promised camp gossip, that is.

Gigi nodded her head solemnly. "I'm not surprised at all this happened to you, Veronica."

"It's *Ronnie*," she said through gritted teeth.

Gigi leaned across the table. "I did warn you."

There had to be nothing worse than letting Gigi think she was right—and she kind of was. But this could be Ronnie's chance to get Jack to take her seriously about maybe, possibly, more-than-one-percent-likely seeing a ghost.

Just when Ronnie decided to admit defeat to Gigi, Jack slapped a hand on her shoulder.

"Sorry, Gigi," he said to Gigi while shooting Ronnie a knowing look—the kind you only share with a best friend. "It's gonna take a lot more than being stuck in the bathroom to convince Ronnie. I've been working on her since we were, like, what?"

"Eight," Ronnie offered.

Jack nodded. "Since we were *eight*. If anyone's gonna bring her to the other side, it's me."

Right. This was her and Jack's thing. And she was about to throw it all away over a one percent?

Ronnie shot Gigi a Jack Park Smirk. "I'm eighty-five percent sure the door's super old with rusty hinges and ninety-nine percent sure you're imagining every bit of your ghost sighting."

Jack's face broke out into a smug grin. "What did I say?"

Ronnie shrugged. "No offense, Gigi."

"Whatever." Gigi waved it off like she was already over it, but Ronnie didn't trust the glint in her eyes. "We already moved on to more important things. After you ran off to the bathroom, we all got to talking about the scavenger hunt, and I thought, *Hey! We should ask Veronica to recite the clue. She's good at rhyming, right?*"

Ronnie's cheeks burned, and she curled into herself like a pill bug. She suddenly wished she was trapped in the bathroom again. That's when she remembered the clue. Straightening, she lifted her chin and looked Gigi dead in the eyes. "Even better. I know where to find the first token."

Gigi crossed her arms. "Yeah, right. No one's figured it out yet."

Ronnie smiled. "While I was in the bathroom, I noticed the bathroom window faces the front lawn. You can see the welcome banner hanging *between two trees* from there. That's when it hit me."

Benji slammed a fist onto the table, making Olivia jump practically out of her seat. "'I was the first to greet you, but you didn't greet me back. Perhaps I should have waved, but I had not any slack. I'm tied up at the moment, in the sun *between two trees*, relaxing in the heat or tense against the breeze!'"

Jack turned to Ronnie with a wide grin. "That's it! You're a genius!"

"But that's just a guess," Gigi said.

Ronnie jumped to her feet. "There's only one way to find out."

🌲🌲🌲

Ronnie, Jack, and Benji raced to the welcome banner with Olivia, Sam, and Gigi following behind. There was no gwishin or strange breeze, but Ronnie did find a small bag tied to one corner of the sign where it met the rope. It could easily be mistaken for a weight, but upon closer inspection, it was the perfect hiding place for scavenger hunt tokens.

Ronnie dug out a handful of pressed pennies from the bag and held them out. "Anyone want the first token?"

Jack, Benji, and Olivia ran up to grab one. Gigi moved slowly and Sam hung back entirely.

Snatching up a penny, Jack peered at the image. "Hey, it's a Chinese character or something."

"What does a Chinese character have to do with camp?" Olivia asked, taking a penny for herself.

"I feel like I've seen it before," Benji said, turning the penny over in his hand.

Sam craned his neck to study Jack's penny instead of grabbing one from Ronnie. As if he'd get cooties from touching her.

Ronnie rolled her eyes. "Here." She dropped the coin into Sam's hand, careful to avoid contact.

"Yeah, that's a Chinese character, but it could be Korean, too," Sam said.

Ronnie smirked at Sam's mistake. "I know what Korean looks like, and that's not it." Everyone turned to her. This was one of those rare moments in which she knew more than someone else about something Korean. The uncomfortable look on Sam's face made it all the more satisfying.

"Um, actually, it *is*," Sam replied, shifting everyone's attention back to him. "Hanja is Korean that comes from Chinese characters. They're just not used much these days."

All eyes bounced back to Ronnie, and her cheeks flamed. "What, do you have a cousin with a Korean stepmom, too, or something?"

Sam shifted on his feet and looked away. "That's not what I'm saying. I don't know Korean or Chinese—just this character."

Ronnie furrowed her brow. "Well, then what—"

"That's where I've seen it!" Benji cried out, pointing his token in the direction of the manor. "In the gallery!"

Gigi wrinkled her nose. "You've been to the gallery?"

Though she wouldn't admit it aloud, Ronnie had to agree with Gigi. Going to the gallery on purpose during summer camp was like doing optional homework during school breaks.

But Benji didn't seem bothered by their judgmental stares. "The counselor in Rooster's Nest said there's a token there."

"Hey—that's not fair," Gigi protested.

"I'm making it fair by telling you guys," Benji said, flashing the entire rainbow of his braces. He nudged Gigi playfully with an elbow, getting a shove and a smile out of her.

"But that's all I've got," Benji added. "The gallery's pretty big and I couldn't narrow down where to look without the actual clue. And Ms. Pavani's no help—well, unless you actually want to learn about Camp Foster's history. She's really into that."

Ronnie thrust her hand back into the bag and pulled out the next clue scrawled on a folded piece of paper. "'Within the collection, you'll find a selection of photos and plaques that hide what you track.'"

Olivia grinned. "That's got to be the clue for the gallery, right? Where else would we find collections and photos and plaques?"

"The plaque!" Benji grabbed Ronnie by the shoulders and gave her a little shake. "That character's carved into a plaque on one of the shelves with a bunch of old pictures of the grounds!" He shook Ronnie again, and somehow it worked to shake off her worries.

Benji's excitement riled everyone up as they ran off to the manor smiling and laughing—even Ronnie. For the first time since arriving at Camp Foster, she was having fun. For the first time all summer, rhyming didn't make her a freak. And for the first time in a long while, Ronnie wasn't thinking about how things were *supposed* to be. The only thing on her mind was finding the next clue.

Maybe rhyming and seeing ghosts didn't have to change anything. As long as she kept it to herself and under control.

TEN

BEWARE

Inside the manor, the front desk was vacant. To the right was a hallway leading to the nurse's station. To the left was a sitting room turned gallery with paintings on the walls. Ronnie wandered over to a cabinet displaying ancient wooden masks with creepy painted eyes, horns, and bared teeth next to other old things like painted tea sets and a handcrafted wooden jewelry box. A tingle shot up her spine and tickled the back of her brain. It was the déjà vu again—the feeling she had seen the jewelry box before but couldn't remember when or where. It was a perfect spot to hide the next clue and some tokens. But when she peeked inside, she found it was filled to the brim with friendship bracelets.

"Over here, guys!" Benji waved everyone over to a table topped with large books and photo albums. Above were two rows of shelves lined with framed photos and a handful of plaques—one that bore the same character as the one on the token.

Ronnie leaned in for a closer look and her eyes grew round like full moons. "I've seen that before."

Jack gave her a funny look. "Yeah, it's on the tokens we just found."

"No, I mean I've seen this before today. I just realized—it looks like the etching on my Korean baby ring."

In keeping with Korean tradition, Ronnie had received a gold baby ring at her dohl—a party celebrating a baby's first birthday. Her dad couldn't remember who got it for her, which usually meant that it was someone on her mom's side. The ring always made Ronnie feel closer to her mom. It also made her feel a little bit more Korean. And every once in a while, she'd take the ring out of its velvet box and put it on, bending it open wider as her finger grew. At its center was a character that looked a lot like the one on the plaque. But she couldn't be sure if it was the same, not without comparing them side by side.

"Why would that be on your ring?" Olivia asked, turning over a framed picture of five young girls doubled over in laughter. Finding nothing on the back, she returned it to the shelf and turned to Sam. "Did you say what the character means?"

Sam scratched the back of his head. "I, uh, can't remember."

"I bet Ms. Pavani knows," Benji offered. "Too bad she's not here."

"I found it!" Sam held up a framed photo of the manor and tugged off an envelope taped to the back. When he dumped the contents onto the table, a slip of white paper fell out with the tokens. But as he reached for the clue, Boo appeared out of nowhere, landing on the table with hardly a sound. Sam snatched his hand back as though it had been burned, even though no one touched him.

"Hey," Ronnie said in surprise to the cat. "Where'd you come from?"

Sam made a shooing motion with his hand. "Get out of here!" Ronnie had never heard his voice so loud or high-pitched. Pulling off his backpack, he began swinging it at Boo. The cat hissed in response, his hackles rising.

Olivia stepped toward Boo with one hand out for him to sniff, signaling Sam to back off with the other. "Hey, kitty, kitty, it's okay." Her movements were as graceful as Boo's, but he was already startled. Leaping off the table, he landed silently on the pads of his feet near the exit. He looked back and met Ronnie's gaze, the scavenger hunt clue poking out of his mouth, before darting out of the gallery.

"Wait! Boo!" Ronnie called out. Before she knew what she was doing, she was running after him.

"Ronnie, where are you going?" Olivia cried out after her, but Ronnie didn't stop. She wanted that clue.

When she reached the front desk, she found Boo sitting by the front door, which had been left ajar. It seemed like he was waiting for her.

"All right, now spit out the paper." Ronnie held out a hand as she approached, trying to mimic Olivia's gentle movements. But when she was nearly within reach, Boo took off out the front door. Ronnie chased after him. Although he was too fast to catch, he wasn't running at full speed. He *wanted* her to follow.

Ronnie looked back over her shoulder. No one had

followed her out. They must be looking for the clue, thinking it had fallen somewhere.

Up ahead, Boo bolted into the forest and disappeared.

Ronnie hesitated. The forest was forbidden. It wasn't worth breaking the rules for a measly scavenger hunt clue, right? It was a terrible idea—eighty percent positive. She should turn right back around—seventy percent certain.

Then, somewhere not too far away, Boo mewed innocently, as if he would offer her the clue if she took just one step into the trees. As if he wouldn't run off again as he lured her deeper and deeper into the woods.

Ronnie peered into the low light, waiting for her eyes to adjust, when a flash of white came into view. The clue! There was another flash of white. This time it lingered, low to the ground, fluttering in the absence of a breeze.

Clutching her backpack straps, Ronnie took one tentative step into the forest. Then another. And another. Until she was completely surrounded by hulking trees. But Boo was gone, and so was the clue.

Then there was the slightest whisper—like paper against paper. And again, a flash of white. But it wasn't the clue. It wasn't paper at all. Her breath caught at the sight of a white nightgown peeking out from behind a wide tree trunk several steps away. Only the bottom corner of the skirt was visible, glowing as though the sun shone through it. But the forest canopy was so dense it filtered out any direct sunlight.

The white fabric swayed, and a pasty-looking foot appeared beneath it. Followed by an ankle, the rest of the skirt, until, at last, the entire gwishin stepped out. Or floated out, actually.

Ronnie gasped and backed away, glancing around for Boo. But she was alone.

The gwishin hovered inches above the forest floor, her toes pointed down. From this close, Ronnie could make out the tinges of purple that bloomed on the tops of her bare, skeletal feet. In contrast, delicate lace along the bottom hem of her skirt fluttered prettily above them. Ronnie wasn't anywhere near as fashionable as Olivia, but as her gaze traveled up the pristine nightgown, she was ninety-nine percent certain it clashed with the red scarf that flowed from around her neck like a deadly river.

Ronnie was still backing away when her heel caught on something, causing her to stumble. With a cry, she fell onto her backside, her hair falling over her face and her backpack slipping from her shoulders.

A subtle breeze swept Ronnie's hair aside, clearing her view and revealing the gwishin closer than ever before— close enough to reach out and touch. Immobilized by fear, she was unable to close her eyes against the gwishin's depthless gaze. Ghost stories didn't do them justice. They were much more terrifying in real life.

The gwishin reached out with one colorless, bony hand to . . . grab her? Strangle her?

Ronnie wasn't staying to find out. Willing her body into action, she shrugged on her backpack and scrambled up to her feet. She was poised to bolt when the gwishin spoke.

"Looking for this?" Her voice was like the wind and felt like it, too. It grazed Ronnie's cheek—warm and soft—not at all cold like she would have expected. The shock of it tugged her eyes up, and her heart gave a lurch.

Although she had managed not to scream, the gwishin must have seen her terror. Lifting a pale hand, she combed long, stringy hair over her face. Still, her pallid complexion and the deathless eyes peeking out from between the clumped strands were no less chilling. Ronnie's throat was so tight she couldn't cry out, but her mind screamed at her to run away.

"Please don't leave," the gwishin—Min-Young—said in her airy voice. "I have something for you." In her bony grasp was the clue.

There was absolutely no way Ronnie was reaching for it. It turned out she didn't have to. The gwishin fluttered a single ashen hand, guiding the breeze like a music conductor guides an orchestra. To Ronnie's silent disbelief, the paper drifted over and tucked itself gently into her palm. She jumped at the sensation.

"Wh-what do you want from me?" she sputtered.

"You're frightened. *Good.*" Min-Young lurched forward with a whoosh, her eyes yawning open like two black holes capable of swallowing a kid whole. Ronnie released a strangled cry, her body trembling so violently she almost fell to the ground.

"Be afraid, for fear will help you to remember." Min-Young's voice shook like a flag caught in a strong gust, growing louder with each word. "A dokkaebi hunts you, little witch. You must beware the scarf of silence!"

The wind screamed in Ronnie's ears. She didn't know about dokkaebi or witches, but she could no longer deny what was staring her in the face. This wasn't her imagination. The gwishin was real.

Ronnie covered her ears and squeezed her eyes shut, but it was too late. She couldn't un-hear the warning. And she couldn't un-see the look on the gwishin's face—both terrified and terrifying. Ronnie spun around and ran faster than she'd ever run before.

ELEVEN

COOKBOOK NOOK

Ronnie ran, clearing the trees, passing the manor, and entering the courtyard. She didn't stop running until she collided headfirst into Olivia.

"Oof!"

"Sorry!"

Olivia and Ronnie cried out at the same time as they ricocheted off each other. Ronnie rubbed her head, and Olivia rubbed her chin, wincing.

"Hey!" Olivia adjusted her mini backpack of the day—a metallic-structured bag that cast rainbow light onto the sides of her smooth brown cheeks. "Where have you been? And why were you running?"

Chasing a cat into a forest forbidden where a gwishin appeared from where she was hidden. She stared without blinking with eyes black as pitch and said I'm being hunted and called me a witch.

It was a good thing Ronnie was too out of breath for that rhyming confession to tumble out. She only managed to huff, "Chasing. Boo," as she worked to slow her racing heart and even out her breathing. Hunched over with her hands on her knees, she looked around the courtyard.

Small groups of campers had gathered to hang out, but she didn't see Jack among them. "Where'd everyone go?"

"Penny from Eagle's Nest found a token during archery. So everyone went there." Olivia's voice grew quiet. "*I* stayed behind to look for you so you wouldn't have to search alone."

Ronnie shook her head. "Oh, I'm so done with the scavenger hunt."

Olivia's eyes flicked down to Ronnie's hands on her knees. When she looked back up, she met Ronnie's eyes with the same hurt look that had been in them during the trust-fall exercise. "It's okay if you'd rather search with Jack. You can just say so."

"What?" Ronnie frowned, confused. "I'm just tired and want to go lie down."

"If you say so." Olivia cleared her throat and looked over her shoulder. "I'm going to catch up with the others."

"Okay." When Ronnie raised a hand to wave at Olivia, a piece of paper fluttered to the ground. Ronnie picked it up and realized she'd been so distressed she'd forgotten all about the clue.

Smoothing out the paper, she read aloud: "'There's so much to cook in this cozy nook. To find the next clue, try vegetable stew.'"

Ronnie groaned. Olivia must have seen the clue in her hand and thought she was trying to keep it from her. But she hadn't been lying when she told Olivia she was done with the scavenger hunt. How could she care about tokens anymore? What she really needed right now was to be alone to think. Because if the gwishin was real, then dokkaebi were real, too. And if dokkaebi were real, then she was being hunted by one. And if the gwishin could be believed . . . then she—Ronnie Miller—was a *witch*.

But those were all one percents. That was almost nothing. *Tiny.*

Then why did it feel so huge?

Nothing was adding up.

🌲🌲🌲

Back at the cabin, Ronnie headed for her bunk. She was too amped for a nap, but she definitely needed to lie down. Her interaction with the gwishin was playing on a loop in her head, and with each replay, she came up with more and more questions. Why did Min-Young's ghost think Ronnie was a witch? What did that have to do with a dokkaebi? Why was Min-Young trying to help her? And what did she mean about fear being good and helpful? Ronnie didn't want to be afraid. She didn't want to see gwishin or dokkaebi. She didn't want to be a witch. She didn't want any of it.

When she reached her bunk, she found Boo waiting for her on her pillow, something trapped between his teeth. Again. Climbing onto the bed, she held out her hand. "Cough up whatever it is you stole this time, Boo. I'm not chasing you again."

To her surprise, Boo immediately obeyed and dropped the object into her hand. It was a friendship bracelet made with orange, blue, and brown threads. Upon closer inspection, she saw a few light tan hairlike threads woven in as well.

"Where'd you get this?"

Boo responded by swatting at the bracelet in Ronnie's hand. His gesture had the distinct quality of *just take it already*.

"But it's not mine. I should get it back to whoever you took it from."

Boo pinned her with his golden eyes and swiped at her hand again—this time with more force. He *really* wanted her to have the bracelet.

"Fine. Maybe whoever it belongs to will see it on me and claim it." She slipped it over her wrist and was surprised at its warmth, like it had been sitting under the sun outside rather than in the cool of the cabin. "Now, please give me my pillow back."

Again, Boo complied, but a strange crackling sound accompanied his movements. He had been sitting on a piece of paper.

"You have *got* to stop stealing clues, Boo!"

But this didn't look like a clue. It looked like it had been torn out of a book. On one side of the paper was an incomplete list of sorts. On the other side was a rhyme, which Ronnie read aloud, *"Take me there, to when and where. A memory that's saved to share."*

A tingle shot up Ronnie's arms, and she shivered at the sensation, which seemed to be happening more often. Was her rhyming problem getting worse? She told herself she was just shaken by her run-in with the gwishin and that the tingle had nothing to do with her rhyming. After all, it shouldn't count as an accidental rhyme when she had read it off a piece of paper.

Ronnie closed her eyes, filled her lungs with a deep breath, and released it slowly.

She felt better already. Though she couldn't explain it, she was suddenly determined . . . and eager. Even the air around her felt different; it smelled different, too. And the pressure of the mattress beneath her faded until it no longer felt like a mattress at all.

Ronnie opened her eyes and was hit with a feeling of dizzying disorientation. She wasn't in her bunk anymore. She wasn't even in the cabin. She was in a library. And as if the sudden change in location wasn't unnerving enough, something else felt off. It was an out-of-body feeling, like she no longer fit quite right in her own arms and legs. Weirder still, she was standing, but could still feel herself sitting up in her bunk back at Sparrow's Nest.

Had she fallen asleep that quickly? This had to be a dream, but it felt like the most realistic virtual reality game ever, except that she couldn't control a thing. She was fully immersed in the body and mind of someone else, experiencing only what that person was doing, feeling, thinking, and sensing.

Standing in a small alcove in a library she had never seen before and trapped in a body that was clearly not her own, Ronnie should have gone into a full-blown panic by how awake—how *real*—everything felt. But she couldn't override the vision's feelings of determination and anticipation. They felt both like her own and not.

A middle-aged Korean woman appeared in the archway

connecting the alcove and the rest of the library. "Min-Young, Lia's waiting out in the gardens for you."

Min-Young? The gwishin?

"Okay, Mom." Ronnie heard herself respond, but in the voice of a teenager. "I'll be there in a sec."

Mom? That meant Ronnie was in Min-Young's head. Ronnie was somehow dreaming about the gwishin's past—something she knew nothing about. Min-Young fixed her gaze toward the large bay windows looking out onto a garden. It was the gardens on Rhee Estates, which meant she was in the library in the manor!

Ronnie caught the hint of her reflection in the glass. Though she couldn't make out details, on the surface, this Min-Young looked very different from the gwishin Ronnie had seen in the forest. Aside from the biggest difference (this girl was very much alive), she looked like a typical Korean American teenager in leggings and a sweatshirt with her hair pulled up into a thick, messy bun.

Min-Young turned her attention to the bookshelves, and Ronnie had no choice but to follow. Oddly, all the volumes were cookbooks, crammed in end to end, floor to ceiling. Cookbooks standing upright. Cookbooks stacked on their sides. Cookbooks stacked on their sides on top of cookbooks standing upright. Despite the obvious lack of space, jars containing roots, small vases of dried plants, and smooth stones were jammed into the stacks on every row.

Min-Young pulled book after book from the shelves and tossed them to the floor, clearly searching for something.

Ronnie read the titles as quickly as she could.

The Joy of Cooking for One. Reject.

Mastering the Roast. Drop.

French Cuisine. Chuck.

Gather Around: Indian Dining. Fling.

101 Air-Fryer Recipes. Dump.

Finally, Min-Young's relief flooded Ronnie's senses. Min-Young had found what she was looking for. She pulled a book to her chest like it was a hidden treasure map rather than a cookbook titled *Korean Comfort Foods.*

Ronnie strained for a better look at the book. She loved cooking with her dad every weekend and had once suggested that they try cooking Korean food. But he'd said Korean cuisine was too tricky because most Korean cooks didn't use recipes. They went on instinct, memory, and taste—things that come with experience, which neither Ronnie nor her dad had much of. He said it was easier to just go to their favorite Korean restaurant, and Ronnie had let the topic drop. Now she wished she had tried a little harder.

Just then, Ronnie felt a familiar press at the back of her tongue just before a rhyme slipped past her lips, "Reveal the spells within this book. For witch eyes only, let me look."

No. She must have misheard. But that wasn't possible because she hadn't just heard it, she'd *spoken* it—the rhyme and the word *witch.* And there was no denying the *tingle, tingle,* followed by a *crackle* and *fizz* that skated over her arms and legs.

This is a dream, Ronnie told herself. *The rhyming and the words don't mean anything.*

She opened the book to a page near the two-thirds mark and the paper transformed from the bright white pages of a contemporary cookbook to the off-white, yellow-edged paper of an antique first edition. Even stranger was the font, which didn't look like a font at all, but rather like handwritten calligraphy.

Ronnie caught the words *Hate to Love: A Curse to Cure* before Min-Young dog-eared the page and slammed the book shut. Again, the impulse to rhyme swelled before she muttered, "Magic potions, spells conceal. Keep it safe, do not reveal." She crammed the books she'd pulled out back onto the sagging shelves and ran out of a back door connecting the library alcove to the gardens.

Ronnie was momentarily blinded by the glaring sun. She blinked her eyes hard, and when she opened them again, the dream—if that was what it was—disappeared. She was back in her bunk—the mattress soft beneath her, Boo napping on her pillow, and the friendship bracelet hot against her skin.

TWELVE

THE SCARF OF SILENCE

The next morning, Ronnie tried to go to breakfast and act like she hadn't had a strangely vivid dream about the camp ghost's past. She tried instead to listen to Gigi talk about the latest camp curse, which involved Emma from Falcon's Nest. Apparently, she burned her tongue on scalding-hot water from her water bottle, which she swore she'd filled with cold water. The thing was, the cold-water knob and the hot-water knob were *right next* to each other. It was hard to care about what was probably a simple mistake.

What Ronnie *should* have been doing was keeping up with Jack and Olivia's arguments, because the next thing she knew, she was in the middle of a discussion about *butts*.

Olivia snapped her head to Ronnie. "So, I totally have a stronger butt than Jack because of ballet, right?"

"I—"

Jack shook his head. "Baseball players have the strongest butts and legs. Everyone knows ballerinas are super skinny and light so guys can lift them."

Olivia ground her teeth so ferociously, Ronnie's jaw ached. "Everyone knows ballerinas have a ton of *lean muscle*," Olivia growled. "And anyway, we're not comparing *professional* athletes here. At least not when it comes to *you*."

"Ronnie." Jack slapped a hand on the table. "You settle this. Who has the stronger butt?" He pointed one finger at his head and the other at his butt. Olivia kept her hands folded, but she stared intently at Ronnie mouthing, *Girl power*. Ronnie made the mistake of turning to Sam for help. He only made things worse by tapping that weird pen of his on the table like a ticking clock.

"Why do I have to be the judge?"

"Because," Jack said. "You know both of us better than we know each other."

Ronnie made a face. "Yeah, but I don't know your *butts*."

Olivia sprang to her feet. "Maybe a visual!"

Jack hopped up, too.

Quick as lightning, Ronnie picked up her tray to shield her eyes. Half-eaten toast and clumps of scrambled eggs tumbled onto the table. "That's a *hard* no. I'm not judging your *butts*. But if you both sit down, I'll give you the next scav hunt clue."

Ronnie peeked out from behind the tray. Seeing both Olivia and Jack back in their seats, she lowered the tray and pulled out the clue from her backpack. "'There's so much to cook in this cozy nook. To find the next clue, try vegetable stew.'"

"Stew?" Olivia cocked her head. "So that's the kitchen, right? Or the dining hall?"

"Maybe we have to wait until they serve us vegetable stew for the answer," Jack suggested.

Ronnie rolled the friendship bracelet between her fingers. "I think I have a better idea."

The group decided to split up. To Ronnie's immense satisfaction, Sam went with Benji and Gigi to search for the clue they got from Penny from Eagle's Nest. That left Olivia and Jack to join Ronnie in searching the manor.

This time, when they entered the foyer, Ms. Pavani greeted them at the front desk. She was a tall Indian woman with bright brown skin, large, wide-set eyes behind oversized wire-rimmed glasses, and long, wavy hair.

"Hello, campers! I'm Ms. Pavani," the woman said with a smile. "You must be here to view the gallery!"

"Well . . ." Ronnie started.

"There's a lot of history here," Ms. Pavani continued, her eyes sparkling with delight. "Haunting, yes, but there's so much more to the Rhees and their story. The albums contain photos of the family line going back generations, as well as newspaper clippings and even journal entries about their mysterious deaths." She sounded like a history audiobook.

"Actually," Jack said, shifting on his feet, "we're here to search the library for a scavenger hunt token."

"Oh." Ms. Pavani's smile dimmed. Even her glasses seemed to droop.

"Wait," Ronnie said. "Did you say photos?"

Ms. Pavani lit right back up. "Why, yes!" She nudged her spectacles up the bridge of her nose. "They're located on the table beneath the plaques."

Ronnie turned to the others. "Why don't you guys start

looking for the token? Search the alcove for a cookbook on vegetable stew. I'm going to check something out first."

Jack and Olivia made their way to the library while Ronnie headed for the gallery. There, she made a beeline for the photo albums. It didn't take her long to find teenage Min-Young. The photo was faded, but the similarities to the reflection Ronnie had seen in what she thought was a dream were undeniable. This picture was proof that what she had seen was the *real* Min-Young—the one who had lived and died on these very grounds.

Take me there, to when and where. A memory that's saved to share.

Ronnie sucked in a sharp breath and stood up so suddenly the album slipped from her hands and fell to the ground with a thud. She had read that rhyme aloud just before the dream. No, not a dream. A *memory*.

Mind reeling, Ronnie staggered out of the gallery and into the foyer. She was glad to find herself alone. She needed to think. She had to make sense of this. But it was impossible! Wasn't it?

Muffled laughter drifted out from behind the double doors leading to the library. Ronnie moved toward the sound. That was it—one way to know for sure. There were no pictures of the library inside the camp pamphlet and no mention of an alcove. There was no logical way she could have known about it before. So if there really *was* an alcove . . . If there really were bay windows with the same garden view . . . If there really was a wall of cookbooks . . . Ronnie rubbed her palms down her shorts before pulling open the door.

The library was the size of a large classroom at school, with leather chairs in its center. The surrounding walls loomed with overstuffed, floor-to-ceiling bookshelves. When she saw an arched opening to an alcove with bay windows looking out onto the gardens, Ronnie's skin hummed like mosquito wings. Her mouth went completely dry as she stepped inside and found herself standing on the exact spot Min-Young had stood in the memory. She couldn't deny it now. Not as her eyes flitted over the shelves overloaded with the same books, jars, vases, and stones she'd seen in the vision—just shuffled around a bit.

"Hey!" Olivia held a book in her hand. The title read *Korean Comfort Foods*. "Isn't it so weird that this entire room is just cookbooks? We're making a stack of all the ones we've checked."

Ronnie barely registered Olivia's voice. Everything—time, space, and sound—ceased to exist. Her disbelief hit an all-time low. It was all real—as real as the cookbook Olivia held in her hand. She handed it to Ronnie and returned to the shelves to pull down another book.

Holding her breath, Ronnie opened it to a random page.

It was a recipe for mujigae tteok next to a picture of the dessert rice cake with pastel green, yellow, pink, and white layers.

She turned the page, and then the next, and the next. There were no old-looking pages. No handwritten calligraphy. Nothing rhymed. Instead, they were filled with recipes with notes written in the margins. Things like *use soup soy sauce instead of salt* and *soak dried seaweed in water for thirty minutes before cooking* and *add radish to*

91

soup base in tidy handwriting. Ronnie wondered briefly if these notes would change her dad's mind about cooking Korean food.

"Found it!" Jack held up an envelope, shaking it in a victory dance.

Ronnie startled. "You did?" Still out of sync with the present, she thought he was referring to the page Min-Young had dog-eared in the memory, *Hate to Love: A Curse to Cure*.

But then Jack pulled out a scavenger hunt clue and read, "'Bring it level to your eye. Steady inhale, even sigh. Nice and easy with the pull. Follow through into the bull.'"

"That's obviously the clue for the tokens Penny found at archery," Olivia said as she accepted a token.

"Well, at least we got another token!" Jack tossed one to Ronnie, but it hit her arm and fell onto the floor. She was too distracted trying to remember what Min-Young had uttered in the memory. She had said a rhyme before opening the cookbook. Like a password. *Or a spell.*

Ronnie slammed shut *Korean Comfort Foods*. "Hey, why don't you guys take the tokens to the others? I'll put these away since you did all the work finding it."

"Cool!" Jack said with a grin. But Olivia shook her head.

"No way!" She grabbed the book from Ronnie. "We'll help and then go together."

Ronnie tugged the book out of Olivia's grasp. "No, really. I insist."

Jack rolled his eyes. "Don't bother," he said to Olivia. "She's super stubborn."

"*And* controlling," Olivia added.

"I am not—" Ronnie clamped her mouth shut and said through clenched teeth, "Fine, I like to do things my way."

Olivia grinned. "As long as you can admit it."

Ronnie crossed her arms with a huff. Watching them leave the library together laughing about *her* made her actually miss their fighting.

Alone, Ronnie sat on the floor among the piles of cookbooks and examined *Korean Comfort Foods*. There were no trick pages, no cutouts, no hidden pockets. As far as she could tell, there was nothing out of the ordinary about that book.

"Here goes nothing," she mumbled to herself. "Reveal the spells within this book. For witch eyes only, let me look?"

She opened the book. Nothing happened. Shutting the book, she tried again. But again, nothing happened. Her disappointment surprised her. It wasn't like she wanted any of this to be real. She didn't actually *want* to be a witch. She wanted to go back to the way things were. Before the gwishin. Before she started rhyming. Back to how things were supposed to be.

The library door opened, and someone walked in. Ronnie closed the book and quickly stuffed it into her backpack. It wasn't stealing—she was only borrowing it for a little while.

A moment later, Ms. Pavani stuck her head into the alcove. "Ronnie, are you finding everything you need here?"

"Yes, we found the scavenger hunt token." Ronnie followed Ms. Pavani's gaze down to the mess of books. "I'm just about to clean up." She picked up *A Soup for All Seasons* from the pile.

Ms. Pavani stepped into the alcove. "Let me help you—it'll be faster."

As Ronnie wedged the book into an open slot, she remembered the question she had been wanting to ask. "Ms. Pavani, do you know what that character means? The one on the plaque in the gallery."

"Those are Chinese characters, which are called hanja when they're adapted for Korean use." Ms. Pavani pushed herself up on tiptoes and tipped a book onto a high shelf.

Ronnie groaned. "That's what Sam said." She picked up another book and shoved it onto an open space on the shelf a little harder than she had intended.

"Well, Samuel would know," Ms. Pavani said with an affectionate smile as she wriggled a book onto a high shelf. "He's such a bright and thoughtful boy. The hanja in question represents the surname Rhee." She picked up another book before pausing to study Ronnie's face. "Why do you ask?"

Ronnie wiped the disbelief off her face and busied herself with another book. "Just curious, I guess." It didn't make much sense that she'd have a ring with someone's else's name on it. Unless the name Rhee had a meaning Ronnie didn't know of. And she was pretty sure all Korean last names had meanings. It'd be too embarrassing to ask an Indian person if she knew something about Korean names that Ronnie—an actual Korean—didn't. It was bad enough that Sam knew more than her about hanja. Maybe she could ask her dad. He could also confirm whether it was the same character on her ring.

Ms. Pavani nodded. "These grounds certainly bring out one's curiosity."

"Yeah, they do," Ronnie agreed. "Especially with that ghost story. Did anyone ever get close to figuring out how the Rhee women died?"

A shadow flickered over Ms. Pavani's face. "Well, no one knows for sure."

"But there are theories, right?" Ronnie squeezed *Candied Confection Creations* between *Beans, Beans, the Magical Fruit* and *The Capsicum Genus: A Chile Story*.

Ms. Pavani stopped shelving books and turned to face Ronnie. "Well, some say it was a coincidence of natural causes."

"No way," Ronnie said. "What about the red scarves? The ones they found around each of their necks?"

"Some do believe it was death by strangulation."

Ronnie shook her head. "There would be marks on their necks."

"Hmm." Ms. Pavani picked up a book and studied the title even though nothing was organized alphabetically. "Others point to poisoning. Perhaps the scarves were laced with something."

"The coroners would have found traces of toxins." Ronnie picked up another book, *Set Your Plate to a Second Date*. "Those are bad guesses."

"I suppose you're right." Ms. Pavani turned to Ronnie, lowering her voice to an eerie whisper. "There is one other theory. The Rhee family believed that cursed red scarves were the dokkaebi's weapon of choice."

The gwisin's warning flashed through Ronnie's mind. *A dokkaebi hunts you, little witch. You must beware the scarf of silence!* A shudder started at the back of Ronnie's head and rattled down to the base of her spine.

"How would you know if you were being hunted by a dokkaebi?" she whispered back.

Ms. Pavani pushed aside some books to open a space on the shelf and gestured at the book in Ronnie's hand. "I don't suppose you would know until you found a scarf wrapped around your neck. But by then, it'd be too late."

Ronnie slid the book into the open space. "Too late as in . . ."

"No one who ever wore the scarf lived to speak of it."

Ronnie's hands flew to her neck, which suddenly felt much too exposed.

THIRTEEN

TREASURE HUNT

Before Ronnie left the manor, Ms. Pavani had given her a stack of Camp Foster–themed postcards. Camp rules limited phone calls to emergencies only, so snail mail was Ronnie's only option for asking her dad about the baby ring.

Now she sat at her usual seat in the dining hall scrawling a note for her dad on the back of a postcard with a picture of the lake on the other side. She kept it short, asking him about the baby ring and reassuring him she was safe and having fun. She was going to leave it at that—just the positive things that she knew her dad would want to hear. But there was something about communicating with him by letter that made her feel bolder.

Before she could chicken out, she wrote something she would never have said to her dad to his face: *I'm not sure if the rhyming problem is getting better. What if it doesn't ever go away?* She wasn't sure what she wanted him to say. She just wanted to talk about it with someone and thought it might help her to stop feeling so bad.

Stuffing the postcard into her backpack to mail off later that day, she hopped to her feet to join her friends. They were huddled around a wooden storage trunk the size of a large shoebox. There had been one sitting open at the center of each table when everyone filed in for lunch.

Jack reached inside and scooped up a pile of plastic gold coins and rained them back down. "Coins—not scavenger hunt tokens."

Olivia held up a colorful beaded necklace pinched between two fingers. "Who knows where these have been," she said with a crinkled nose.

"What's this?" Ronnie asked as she reached for a bundle of burlap bags. Separating one from the rest, she smoothed it out on the table to reveal a picture of a parrot sporting a black eye patch.

"I think it's a treasure hunt!" Olivia cried out. "I be off to collect me loot!"

Jack tugged a burlap bag free and shook it out. "Aye, me faithful parrot!"

Olivia squeaked, dodging the bag. "Keep that away from me! Birds are creepy!"

"Even parrots? They can *speak*!"

"You don't see how that makes it *worse*?" Olivia shuddered from head to toe. "Their beady eyes . . . their pointy beaks . . . their taloned feet . . ."

The entire dining hall was abuzz with theories about what the treasure chests meant. By the end of lunch, half the campers were decked out in colorful bead necklaces and the other half were sneezing due to the burlap fibers.

At last, Robbie stormed into the dining hall wearing a pirate's costume—complete with a pirate's hat, eye patch, and hook—along with another counselor in a full-body parrot costume. A bunch of the campers hooted and hollered at the duo. Olivia released a horror-movie scream.

Parrot Suit spoke first. "I hope all ye landlubbers filled yer bellies to the gills, 'cause ye be needing yer energy for—"

Robbie provided a drumroll on his lap.

"A treasure—"

"Or painted rock," Robbie cut in.

"—hunt!"

The campers roared with excitement. Peace signs quieted the crowd, and Robbie continued. "The hunt takes place on the front lawn and courtyard. It will be played as a competition between cabins."

At the far end of the dining hall, Willa cupped her hands around her mouth. "Let's go *Spar-rows!*"

Someone shouted in response, "Eagle's Nest! Beats the rest!"

"Whoooooo's gonna win? Owls—hoot, hoot!"

"Cock-a-doodle-*ROO*-ster! Cock-a-doodle-*ROO*-ster!"

The peace signs took longer to take effect after that.

"To win," Robbie continued, "collect rocks!" He jabbed his hook into the air. "But not all rocks are created equal. Blue rocks—"

"Diamonds," Parrot Suit interrupted.

"Blue *diamonds*—are worth a whopping ten points, followed by red rubies worth three points, and lastly green emeralds at a sad, single point. The cabin with the most points will win a special surprise activity."

Parrot Suit cawed, and Olivia flinched. "All ye scalawags will agree it be worth yer while!"

Robbie held up his hook. "Oh, and one more thing. If one of us catches you, we get to take *all* yer loot." He smiled wickedly. "And the hunt begins—"

Parrot Suit flapped his massive wings and jerked his beaked head from side to side. *"Now."*

It was instant chaos.

Kids snatched up burlap bags and ran for the door.

Kids ran for the door without bags, only to turn around and run back to their table, colliding with kids running for the door.

Kids shouted orders at other kids in their cabin to go for only blue rocks because they were worth the most. Others thought the blue ones would be too rare and so a waste of time. Still others planned to grab rocks indiscriminately.

Olivia practically vibrated as she tugged on Ronnie's arm. "Come on! Let's go!"

"But we need a plan," Ronnie yelled out over the commotion as she ran to keep up with Olivia.

"How about, get as many rocks as you can?" Olivia expertly dodged a kid who abruptly dropped in front of them to pick up a rock—all without breaking stride.

"Follow me." Ronnie surged ahead, leading Olivia out of the crowded courtyard and onto the quiet front lawn. "The ratio of kids to rocks in the courtyard is probably not in our favor. Plus, I'm estimating the likelihood of finding a blue rock without fighting someone else for it somewhere around fifteen percent. Meanwhile, we'd be losing out on all the red and green rocks, which there are probably a

ton more of. And we don't have as much competition out
here." Ronnie grinned as she pointedly glanced around the
relatively empty lawn.

Olivia beamed at her. "I knew your controlling and over-
analytical mind would come in handy!"

"Thanks!" Ronnie's grin twitched. "Wait—my what?"

But Olivia had already run off to the left side, leaving Ronnie to search the right. At first, she meticulously
scoured every inch of ground, pushing aside the tall grass
and checking every stone in the stacks that littered the
grounds. But when she heard the voices of other campers
making their way over, she opted for speed over accuracy.
If she covered enough ground first, she was bound to find
at least one—

"Argh!" Ronnie pulled her foot back from whatever it was
she had stubbed her toe on. She should have worn tennis
shoes instead of flip-flops. Glancing down, she picked up
the offender—a blue painted rock. Although she wouldn't
exactly say the pain was worth the find, she placed the rock
into her bag.

"Ronnie! Run!" Olivia called to her from behind.

Ronnie glanced over her shoulder to find Parrot Suit
gunning for her. Maybe it was his unexpected speed and
agility. Maybe it was his gaping, pointy beak. Or maybe
those unblinking, beady black eyes had taken on a menacing quality. But Ronnie suddenly understood how a large
bird costume could be absolutely terrifying. Plus, there was
something about being chased that made her feel like she
was going to *die*.

Spinning around, she ran in the opposite direction—away

from the camp buildings, across the lawn, and past the manor. She *really* should have gone with tennis shoes that morning.

When she dared to peek back, she saw Parrot Suit on her tail and drawing closer. She pressed forward, but she was quickly nearing the edge of the lawn. The scent of fresh pine wafting from the looming forest stung her nostrils. She was done for. This was the end. That feathered monstrosity was going to chomp on her like she was an overgrown worm!

But then a flash of unexpected color cut through her panic-induced visions of being stabbed by the pointed tip of a gigantic beak. It was another blue rock just beyond the tree line. It must have been kicked in there by accident. But there was no point in collecting blue rocks now. It was too late. She was caught. With nowhere left to run, she came to a halt and turned to face her defeat.

Panting, she thrust her bag out toward Parrot Suit. "Here. Take it!"

But instead of grabbing the bag, Parrot Suit stood just an arm's reach away. With taloned feet planted, his costumed face looked just past her. He must have seen the blue rock, too.

"Just take it all!" Ronnie called out to him. But he didn't say a word as he continued to stare. She was about to offer to grab the rock for him when he suddenly shook his head around like a dog after a bath. Then he pivoted and ran off after another girl trying to sneak past them.

Ronnie slumped with exhaustion from running for her life. Wiping sweat from her forehead, she slipped into the forest—just enough to duck under the shade, where it was nice and cool. And since she was there, she figured she might as well grab the blue rock. It was only a few steps away.

But when she bent down to pick up the rock, she spied a glint of red deeper in the forest. Another painted rock? She squinted into the distance, but her view was obstructed by some brush. Tossing the blue rock into her bag, she straightened and stepped closer. She had already entered the forest—what was a few more steps?

Having closed half the distance, she could see it was a few red rocks piled together at the base of a tree. They might not be worth as much as blues, but four reds were worth more than a single blue. Ronnie shot a nervous glance over her shoulder as Ms. Hana's rule about the woods rang sharp between her ears. But these rocks were planted here, so they were clearly meant to be found. And she'd be quick about it.

Ronnie had nearly reached the rocks when a vicious snarl made her jump back.

Boo loped toward her with wide, feral eyes and puffed-up fur. Ronnie was once again struck by the instinct to run for her life. But as he neared, she realized he wasn't after her; he was after the rocks.

"They're just rocks, Boo," she called out.

But when she pushed the brush aside, she realized she had been wrong. There were no rocks. There was only Boo attacking a red scarf entangled in his mouth and sharp claws.

And the scarf *fought back*. It thrashed around with a life

of its own. Ronnie blanched, recognizing the scarf. It was identical to the one around the gwishin's neck. But this one didn't drape or ripple like a gentle river. It coiled and struck like a very hungry, very angry cobra.

One end of the scarf tore free of Boo's claws and shot out toward Ronnie like an arrow released from a bow. The other end was still firmly in Boo's grasp, and the scarf snapped taut just inches from Ronnie's throat.

Dropping the bag of rocks, Ronnie staggered back. Her throat closed up, cutting off her scream. The scarf hadn't touched her, but she couldn't make a sound. She wanted to turn and run, but her legs were as stiff and wooden as the trees that surrounded her, isolating her from the rest of camp. Meanwhile, the gwishin's warning echoed in her mind: *A dokkaebi hunts you, little witch. . . . You must beware the scarf of silence!*

"Ronnie!" Two hands grabbed her from behind.

Ronnie's heart, which had stopped cold, began to beat again when she recognized Olivia's voice. She whirled around and choked out, "What are you doing in here?"

Olivia's eyes looked more feral than Boo's had.

Boo!

But when Ronnie looked back, he was gone. Along with the scarf.

"What are *you* doing?" Olivia hissed.

"I, um, found a rock in here!" Ronnie picked up her bag and showed Olivia the two blue rocks still nestled inside.

Olivia's shoulders relaxed slightly at the sight of the rocks. "Why was it in here?"

To lure me in, Ronnie thought. "Must have gotten kicked in by accident."

Olivia grabbed her by the arm and began pulling. "Well, that's no excuse to break the rules! Let's get out of here before Ms. Hana sees us."

Ronnie didn't need Olivia to tell her twice. She ran out of the forest as fast as she had run toward it. Only this time, her life really was in danger.

The gwishin was right.

Ronnie was being hunted by a dokkaebi.

FOURTEEN
STARS

Parrot Suit took the stage in the courtyard to announce Sparrow's Nest as the winning team. It turned out Ronnie had found two of only four planted blue rocks. Olivia joined the rest of their cabinmates in jumping up and down while shouting, "Let's go, *Spar-rows*!" It took Ronnie a little longer to shake off what she'd seen in the forest. It didn't help that Parrot Suit's eyes seemed to follow her no matter where she moved. A shudder shook her shoulders. Parrots—and all large birds in general—would forever haunt her nightmares.

The prize for winning the treasure hunt was stargazing on the lake after lights-out. But as Ronnie and her cabinmates followed Willa out into the pitch-black with only a single lantern, she couldn't help but wonder how this was in any way a win. To make matters worse, Willa decided the eerie walk to the lake was a good opportunity to do a trust exercise. So Ronnie fell into line, closed her eyes, and held the hands of the kids in front of her and behind her.

Usually, Ronnie had no problem with the dark. But after being chased by Parrot Suit and that run-in with the scarf, she found herself peeking through her lashes during the whole exercise.

"Does it have to be so dark?" Olivia asked once they'd arrived at the lake. She gave a shaky laugh to cover up her fear, but by the sound of everyone else's forced laughs, she wasn't the only one who was afraid.

"I know it's super dark," Willa said. "But you'll be glad for it once we get out on the water."

Ronnie climbed into the back seat of a double kayak behind Olivia and paddled out to the middle of the lake. Her nerves frazzled, she jumped and startled each time the kayak rocked or a breeze blew past her neck—cold and silky. Whispers in the air curled warnings against one ear and bid her closer in the other.

Willa situated the group so they formed a linked circle. "Now I'm going to turn off my lantern, and I want everyone to look up into the sky."

Once the lantern was off, Ronnie couldn't see her own hand in front of her. At first. Then, slowly but surely, the stars above grew big and bright as her eyes adjusted. A hush fell over the group, and Ronnie's racing pulse steadied.

She had never seen stars like this before in all her life. They were the size of softballs. In that moment, she could understand why people wished upon them. It was such a one percent thing to do, but when they glimmered like this, it was easier to believe in magic.

"Didn't I tell you guys it'd be worth it?" Willa asked. There was a murmur of agreement among the campers, their heads tilted back and their eyes fixed on the radiant night sky.

"How about we go around and share one thing that's been hard about being here at camp and one thing that's been good. I'll start. It's been hard to be away from my dog, Beans, because he's been my best friend since I was ten and this is my last summer at home with him. I'm going to college next year, and I'll be living in a dorm. I'm really going to miss him."

This was exactly why Ronnie didn't want a pet.

"There are so many good things about being here this summer," Willa continued. "It's hard to choose, but if I have to pick one thing . . . I guess it'd be that because this is my last summer at Camp Foster, I've decided to make it the best and I'm really soaking up everything I love about this camp. I guess that technically wasn't *one* thing." Willa laughed. "Who wants to go next?"

"I can go," Olivia called out from up front, her voice shy. "Something that's been hard is I miss ballet. I can't remember the last time I didn't have class or lessons or rehearsals every single day. I thought I'd feel free. And there's some of that. But I also feel like a big part of *me* is missing. I guess I didn't expect that."

Ronnie could definitely relate. This was why she was such a stickler for routines—you always knew what you were going to get.

Olivia shifted in her seat, rocking the kayak back and forth. "One thing that's going well at camp is making friends and getting to hang out all day every day!" She turned back to Ronnie with such a genuine, open smile that Ronnie couldn't help but return it. It felt kind of like one of those unspoken agreements between her and Jack—neither had said a word to one another, but they both understood that they were *friend* friends now and not just camp friends.

As everyone took turns speaking, Ronnie gazed up at the stars. She was determined to hold on to this moment of peace. This slice of time where nothing else mattered but the glow of the stars.

Besides, she had nothing to say. Well, at least not anything anyone would understand—not even Olivia, who Ronnie *wanted* to tell. It would be such a relief to talk about the secrets she'd been keeping. Maybe it would feel like closing her eyes, letting go, and falling back.

But how could she expect anyone to catch her with all the baggage she carried? How could she even begin to explain the weight of it all? Like how she was here at camp because she couldn't stop herself from rhyming. Or how she was glad Olivia was her friend but also worried about how to be a *friend* friend to Olivia when she was already struggling to be the kind of kid her dad needed and the very best friend Jack wanted. Losing her mom had taught Ronnie you can't hold on to everything and everyone all at once—so you had to choose. And she only had two hands.

Or how about the fact she was being haunted by a gwishin—for real. Or that she just found out dokkaebi were also real and one wanted to silence her—and not with a peace sign.

No, she couldn't tell anyone. Not Jack. Not her dad. And definitely not Olivia. She needed them now more than ever, and her problems would only push them away.

"Thank you to those who shared tonight," Willa said gently. "For those who weren't ready to share, I want you to know that's okay. But you should also know your cabin-mates are here for you. You don't have to do anything alone."

Willa was right. Ronnie needed answers. She needed help. Lucky for her, she wasn't alone. She had the gwishin.

FIFTEEN
LIVE BAIT

The next day, Ronnie was on a mission to get herself out of not one but *two* life-threatening situations with a single plan that involved a little white lie, her best acting, and the cookbook she'd borrowed from the library.

Threat of death number one: the ropes course. Having reluctantly graduated from the low ropes course, Ronnie was moved along to the midlevel challenges, which involved various nets and wobbly wood-plank bridges to cross. When she and Olivia reached the front of the line to cross a tightrope suspended thirty feet in the air, Ronnie decided it was time to put on a show. Bending over, she grabbed her stomach and released a pained moan.

Olivia turned to her. "What's wrong?"

Ronnie twisted her face into a grimace. "Stomach. Hurts. Bad."

"This is why breakfast burritos are never a good idea! I'm going to find Willa."

For a fleeting moment, Ronnie was proud of her performance for getting such an immediate reaction from Olivia. But then she realized Olivia's response probably had less to do with Ronnie's acting and more to do with Olivia being a good friend.

"Can you make it down the rope ladder?" Olivia asked when she returned. "I'm going to walk you to the nurse's station."

Ronnie nodded and gingerly made her way down. Once on the ground, she grabbed her backpack, which she wasn't allowed to carry with her on the course. "You should stay here and do the course. I can make it to the nurse's by myself."

Olivia gave a firm shake of her head. "You're not carrying this when you're in pain."

"Thanks, but I'm fine. Really. I got it." Ronnie tugged. Olivia had been really excited to get to the midlevel course, and Ronnie didn't want her to miss it for a fake stomachache.

Olivia tugged back, her lips pressed into a hard line. "I insist."

Ronnie tugged even harder, pulling Olivia forward. "But this bag totally clashes with your top, don't you think?"

Olivia glanced down at her bright pink blouse with black trim and then at the olive-green backpack. She bit down on her lip as if it pained her to witness the two in proximity. With a small victory smile, Ronnie pulled the backpack onto her shoulder.

But Olivia's protective instincts must have won over her fashion sense because she snatched the backpack off Ronnie's shoulder and slung it over her own.

"I can pull it off," Olivia said, her nose in the air. "Besides, you're sick."

That was right. Ronnie had almost forgotten. Scrunching

up her face into a miserable grimace and clutching at her gut, she allowed Olivia to take the backpack and the lead.

Once they arrived at the front of Rhee manor, Ronnie straightened and made a grab for her backpack. But Olivia was too fast, and she pivoted out of reach. "Why are you so obsessed with the backpack?" she asked. "Can you just let me help you?"

"Olivia, I'm not sick."

"Really? Let's go back to the course, then." But before Olivia could turn around, Ronnie grabbed her arm.

"Actually, I'm not going back."

Olivia frowned. "You still want to go to the nurse?" Then her mouth formed a small O, and she winked. "You need to use the bathroom, huh? I get it. More privacy in the manor than the cabins."

"No, I don't need to poop."

Olivia's eyes bulged. "Oh. Em. Gee. Ronnie. Just call it number two already!" She reached for the door, and Ronnie stepped in the way.

"Wait." Ronnie pressed her back to the door. "I can't go in there."

Olivia gave her a quizzical look. "So, if you're not going back to the ropes course and you're not going to the nurse's . . . where will you be instead?"

"I just need to go do something." Ronnie's mouth pinched to one side. "And I can't tell you what."

"But—"

"Please, Olivia," Ronnie pleaded, her hands clasped together.

Olivia groaned. "I hate breaking the rules!"

"That's why I owe you big." Ronnie did her best puppy-dog eyes. "Pleeeeease? Sneaking around is all part of the camp experience! We're making a memory here!"

Olivia bit down on her lip. "Something *friends* do for each other, right?"

Ronnie suddenly felt queasy. It felt wrong to use the friendship angle to get Olivia to agree, but she had no choice. This was literally a life-and-death situation. Ignoring the roiling in her gut, Ronnie nodded. "All the time."

"And I guess it's not that different from when my sisters and I cover for each other with our parents."

Ronnie's face split into a relieved smile. "Exactly!"

"And you'll tell me everything later?"

"Of course!" Ronnie eyed her backpack, which was still on Olivia's back. "Oh, and I'll need—"

"OMG, here's your precious giant backpack." Olivia shrugged it off, and Ronnie took her *average*-sized backpack gratefully. It made sense that regular-sized backpacks looked huge to Olivia next to her mini non-backpacks.

When Olivia was no longer in sight, Ronnie jogged over to the nearby tree line. She stopped just short of stepping off the grass lawn and onto the dirt forest floor. She stood there, the sun hot on her back, unsure if she wanted to find the gwishin—not even close to a manageable eighty percent sure. She was at most at seventy-two percent on the certainty meter.

But it was now or never. She needed Min-Young's help if she was going to survive threat of death number two: the dokkaebi.

Ronnie marched into the forest several paces, cleared

her throat, and then said nothing. She didn't know how to call upon a gwishin. Maybe there was a ritual or a special summoning chant. She knew neither.

"Min-Young?" she tried. "Are you there?" She was met with silence. "I'm sorry I ran away last time. I won't do that again. I brought a peace offering—the cookbook you were looking for when you were, um, alive." She wasn't sure if it was bad manners or not to bring attention to the fact that a gwishin was dead. "I saw your memory of it, and it seemed important to you."

A warm breeze swept over Ronnie and tousled her hair. The gwishin stepped out, the red scarf around her neck swaying gently. Now that Ronnie knew it wasn't blood, it was kind of pretty. In fact, she wouldn't mind focusing her gaze on that rather than the gwishin's face.

"Hello," Min-Young breathed.

Ronnie gulped and forced herself to look up. *It's just a little eye contact*, she reminded herself. *You do it with adults all the time. So what if this one happens to be dead?*

"So, you know my name," Min-Young said, "but I don't know yours." Her hands went to her scarf, running the length of it through her fingers tenderly and repeatedly, as though it soothed her.

"I'm Ronnie." She looked into the gwishin's eyes, flinched, and then focused on the side of the gwishin's head instead. "But if you don't know who I am, then why are you haunting me?"

"I'm *not* haunting you, Ronnie. But I suppose I have been watching you." Min-Young stepped closer, and the movement caused the hair draped across her face to brush aside.

Ronnie's stomach lurched at the sudden appearance of an entire half of the gwishin's face. No matter how many times Ronnie saw it, there was no getting used to her ghoulish eyes, the grayish tint in her cheeks, or those bloodstained lips. "I believe we can help one another."

"Why me?" Ronnie held her breath, expecting an answer she wasn't sure she was ready to hear.

A line formed between Min-Young's brows. "Because you're a witch, Ronnie."

Ronnie shook her head, a crooked smile of disbelief on her face. "Witches are old. I'm only twelve. I don't own a broom—I just vacuum. And I'm not even a little superstitious. Show me a ladder and I'll walk under it!"

"Come now, Ronnie. You can't determine a person's identity from their looks alone or checking off a few boxes."

"But . . . you're a gwishin, and you definitely *look* like a gwishin."

"And you look Korean, but is that all you are?"

Ronnie's eyes snapped to the gwishin's in surprise. No one had ever assumed she was *too* Korean. Rather, it seemed she was never Korean enough. "No. I'm hardly Korean at all."

The gwishin frowned. "What do you mean, 'hardly Korean'?"

"I mean I don't have a Korean-sounding name. I've never even been to Korea, and I can't speak the language much at all." She dropped her gaze, embarrassed to admit her shortcomings.

"Hats and brooms don't make a witch, and those things

you listed aren't what makes a person Korean. Being Korean is in your blood and soul. And so is being a witch."

Ronnie's spirits lifted at being told she was enough just as she was, even without speaking Korean like Jack or possessing his vast knowledge of Korean lore. Her Korean heritage was in her blood.

Just like being a witch.

Her spirits deflated like a popped floatie.

The gwishin peered at Ronnie with those dark, dark eyes. "In fact, your witch instinct should be kicking in with a vengeance at this point. Have you been rhyming when you're emotional?"

Yes.

"Have mosquitoes been particularly attracted to your blood?"

Ronnie's hand instinctively found the bite on her neck.

"There's also the energy exchange—heat or tingle or simply a gut feeling—upon contact with or nearness to magical objects. They're all over these grounds."

Déjà-vu.

"No," Ronnie whispered. "No, no, no. I have enough problems. I can't be a witch, too!"

The gwishin hesitated briefly at Ronnie's reaction, then drifted closer. "I'm afraid it's not a choice." A light wind swirled dead leaves and pine needles beneath the gwishin's toes. "The magic has always been in your blood. It just didn't activate until you turned twelve."

"That was when my rhyming started." Ronnie groaned. "When *all* the problems started."

Min-Young tipped her head to one side. It was probably just a response to thinking, but with a gwishin's face, she looked like she was contemplating how best to draw out Ronnie's most tortured scream. "Rhyming was a problem?"

"It's not normal for a twelve-year-old to speak in rhyme uncontrollably."

"Hmm," Min-Young said, sounding unconvinced. "You'll be happy to hear that the compulsion will fade."

Ronnie felt a glimmer of hope. "It will?"

"As you gain control of your witch magic, you will be able to control the impulse to rhyme."

"I don't want to get *better* at being a witch. I don't want to be a witch at all! I want to be *normal*. I just want everything to go back to how it used to be and forget any of this happened—"

Min-Young swooped in close—so close Ronnie could see tiny cracks in the bruised skin beneath her recessed eyes. "Memories are sacred!" Her windy voice was a scream that fractured like broken glass.

Ronnie recoiled. "I—I'm sorry."

Min-Young swept back. "No, I'm the one who's sorry, Ronnie. As a gwishin, I've lost most of the memories of my life, and I would do anything to get them back . . . anything." She dropped her head between her hands like she was trying to hold memories inside by force. "So as you can imagine, I can be quite passionate about them."

Ronnie tucked her hair nervously behind her ear, feeling compelled once more to offer comfort. "I bet you're glad to be rid of some memories, right? Like the bad ones?"

Min-Young's head snapped up, her scarlet lips pulled into

a small smile. It looked downright menacing. Gooseflesh flashed along Ronnie's arms. But she was starting to understand that the gwishin wasn't at all how she appeared.

"There are few memories so bad that I would not want them," Min-Young replied. "In fact, some of the worst ones are inexplicably tied to some of the very best. You cannot have one without the other, Ronnie, and I would have it no other way." Min-Young blinked, and Ronnie realized that it was the first time she had done so. "Speaking of memories, you said you have my cookbook?"

"Um—yes. *Korean Comfort Foods*?"

The gwishin's face brightened. Okay, maybe *brightened* was a stretch, but she did look slightly less wan. "I didn't know what was in the memory. I can't access the Rememberings without witch magic, and I lost that when I died. But clearly some magic lingers, because my spirit knew that specific Remembering was important—which was why I had Boojuk deliver it to you."

Ronnie tugged her backpack to her front and pulled out the book. "You know Boojuk?"

"He was my familiar. He hasn't forgotten me, nor will he allow me to forget him." Min-Young gestured toward the book, and the pages rippled. "Go ahead and crack it open."

"Are you hungry?" Ronnie asked.

"Hmm? No, I don't eat, though I do miss it sometimes," Min-Young answered distractedly. "Why do you ask?"

"It's a cookbook?"

"Oh, but it is so much more," she breathed. "It's also a grimoire, a textbook of magic. But you'll need a spell to bring that out."

Ronnie flipped through a few pages of recipes. "It looks just like a real cookbook."

"They're all real cookbooks. In fact, all cookbooks hide grimoires within them. They give the best cover if we're ever caught in the midst of spelling or brewing."

"*All* cookbooks? Even the ones at my house?" Ronnie and her dad actually *used* cookbooks at home, which meant she had spells and potions in her possession without ever knowing it! "How do you know which book will have what you're looking for?"

"Witch instinct—arguably the most magical thing about being a witch." Min-Young rose and clasped her hands before her. "Now, to reveal the grimoire in this cookbook, you will use the standard spell. Reveal the spells within this book. For witch eyes only, let me look." She nodded at Ronnie. "Go ahead and give it a try."

Ronnie shook her head. "I—I can't. I don't know how."

Min-Young threw her head back and let out a laugh that reminded Ronnie of wind chimes. It was so pretty she could almost forget about the black pit eyes, sanguine lips, and cadaverous skin. Almost. "Don't be silly, Ronnie. Of course you can. How do you think you got into my memory?"

Ronnie thought back to when she had put on the friendship bracelet. She hadn't seen the memory right away. She had read a couple of lines of rhyme. *Take me there, to when and where. A memory that's saved to share.*

Ronnie's mouth dropped open. She had cast a spell without even realizing it.

"It's possible you've cast quite a few spells without your knowing," Min-Young said, confirming Ronnie's thoughts.

"Now, go on." She gestured with her gaunt hands, causing the wind to blow gently over Ronnie's face and ruffle her hair.

Ronnie cleared her throat. "Reveal the spells within this book. For witch eyes only, let me look?"

Nothing happened.

"Don't ask. *Demand*."

Ronnie drew in a deep breath. "Reveal the spells within this book. For witch eyes only, let me look!"

A tingle started at the top of her head and trickled down to the tips of her fingers and toes. It lingered there, the sensation crackling and fizzing. And when the words on the page began to wiggle and move about in a fluid dance, Ronnie nearly dropped the book.

The letters spelling out *Samgyetang* rearranged themselves until they read *Rememberings* in calligraphy. Then, slowly but surely, the page yellowed and aged right before Ronnie's eyes.

There was no denying it now—not when she was seeing it with her own eyes and touching it with her own hands. This was magic. Magic that came from her own mouth.

"I'm a *witch*," Ronnie whispered.

"Now, be sure to always conceal the grimoire when you're done with it." Min-Young cleared her throat. "Magic potions, spells conceal. Keep it safe. Do not reveal."

Ronnie repeated the spell. This time, it worked on the first try.

"It's a good start. Now, if you want to become a proficient witch, you'll need to begin with the basics," Min-Young said decisively as she began to hover-pace. "In the library alcove, you'll find a cookbook, *Essential Oils in Cooking.* The grimoire within it contains many basic lessons and spells, as well as protective measures against witch-hunting dokkaebi." A wistful note entered her voice. "It's one I referred to many times as a young witch."

"You sound like you miss it."

Min-Young released a mournful sigh that rustled the nearby branches. "Oh, I do. I miss it sorely. I miss a life I can hardly remember."

"Don't you think it might be easier to just forget it all?" Ronnie braced for Min-Young's "passion about memories" to burst forth, but when it didn't, she continued. "If you don't remember at all, then you would have nothing to be sad about."

Min-Young looked at Ronnie for a moment. She seemed to be considering her next words carefully. "You are right that this causes me great pain. But that pain is a measure of how much I had lived and loved. Without that, I am nothing but a gwishin, trapped in a world I have forgotten."

Ronnie marveled at how differently Min-Young thought from her dad. Maybe it was a gwishin thing to be so open and accepting of sadness and pain. To appreciate it, even. Oddly, it was exactly this quality about Min-Young that made her less scary and more human. And it was this that convinced Ronnie that Min-Young was so much more than some ghost story.

Min-Young's expression darkened. "The moment I became a gwishin, I began losing memories of my life— including the identity of the dokkaebi that silenced me with this scarf." She hooked the fingers of both ghastly hands around the scarf that encircled her gaunt neck. Ronnie thought Min-Young might tug at it, but she merely gripped it. "I believe it is this scarf and the dokkaebi magic it contains that tether me to this forest. So, it follows that the dokkaebi who murdered me is the only one who can release me—by his own will or his banishment. Once the magic in the scarf is gone, I'll have my memories back. I'll be free." Releasing the scarf, she fanned her hands out to Ronnie. "That's where you come in."

Ronnie shook her head. "But I don't see how I'm supposed to find a dokkaebi."

Min-Young pinned Ronnie with her fathomless eyes. "That is just the thing, Ronnie. I have not seen a dokkaebi on these grounds since I became a gwishin. It's almost as though dokkaebi avoid coming here. But shortly after your arrival, I saw another scarf of silence dart through the woods. When I moved toward it, my own scarf began to jump and jerk like a poorly strung marionette. The movements were weak and disjointed, but it was the first time my scarf moved without the force of my wind. At first, I wondered if I had imagined it all, but then I saw yet another scarf and felt the tug from its owner a second time. And that was the time you nearly jumped out the bathroom window right into its trap. That's how I know you are a witch. That's how I know you *don't* have to find him. He'll find you."

Ronnie released a strangled cry, a hand flying over her mouth. She had forgotten all about the bathroom door incident. "That was a trap?" she choked out. "But what would a dokkaebi want with me?"

"Only your eternal and irrevocable *silence.* Witches are immune to dokkaebi Persuasions, so they'd like nothing more than to be rid of us all. But I can teach you spells for protection. And for fighting back." Min-Young pushed forward, the black of her eyes intensifying against the sallowness of her skin. "Listen, Ronnie. We can help one another. Because if I'm right, then the dokkaebi hunting you is the same one who silenced me."

Understanding struck Ronnie like a belly flop on the lake. Min-Young wanted to use her as live bait.

SIXTEEN

GRIMOIRE

That night, Ronnie waited for the girls of Sparrow's Nest to fall asleep. When the sounds of breathing evened out, she wiggled deep into her sleeping bag, where she'd stashed a flashlight and *Essential Oils in Cooking*, which she'd borrowed from the library after leaving Min-Young's clearing.

"Reveal the spells within this book," she whispered. *"For witch eyes only, let me look."*

Tingle, tingle, crackle, fizz. The now-familiar sensation ran through her like sparklers.

While the cookbook was about fifty pages long, the grimoire was more than three hundred. Ronnie flipped the yellowed pages until a heading caught her eye:

FOUR COMMON MAGICAL HOSTS

Witch Blood Magic: Temporary once it leaves the body of the witch in the form of spoken spells. Lasts as long as short-term memory. Can be extended when transferred to a stable host via spoken spells.

String Magic: Connects two magical hosts. Ideal for psychic exploration of unknown magical objects. Wears down over time—duration varies depending upon the quality of the string and the connected hosts. Effect dependent upon witch instinct.

Tree Magic: Ancient, powerful magic. Hosts layers upon layers of Witch Blood Magic by absorption of spoken spells. Also fortifies spoken spells. As such, magic is often carried out in the presence of trees. However, Tree Magic is unpredictable due to the passive nature of both absorption and release of magic within the environment.

Everlasting Magic: The oldest and most enduring magic on earth. Found in both known and unknown objects all over the world; everlasting hosts contain an eternal magic with no time limits so long as the hosts themselves remain intact. (See: "Cookbooks and Other Common Everlasting Hosts" in *So You're Makin' Steak 'n Bacon*)

Ronnie flipped through the grimoire, stopping on spells that caught her attention. There was one for invisibility: *Out of sight, but I'm still here, hold my breath and disappear.* According to the grimoire, if she recited the spell, she would remain invisible as long as she held her breath.

Another was levitation. It required a potion made with

stiff whipped egg whites and powdered dragonfly wings as the main ingredients. There was a warning about the potion staining porous surfaces. That seemed like a small price to pay to levitate.

She fell asleep that night and dreamed she was floating up in the treetops with Min-Young. When she spotted her dad on the ground, she swooped down before him and waved her hands in front of his face. But her hands were invisible, just like the rest of her, and he looked right through her.

🌲🌲🌲

The next morning, Ronnie ducked out of breakfast with *Essential Oils in Cooking* tucked away in her backpack. She plopped down onto a log bench in the courtyard and pulled out the cookbook. Feeling conspicuous, she glanced all around her. But Min-Young was right. Cookbooks really *were* the best cover. They were perfectly normal for someone to study carefully, but also too uninteresting to ask much about. No one gave Ronnie or the book a second glance.

With the book on her lap, she recited the spell under her breath. *"Reveal the spells within this book. For witch eyes only, let me look."*

Tingle, tingle, crackle, fizz.

This time, Ronnie went straight for the section on banishments.

HOW TO BANISH A DOKKAEBI IN TWO STEPS

A Basic Overview

Dokkaebi banishments are arduous affairs not many witches live to boast of performing. The Rhee witches completed the highest number of successful banishments: They fully banished five different dokkaebi and partially banished one dokkaebi a total of nine times before the last Rhee witch was silenced. (For complete history, see "A Complete History of the War Against" Dokkaebi in *Grandma's Secret Recipes*.)

Partial banishments are most common but are also the costliest for witches and their human allies. Because partial banishment by spell casting requires (at minimum) three skilled witches in close proximity to the targeted dokkaebi, there is a high risk of silencing. (For banishment spells, see "Advanced Attacks for the Advanced Witch" in *Finger-Licking Finger Foods*.)

Dokkaebi may also be banished by human wrestling. In these cases, losing a match to a dokkaebi almost always results in the loss of the human's memories. (For tips on how to successfully wrestle a dokkaebi to submission, see "So You're Training to Wrestle a Dokkaebi" in *Edible Art with Fondant*.)

When a dokkaebi is successfully banished, he loses his human form, and his spirit is forced back into his touchstone for safekeeping until he can return to full human force. This can take, on average, four to seven years. As such, it is in the dokkaebi's best interest to keep his touchstone well hidden. (For more on everlasting magic, see "Four Common Magical Hosts" in this grimoire, *Essential Oils in Cooking*. For more on touchstones, see "Touchstones and Tethers" in *Paleo Please and Thank You.*)

"There she is!"

Across the courtyard, Olivia waved her arms as she strode toward Ronnie, Jack and Sam in tow. Slamming the grimoire shut, Ronnie muttered the concealing spell. She jumped up at the *tingle, tingle, crackle, fizz*—frantic her friends would pick up on it. But unlike her rhymes, there was nothing to give her away. She shoved the cookbook into her backpack.

Olivia stopped before Ronnie, grinning triumphantly. "I told you she'd wait for us." Lifting her chin, she peered at Jack from the corner of her eye.

Ronnie stood up and hefted her backpack over her shoulders. "Why wouldn't I?"

"Jack was saying that you're so checked out of camp that you'll probably find a way to get out of swim like you did with the ropes course and the scavenger hunt and stuff."

Ronnie flinched. Had she been acting checked out? She wanted to defend herself and explain that if she was trying to get out of anything, it was being haunted by a gwishin, being a witch, and being targeted by a murderous dokkaebi. But how could she explain that? So she bit her tongue.

"But *I* said that you wouldn't flake out on swim," Olivia continued. "It was one of the activities you were most excited about, right?"

Ronnie nodded, her lips pressed tightly together to prevent any confessions, especially rhyming ones.

"So I was right!"

Jack scowled. "*Technically,* she only waited for us halfway." He gestured to the distance between their location in the courtyard and the pools.

"So," Sam said loudly, interrupting what would have probably turned into an argument about the definition of halfway. "Who's excited to go swimming?" He waved Olivia and Jack along, as if Ronnie wasn't there.

She trailed behind them, for once not minding being left out by Sam. If he wanted to deal with Olivia and Jack's fighting, he could be her guest. Ronnie tuned them out, and her thoughts slipped back to dokkaebi banishment. But a flutter of white in the treetops jolted her back to the present.

It was Min-Young, hovering among the trees again. Slowing to a crawl, Ronnie gave a tiny wave, but Min-Young didn't seem to notice. She looked past Ronnie, far into the distance.

"Ronnie!"

Ronnie's head snapped down to Olivia, who had stopped up ahead.

"What are you doing? One minute you were next to me, and the next, you're just standing there spacing out." Olivia turned her head to where the gwishin was. "What is it?"

Min-Young was gone.

"Sorry," Ronnie mumbled as she caught up. "I'm just tired. Didn't sleep much."

Olivia gave her a sympathetic nod. "Was it the gwishin?"

"What?" Ronnie startled.

"I totally get it." Olivia nodded her head a bunch of times. "I heard all her victims are having trouble sleeping."

The word *victim* made Ronnie think of another word: *prey*. That made her think of hunting, which then reminded her of the dokkaebi. "I actually forgot all about that." This was mostly true. Ronnie had forgotten about the fake camp curse. But Olivia must have picked up on Ronnie's unease because she gave Ronnie a pitying smile and an I'll-pretend-to-believe-you head tilt.

Olivia wasn't entirely wrong. The reason she hadn't slept well *was* thirty-three percent due to the gwishin. And another thirty-three percent due to a dokkaebi. And another thirty-three percent due to the fact that she had just learned she was a witch.

🌲🌲🌲

Refreshing laps in the crystal-clear pool was exactly what Ronnie needed to take her mind off ghosts, witches, and goblins for a little while. What she didn't need was to be placed in the same advanced-level swim class as Sam. Olivia and Jack were placed there, too, but then Jack slipped and fell as he was climbing out of the pool and was sent to the nurse to check out a gash on his elbow. That meant one less person to function as a buffer between her and Sam.

Still, Ronnie was determined to enjoy swim class, especially when Robbie, the counselor in charge of their group, set up a contest of diving for rubber squid. Ronnie always beat Jack and her dad at that game. The whistle shrilled, and she dove for a lime-green squid near the wall. But just as she wrapped her fingers around the tentacles, it slipped out of her grasp. The moving water distorted her view. When it cleared, Sam was clutching the squid, the green flecks in his eye winking at her in triumph.

Ronnie pushed up to the surface and sent a splash in his direction. "I had that one!"

Sam wiped water from his eyes. "I'm pretty sure I got to it first. Not to mention I have it now."

"I'm pretty sure you snatched it out of my hands!"

Olivia gently grabbed her arm, but Ronnie jerked away.

"Guys," Olivia pleaded, "it's just a silly game."

"You're right, Olivia," Sam said in that gentle voice that was really starting to irritate Ronnie. Then he turned to her. "You're being a sore loser about it, Ronnie."

She whirled on Sam, slapping herself in the cheek with her drenched hair. "It's not losing when the other person's a cheater!"

"Fine. You want it so bad, have it." He tossed the green squid at Ronnie, but she lurched away like it was oozing ink. The squid hit the water with a slap and sank.

"It's not about the squid! I wanted a fair game."

Sam shrugged, his expression bored.

The less he seemed to care, the more Ronnie did. And she hated that. "I'm leaving." She swam to the edge of the pool.

"Wait, where are you going?" Sam called out after her.

Ronnie glared down from the pool's edge. "What do you care?"

"Well, you can't just leave," Olivia said, anxiously scanning the pool. "You have to tell Robbie!"

"Just tell him I feel sick and went back to the cabin."

"No!" Sam cried out, his tone strangely panicked. "You can't go by yourself!"

Olivia and Ronnie turned to one another with matching stunned expressions.

"I mean, it's against the rules," he quickly added. "You have to get permission first." He looked all around until he spotted Robbie, who was watching three swimmers grappling over an electric-blue squid. "Robbie! Robbie! Ronnie's trying to leave!"

"I—I'm not—" Ronnie sputtered as Robbie made his way over.

"Hey, what's going on?" Robbie's forehead crinkled in concern.

"I just . . ." Ronnie blinked several times, struggling to form words. "I think I swallowed too much pool water. My stomach hurts." She wrapped her arms around her middle.

Robbie winced. "Been there. Why don't you hang out on a bench? Or I can find a volunteer to take you to the nurse if you want."

Ronnie shook her head. "I'll sit and watch the class." She met Olivia's eyes and they both turned to Sam, but he was gone.

Ronnie spent the rest of the class sitting on a bench with the sticky humidity, the smell of chlorine, and the echoes of voices bouncing off the walls. She went over what had happened in the pool with Sam, trying to make sense of it.

First, he ignored her.

Then he picked a fight with her.

Now he was worried about her breaking the rules?

It made no sense. Just like everything else lately.

SEVENTEEN

FORGETTING

After class, Olivia rushed over to Ronnie, squealing with excitement. She bent her head in close to whisper, "OMG, Sam totally likes you!"

Ronnie drew back in disbelief. "What? Did *you* drink too much pool water?"

Olivia giggled and bounced on her heels. "Oh, come on, Ronnie! It explains why he acts so different with you."

If this was what it was like to be crushed on, she didn't want it. Ever. "I give your theory no more than a three percent likelihood. I'm ninety-seven percent sure he absolutely hates me."

"Not a chance." Olivia shook her head. "Sam's super sweet. He's just confused about his feelings for you. And come on—he's totally cute, right? Those hazel eyes with the green? *Right?*" Olivia squealed again, making Ronnie laugh.

But it wasn't so funny when Sam held the door to the dining hall open for Olivia but let it slam into Ronnie's shoulder. Or when Sam told Jack how fun their swim class was, especially the second half—the half Ronnie had sat out. Or when he soaked Ronnie during the water balloon toss claiming he simply "missed."

Even so, Olivia kept shooting Ronnie secret glances while mouthing, *Three percent*. And for the rest of the day, anytime Sam was rude or strange toward Ronnie, Olivia would make one of those faces people made while watching cuddly kitten videos.

Whatever that meant.

All Ronnie knew was that Olivia nudging her every time Sam acted peculiar only made it harder to ignore him and that bizarre pen he kept pulling out and spinning. The way he held on to that thing, you'd think it possessed some sort of magic. Even as they stood in line for the egg-and-spoon race during cabin competitions, he kept that pen in hand.

Olivia, who had gone to the bathroom, jogged back into the line next to Ronnie.

"Tell me it's not weird that Sam treats that old pen like a blankie or something," Ronnie said, jutting her chin at Sam across the field. Instead of answering, Olivia passed Ronnie a piece of paper folded in half. It was much too big to be a scavenger hunt clue and had her name written on the outside. "What's this?"

Olivia shrugged, her eyes not quite focused on Ronnie. She seemed distracted. "I found this note in the bathroom. It had your name on it."

"In the bathroom?" Ronnie was surprised at how casually Olivia had handled a piece of paper that had come from the bathroom. But she supposed it looked clean enough—no stains. Just a bit of water. At least she hoped it was water.

Olivia nodded. "I knew the moment I saw it that I must give it to you." With that, she stepped to the front of the line, stuck the end of a spoon into her mouth, and prepared to accept an egg.

Ronnie opened the note. It read: *Meet me in the forest.*

Ronnie glanced around hoping to spot whoever had written her that note. Then she remembered seeing Min-Young earlier that day in the treetops. She had thought Min-Young hadn't seen her, but she must have. The note had to be from her!

She looked around again, this time wondering if she could slip away just for a little while. Like a bathroom break. She accidentally made eye contact with Sam, and he didn't seem happy about it. Ronnie decided to ignore him. Everyone else seemed plenty distracted, making it the perfect time to leave unnoticed.

🌲🌲🌲

"Min-Young?" Ronnie whispered as she stepped into the woods. "Are you here?" She held her breath, waiting for the wind to announce Min-Young's arrival.

Nothing.

"Min-Young?" Ronnie tried again. The crack of a twig rang out in the silence. She spun around, a half-formed smile on her face.

But again, no one was there.

A blur flashed in Ronnie's periphery—something had darted past, like a long-tailed bird. She turned in its direction, but she was too late. She saw nothing.

Next came the sound of muted footsteps—slow and

careful. "Who's there?" she called out. There was no response, but she couldn't shake the feeling she was being watched. Her breathing was suddenly shallow, and she began backing out of the forest.

Then she saw it. Someone with short honey-blond hair staggered backward out from the trees, bent over as if he'd accidentally caught a football with his gut.

"What are you doing?" Sam snapped at her, his hands still clutching his stomach. His shirt was lumpy beneath his hands. "You're not supposed to be here."

Ronnie put her hands on her hips. "If I'm not supposed to be here, then neither are *you*. Are you following me?"

"I— N-no," he stammered. "I can't help that I saw you sneak in here." Sam set his jaw. "We need to leave. Now."

"I'm not going anywhere with you."

"I'll *tell*."

Ronnie planted her feet. Sam grimaced and tightened his grip around his middle. Ronnie wondered if he was going to be sick. When his face started losing its color, Ronnie was ninety-nine percent certain he was going to hurl. She leaned away from him just as Boo leaped into view.

"L-leave me alone!" he yelled at the cat. Ronnie couldn't understand the look of sheer terror on Sam's face. She would have felt bad for him if he hadn't followed her and then threatened to tell on her.

Boo's eyes glowed gold, and his tail swished languidly as he stalked forward a few steps. Then he paused midstride, arched his back, and hissed. Sam spun around and ran away.

Grinning, Ronnie bent to smooth down Boo's fur. "Any chance you can help me find the gwishin?"

He didn't answer—he wasn't a talking cat. Ronnie was glad for that because she had more one percents than she could handle right now. Boo glanced over his shoulder at Ronnie to indicate she should follow and then prodded deeper into the trees.

A few minutes, two cobwebs in the mouth, and seven sticker bush scratches later, Ronnie found herself at the edge of a wide clearing. *There.* Min-Young was at the center, her back to Ronnie.

Ronnie opened her mouth to call out. But her voice lodged in her throat at the sound of pained moans and agonized wailing. Like the gwishin's voice, it sounded like the wind playing tricks on her ears. Ebbing and flowing, it came from both right against her ear and clear across the forest. There were no words, just cries with a devastating human quality to them—one that made her heart ache. Boo dropped low to the ground, his ears pressed to the sides of his head.

Ronnie took a step forward, and a branch crackled under her foot.

The cries stopped suddenly, and Min-Young spun around, her nightgown twisting against her haunting form. "Ronnie? Boo?"

Boo sauntered over to Min-Young. When he reached her, he walked figure eights beneath her feet and then planted himself up against the side of a tree stump with light green moss sprouting on the surface.

Ronnie shrank into herself, suddenly feeling like she was intruding. "I got your note to meet you here." She glanced around the clearing and noticed stones—like the ones stacked around the campgrounds—scattered along the perimeter.

Min-Young frowned. "Did you? I don't recall leaving a note . . . or know how I'd write one, for that matter." Her all-black eyes rolled around their sockets as she searched her memories. Ronnie tried not to show her revulsion on her face. After a long moment, Min-Young pressed her hands to her temples. "I'm sorry, Ronnie. I must be forgetting."

Ronnie winced. "Does it hurt? The forgetting?"

Min-Young blinked a few times. "The best way to describe it is that it feels like my soul is being torn apart. It's a mental agony with no physical equivalent."

The sound of Min-Young's anguished cries echoed in Ronnie's ears. She wondered how much of Min-Young's time as a gwishin had been filled with such misery. It was no wonder she wanted to be free.

But then Min-Young grinned, her ink eyes brightening, her suffering seemingly forgotten. Even the air felt lighter, and the surrounding trees stood taller. The shift was sudden, and it was hard for Ronnie to believe the smiling gwishin before her was in any kind of pain. She wondered if Min-Young had actually forgotten it.

"But I'm glad you're here." Min-Young guided Ronnie to the stump in the center of the clearing and motioned for her to sit. "You must have so many questions, and we have so much work to do. Did you find the grimoire?"

Ronnie nodded and pulled out *Essential Oils in Cooking*

from her backpack and placed it on her lap. *"Reveal the spells within this book. For witch eyes only, let me look."*

Tingle, tingle, crackle, fizz.

She'd never get over the sensation of magic running through her body.

"Very good," Min-Young said, making Ronnie flush with pride.

"So I get witch blood magic—they're spoken spells like the one I just used, right?"

Min-Young nodded.

"And tree magic seems pretty obvious. It's like a booster that enhances magic."

Min-Young nodded again.

"But I don't get string magic or everlasting magic."

A breeze picked up, and Min-Young glided to the edge of the clearing, the crimson scarf and her long black hair entangling as they trailed behind. She hovered above one of the stones at the perimeter for a moment before moving on to the next one and the next until she had gone around the entire clearing. "The stones are the most common everlasting hosts you'll find on the grounds.

"They can hold magic so long as they remain intact," Min-Young continued. "Layers of protective spells have been placed upon the manor in this way by elder witches in my family line. It's not something a single witch can accomplish—not even over the course of her entire life."

"How does it protect against dokkaebi?"

"It renders dokkaebi magic ineffective. Enough stones can snuff out their Persuasions or wipe out their telekinesis, which they rely on to silence witches." Min-Young ran a hand down the length of the scarf. Like it was a pet snake and not a murder weapon.

Ronnie shuddered. "And the scarf? How exactly does it work?"

"For a non-witch or a pre-witch," Min-Young said, turning her ink-pool eyes onto Ronnie's, "the scarf is just a scarf. But its danger begins the moment the witch turns twelve, at which point the severity of injury increases from causing rashes or burns to temporary loss of voice or fever spells. The scarf becomes deadly in a matter of weeks or months—it's different for everyone. But once the scarf can kill, proximity alone can weaken a witch's magic."

Ronnie's mouth ran dry. "So, what can I do?"

Min-Young pointed a finger at the cookbook in Ronnie's lap. A ribbon of wind slipped under the cover of the book and flicked it open with the physicality and dexterity of a finger. Then the pages lifted at the corners and flipped over one after another as if being kicked up by two invisible feet running along the edges.

"We can start with a repellent," Min-Young announced. "It won't be enough in a direct attack with a scarf because, as you may have guessed, the scarves are everlasting hosts. But it can help keep other, temporary dokkaebi magic at bay." The wind died down and the pages settled. "Here."

BASIC REPELLENT

USES: Repels nuisances found in nature such as insects, smoke, humidity, and body odor (of others). Serves as base for more complex repellent spells.

INGREDIENTS:

coconut oil
pinch of salt
pinch of ginger (fresh or powder)
dead skin-cell dustings from witch's hands
garlic breath
metal stirrer

INSTRUCTIONS:

1. Place coconut oil in bowl, any amount.

2. Add salt and ginger to oil.

3. Stir in figure-eight motions five times using metal stirrer.

4. Rub clean hands together over bowl twelve times, then hit palms together three times.*

5. Stir in figure-eight motions five times using metal stirrer.

6. Blow garlic breath into bowl for ten continuous seconds.**

7. Stir in figure-eight motions five times using metal stirrer.

8. If available, add fresh or ash essence*** of nuisance being repelled.

9. Allow potion to stand for at least thirty minutes before using. When ready, rub pea-sized amounts onto both temples, nape of neck, inside each elbow, on both wrists, and behind both knees. While massaging into skin, recite unispell.****

FOOTNOTES:

*Clapping hands should sting slightly, but only briefly, for optimum results.

**Chewing of one raw garlic clove is recommended.

***Essence for living nuisances include blood, sweat, or tears.

****Specify nuisance for peak potency.

Ronnie scratched at a new bite on the side of her knee. It was the size of a tennis ball with an angry red center. "Could I use the repellent potion on mosquitoes?"

"Yes," Min-Young said. "And that would be a great test for your base. All the ingredients are common kitchen items."

"But what about the essence? Where can I find that?"

"You don't need it for the potion to work, though it would give it more power. What you *will* absolutely need is a unispell, which is a spell that is unique to you," Min-Young explained. "One you create. It comes with magical maturity and power, as well as practice. You see, the magic lies in the intention spoken into the unispell." Min-Young pressed a hand down on the base of her throat, where the scarf had twisted onto itself. "Words have great power."

"But I've spoken dozens of bad rhymes." Ronnie clamped a hand over her mouth. "Have I been casting spells without knowing it?"

"Not all unispells result in a magical act. And for young witches especially, the magic in the words is too fleeting to effect change. But as your power grows, you will need to watch your words carefully."

"You mean control the rhyming?" Ronnie made a face. "That's what I've been trying to do this whole time, but it's really hard."

Min-Young tapped Ronnie's nose with a finger. It felt like the press of the wind. "That is because you have been resisting. It'll get easier to control your words as you lean into your magic."

Excitement fluttered beneath Ronnie's ribs. She told herself she wasn't excited about being a witch, but rather about the promise of controlling her rhymes.

Min-Young's bright lips pulled down into a hesitant frown. "But you should know that the strengthening of your witch blood places you in danger of witch-hunting dokkaebi. They, like all magical creatures, are drawn to magic, and a witch is full of it in her very being."

Ronnie wrapped her arms instinctively around herself. "So there are other creatures besides the dokkaebi hunting me?"

"Not necessarily. What I mean to say is that there is a far greater potential for magic in this world than we see realized. Much magic remains dormant until it is provoked—triggered by the awakening of other magic in its proximity."

Ronnie nodded slowly as she made sense of what Min-Young was saying. "Like remembering. Sometimes all it takes is recalling one tiny detail for the rest of a memory to come flooding back. Like it was there all the time, just hidden beneath a bunch of . . . a bunch of . . ." She couldn't think of an analogy.

"Fear?"

"I—I've never thought of it that way." Ronnie spoke slowly, mostly to herself, a connection forming rapidly in her mind. "I wonder if that's why Dad forgot all about Mom and why he put all of Grandpa's pictures into storage boxes after he died." She stopped abruptly, remembering she wasn't alone. "Sorry."

"For what?"

"For bringing up such a depressing topic," she said with an apologetic smile.

"It sounds like an important topic to me." Min-Young floated down low to the ground and folded her legs beneath her so she was "sitting" just above the forest floor in front of Ronnie. "Go on. Why do you think your dad hid the pictures away?"

Ronnie hesitated, but it was hard to deny an unblinking gwishin. "Maybe it wasn't just that they made him sad. Maybe he was afraid that being sad about one thing would remind him of other things that made him sad, too—things he had forgotten. Like my mom. So forgetting one thing meant forgetting it all." Tears sprang to Ronnie's eyes, and though her heart was sinking, it was also racing at her confession. She never talked to anyone about being sad about her mom or grandpa dying. Not her dad. Not Jack. And here she was now, pouring her heart out to a gwishin. Ronnie peeked up at Min-Young, remembering what the gwishin had told her about memories.

There are few memories so bad that I would not want

them. *In fact, some of the worst ones are inexplicably tied to some of the very best. You cannot have one without the other, Ronnie, and I would have it no other way.*

"I guess I can't remember how the people I loved lived without remembering that they died," Ronnie murmured, feeling a strange mixture of grief and hopefulness. She wanted to remember, but she didn't want the pain that came with it.

"This is true," Min-Young said. "Memories beget memories. Magic begets magic. And this is true in every way. The more powerful you become, the more magic will be drawn to you and out of you. You will become more visible to your enemies, but you will also attract allies. Your witch instinct will blossom—" Min-Young's eyes glazed over, and she was no longer looking at Ronnie. She floated up, her legs straightening beneath her, and drifted away toward the edge of the clearing like a boat without its anchor.

Ronnie set the cookbook down on the stump and followed Min-Young to a stone at the edge of the clearing. Something was poking out from beneath it. She squatted down for a closer look. It was a friendship bracelet made with purple, yellow, and black thread. Min-Young crouched down and pressed a pale finger to the bracelet. Her finger passed right through the threads, but the bracelet shuddered against her wind.

"Sometimes, I experience a wisp of witch instinct and it triggers a memory, or at least the presence of one." Her whisper-thin voice carried over on a weak breeze that grazed Ronnie's cheeks. "This is an example of string magic."

Ronnie ran a finger over the friendship bracelet on her wrist. She had never taken it off. "Like the memory?"

"Rememberings are the most commonly used, but the possibilities with string magic are endless. It can connect time, place, and even thoughts. Rememberings are bridges, ladders, and sometimes lassos. With simple Rememberings, ginseng-root fibers are woven into friendship bracelets cast to hold the wearer's memories to be replayed by any witch at any time."

Ronnie peered closer at the bracelet under the rock and confirmed the distinct ginseng-root fibers among the threads. "How did you get that bracelet?"

Min-Young glanced back at the center of the clearing, where Boo was napping next to the stump. "Although our spiritual connection was lost with my silencing, Boojuk has remained committed to me these past seven years, bringing me gifts he believes will be of use."

It dawned upon Ronnie that each stone surrounding the clearing held something down. There were friendship bracelets, newspaper clippings, photographs, and pages torn from grimoires, among other items.

"Every once in a while, I'll get this sense I'm ready for a memory and will be drawn to one of these clues. In fact . . ." Min-Young pointed to a stone just beyond reach. It pinned a roughly torn and folded piece of paper to the ground. "Shortly after you arrived, I was drawn to a journal entry Boo had rescued in which I wrote about the dokkaebi hunting me at the time. He enjoyed making a spectacle of his hunts. Unlike most dokkaebi that fear discovery—and so silence witches in private—my dokkaebi thrived on the attention. Nothing would please him more than to become a trending headline." She pulled the length of her scarf through her fingers. "He wants witches to know what he's capable of. He wants me to *witness*."

"You think he'll try to silence me in front of you?"

"I am certain of it." Min-Young's lips turned down into a determined frown. "But we'll beat him at his own game. We will discover him before he discovers us."

The bracelet trapped beneath the stone flapped against a sudden flash of wind. Ronnie reached out and tugged it free. Taking a seat on a patch of wild grass, she tied the bracelet to her empty wrist.

"Take me there, to when and where. A memory that's saved to share."

EIGHTEEN
THE LOVE CURSE

Ronnie blinked and found herself on the lake, a paddleboard beneath her and her feet dangling in the water. The hazy glow of the summer sky at dusk slowly retreated from the golden light of the lanterns floating gently on the water's surface. On the shore, people lounged on blankets under linen canopies. The sound of music, soft and lazy, drifted over the scene.

This time, Ronnie was seeing from the perspective of a young woman anxiously looking between two others on paddleboards next to her. She recognized one as Min-Young, but the other person was a young man she couldn't place. Both wore baseball caps that shrouded their eyes.

"You didn't think you'd actually be able to Persuade me, did you?" Min-Young's tone was haughty. From this perspective, she looked older than the last memory by a few years.

"I wasn't trying to—" the guy started.

"I saw your eyes do that dokkaebi flash."

He scratched behind his ears. "That happens a lot when I'm trying to convince anyone of anything. I don't have full control over it yet."

Min-Young threw her head back and laughed, loud and harsh. "Will that be your excuse after you silence us?"

Ronnie's gaze cut to Min-Young. "Min, that's not fair—" she heard herself say in a voice she didn't recognize.

Min-Young's head snapped to Ronnie. "Not *fair*? Lia, what are you talking about? Did this dokkaebi actually manage to Persuade you?"

Ronnie felt Lia's heart sink. "Of course not! It's just . . . did you set all this up just to trap him?" She glanced around at the floating lanterns on the water and the people on the shore.

"Of course," Min-Young said without hesitation. "I wasn't going to confront him on his terms—alone with a scarf and no human witnesses."

"This was supposed to be a college graduation party." Lia threw her head back and groaned. Ronnie's vision was filled with familiar softball-sized stars. "Not one of your dokkaebi banishing attempts."

"B-banishing?" the guy stuttered.

Lia grimaced. "Don't worry, Ambrose. No one's being banished. Right, Min?" She shot Min-Young a hard look, which Min-Young pretended not to see.

"Whatever." Min-Young swept her fingertips through the water, splashing her legs. "I don't need to banish you to stop you."

Ambrose backed away on his paddleboard. "Hey, I'm not trying to silence anyone. I don't even have a scarf yet." He winced, shaking his head. "I mean I don't have one and I don't want one. Ever. I swear."

"Really?" Min-Young cocked her head. "And yet you're

part of a witch-hunting faction. You even have a witch-hunting mentor."

"Is that true?" Lia asked in a whisper. Ronnie could have shuddered at how normal the guy looked. Nothing about him screamed *dokkaebi*.

"I—I was looking for others like me . . ." he stammered. He didn't meet Lia's gaze, but she kept staring at him, her heart tearing apart, willing it not to be true.

Min-Young sighed. "Lia, you always trust too easily." She casually reached into the pocket of her shorts and pulled out a small, corked vial.

"Min . . ." Lia eyed the vial.

"Wait." Ambrose's voice shook. He held out his hands like a shield. "What is that?"

Min-Young pulled out the cork and held it up before her. "It's nothing you need to worry about if you have no plans to hunt witches. Which you don't, right?" She raised her brows.

Ambrose's chest heaved. His hands twitched. And then there was a distinct green flash of his eyes beneath the brim of his hat. It looked like the sun reflecting off a green gemstone.

Min-Young's board lurched back, her eyes widening a half second before she crashed into the water—vial and all. Quick as lightning, she resurfaced next to Ambrose. Gripping his board with both hands, she bore down using her entire weight. The board tipped, and he fell into the water. Min-Young didn't wait for him to resurface before she began to speak.

"When next you hunt a witch, take heed—"

Ambrose broke through the surface and gulped in mouthfuls of air. Ronnie felt Lia's panic build.

"For she is all that this curse needs—"

"Wait—" Ambrose sputtered, his gaze darting down to the water he was submerged in. The surface had the unmistakable sheen of oil from Min-Young's vial.

"—your hate will die; your love will rise. This love will lead to your demise."

Ronnie felt Lia's devastation, and though Ronnie couldn't make sense of it, she knew that Min-Young had somehow cursed not only Ambrose but Lia as well.

Without another word, Min-Young ducked her head under the water and swam toward the shore, where the soothing music continued to play. Dulcet notes drifted over the lake, the sound ebbing and flowing like a gentle current.

🌲🌲🌲

Ronnie blinked out of the Remembering and described everything she saw and heard to Min-Young. She could tell when memory sparked in Min-Young by the widening of her eyes or a twitch in her hands as she stroked her scarf.

"Ah, Lia and Ambrose . . ." Min-Young muttered mostly to herself. "I remember now. A witch and a dokkaebi." She adjusted her scarf, but it fell into place in the exact same position as always. "I cursed him to fall in love with the next witch he hunted."

Ronnie thought of the curses from books or movies, from burning to death under the sunlight to reliving the same day over and over. But she had never heard of a curse that made you fall in love. "That's a curse?"

"For witch-hunting dokkaebi, yes." Min-Young folded her legs and floated down so she was level with Ronnie. The ends of her glossy red scarf and limp strands of her long black hair pooled in her lap. "You see, it's difficult to stop a dokkaebi from silencing a witch. Now, should he fall in love with that witch, then he will not be able to silence her. They cannot give up something they love."

"What about the witch? Is she cursed to love him back?"

"Therein lies the beauty of the curse." Min-Young winked, which was a little unnerving coming from someone who rarely blinked. "If somehow the witch can love the dokkaebi, then the dokkaebi will become grounded in his human form. Over time, if he lets himself, he will become increasingly human. He will lose his Persuasions and even begin to forget he ever was a dokkaebi at all. For all intents and purposes, he would be human."

"And if the witch can't love a murderous witch-silencing goblin?"

Min-Young twirled the scarf in her fingers. "He would suffer the heartache of unrequited love for the rest of his life and would be vulnerable to banishment by that witch." Her eyes went distant for a moment and then snapped to Ronnie's when they came back into focus. "But Lia and Ambrose fell in love. They got married and she left the coven."

"And you were silenced," Ronnie said hesitantly. "Does that mean he wasn't the one who silenced you?"

"Possibly. More likely, however, is that something went

wrong with the curse." Min-Young ran the scarf through her fingers, the silk strands rippling like gushing blood. "But that's enough for today." She looked exhausted, but her cheeks lifted with a smile. "Thank you. I'm so grateful for these memories."

"You're welcome." Ronnie looked away, suddenly feeling shy.

"You'll bring the repellent potion next time?" Min-Young asked.

Ronnie nodded, a smile stretching across her face at the thought of a next time. She made her way back to camp, her arms swinging at her sides and a bounce in her steps.

By the time she reached the edge of the forest, she had a half-formed plan for the next opportunity to sneak away from camp. That plan came to a grinding halt when she saw Ms. Hana waiting for her just beyond the tree line, her sleek black hair glinting blue under the sun. Stomach twisting, Ronnie trudged through the remainder of the woods.

Ms. Hana paced, her steps slow and deliberate. "The forest is off-limits without permission." Every syllable was clipped. "Did you have permission, Veronica?"

"No," Ronnie admitted, wiping the beads of sweat that formed across her forehead. It was hot without the shade of the trees. Or maybe it was the heat of Ms. Hana's burning stare.

"Then what were you doing in the forest?" Ms. Hana's eyes were full of knowing, but there was no way she could actually know about Min-Young. It was probably an adult trick to get kids to spill their guts.

Ronnie thought fast. "I followed Boo in and got lost."

Ms. Hana didn't say anything for some time as she continued to pace a strange path. It took Ronnie a moment to notice the small stone piles on the ground hidden among the overgrown grass. Ms. Hana had been walking around the stacks to avoid toppling them. Ronnie was ninety-five percent sure those stones hadn't been there when she had passed that very spot on her way into the forest.

"And where is he now?"

"I lost him." Ronnie swallowed and forced herself to meet Ms. Hana's penetrating gaze. "I hope he's okay."

Ms. Hana stopped pacing and stood before Ronnie. "He'll manage just fine. As for you—you are very lucky to have found your way out. It isn't safe to go wandering in the forest alone."

Sensing a thawing in Ms. Hana's demeanor, Ronnie nodded dutifully. "I'm sorry, I won't go into the forest again." *Today,* she added to herself.

After a beat, she took a step away, but Ms. Hana stopped her with a raised hand. "A rule was broken, and there must be consequences. The kitchen staff will be notified of your arrival tomorrow morning at six to help with breakfast preparations."

Ronnie made a face. "Six in the morning?" She couldn't think of anything crueler than waking a kid that early during the summer.

"Perhaps toilet-cleaning duty this evening is more acceptable to you?" Ms. Hana raised a brow. "The bathrooms do get filthy so quickly."

Ronnie sucked in a breath. "No! I'll be in the kitchen tomorrow morning at six. No problem."

Ms. Hana bared her teeth in her signature nonsmile. "Good. Then off you go, now."

Ronnie speed-walked all the way to the ropes course, the director's gaze hotter than the overhead sun on the back of her head.

NINETEEN
WILD&FREE

Waking up before six the next morning was torture. But there was something soothing about refilling the condiments at the breakfast bar in complete silence. It helped Ronnie organize her thoughts about spells and curses and murderous dokkaebi.

Noting the fill levels on the remaining condiment trays, she made a mental list of things to grab from the pantry. "Butter, syrup, and honey," she muttered to herself repeatedly as she made her way through the kitchen.

The pantry door was slightly ajar. She began to push her way in, when a shuffling sound from inside stopped her midmotion. Peering into the opening revealed dark shadows within, which Ronnie's imagination transformed into silencing scarves. Then came a thud that was only slightly louder than the hammering of her heart in her ears.

She glanced around the kitchen, but no one else seemed to have heard the noise. One of the cooks was scrambling eggs, and another was running dishes out to the buffet. Both were close enough to hear Ronnie if she called out for help, but their presence wasn't much of a comfort knowing that the dokkaebi liked attention. He could probably easily Persuade two people of his innocence while silencing Ronnie at the same time. But she couldn't just stand there, and the witches had told her that the camp buildings were heavily protected.

Bracing herself, she reached into the pantry, flipped the light switch, and snatched her hand back. Light flooded the space, revealing a container of ginger powder tipped over on the floor and a black cat languishing on a high shelf next to a jar of coconut oil.

"Boojuk!" Ronnie's body went limp with relief. The muscles in her arms wobbled weakly like gelatin as she reached up and pulled the cat down. "I don't think cats are allowed in the kitchens." Boo gave an indifferent twitch of his whiskers. "Especially when they make a mess of the pantry." When she reached down for the ginger, Boo jumped out of her arms and began swiping at a string of garlic cloves hanging from a low hook on the wall.

Ginger.

Coconut oil.

Garlic.

These were the ingredients she needed for the repellent base! Ronnie scanned the shelves for some salt, a metal stirrer, and a lidded plastic cup.

"Boo," she whispered, interrupting his game with the garlic. "You're a genius!" He blinked slowly at her as if to say *duh.*

"Will you watch the door to make sure no one comes in?" Ronnie gave him a little scratch behind the ears, and he padded over to the door, sighed, and plopped down to keep watch.

As Ronnie got to work brewing her first witch potion, she racked her brain for a unispell. Now that she actually wanted to rhyme, it turned out she was bad at it. It wasn't until she remembered that unispells came from witch instinct rather than human will that she came up with the right one. It wasn't pretty or perfect, but the magic of the words hummed in her blood and bones.

Pesky mosquitoes, don't you come near. There's room for only one of us here.

The *tingle, tingle, crackle, fizz* confirmed that she'd found a spell. Now she just needed to see if it worked.

🌲🌲🌲

"Hellooooo . . ."

Ronnie blinked at the hand waving inches from her nose.

"You've been spacing all day," Jack complained, speaking loudly over the chatter and laughter all around them. "What's up with you?"

Ronnie squeezed her eyes shut against visions of green-eyed goblins and possessed scarves. When she opened her eyes, the crowded scene inside the Lodge came into focus. Jack and Olivia sat to her left and right as they waited for the surprise guest speaker to make their appearance.

Ronnie shrugged. "Nothing's up. Why?"

Jack quirked a brow, not convinced. "I was asking you if you have any idea who the guest speaker is."

Benji, in the row ahead, twisted around in his seat. "I

know who it is." Of course he did. He held up two fingers. "Two clues. Pocketknife. Compass."

"A Girl Scout?" Ronnie asked.

Jack leaned forward, his eyes wide. "Guy Lobing? From *Wild&Free*?" Benji pointed at Jack, flashing his rainbow grin.

Ronnie's mouth dropped open. "How in the world did you get that from a pocketknife and compass?"

Olivia's brows knitted together. "Who's Guy Lobing? What's *Wild&Free*?"

"The internet reality show? He's got, like, four million followers?" Benji's eyes grew wider by the second.

Olivia continued to stare blankly, and Jack jumped in. "He gets dropped off in the middle of nowhere with nothing but a broken compass—his good-luck charm—and a pocketknife."

Ronnie patted Jack's arm. "Is he the one who speared a squirrel while it ran up a tree from, like, fifty feet away?"

Jack stabbed a finger to his chest. "Dead center."

Olivia's mouth fell open in horror. "The poor animal!"

"Sorry," Jack said, not sounding sorry at all. "Guy's gotta eat."

Benji nodded. "In the wild and free—"

"It's eat or be eaten." Jack flashed a wicked grin.

The topic of being eaten reminded Ronnie about her mosquito bites. She checked her arms to confirm she had no new ones since she started using her repellent potion. When she reached down to check her legs, she found Boo under her chair, his nose low to the ground.

"What are you doing, Boo?" she whispered to the cat.

He hissed softly in response and swiped at something on the ground. It rolled toward Ronnie's foot.

It was Sam's weird old pen. It must have fallen out of his backpack. Ronnie picked it up and took a closer look. The wooden barrel was hollow—no ink, no pen tip. It was completely useless, so it must hold some sort of sentimental value for Sam.

"Argh!" Sam suddenly cried out, jumping up from his seat.

Ronnie bolted up, reflexively sliding the pen under her lap. She didn't want Sam to see she had it.

Boo jumped up onto the empty seat next to Sam and hissed at him, his fur standing on end. While everyone was distracted by Boo, Ronnie pulled the pen out from under her lap to sneak it into Sam's backpack without him seeing. But before she could, he grabbed his backpack and began using it like a shield/weapon to shoo Boo away. Thinking fast, she shoved the pen into her pocket instead.

"Hey!" she cried out as she scooped Boo up in her arms. "He's just a cat."

Sam's face was bright red, his eyes round with pure fear. "I'm . . . allergic . . . to cats," he muttered. "I swear he knows it, too."

Tossing a disapproving look in Sam's direction, Ronnie ran a hand soothingly over the top of Boo's head. He purred with satisfaction before bounding out of her arms. But once he landed on the floor between Ronnie's and Sam's chairs, he took his sweet, sweet time leaving, his tail swishing from side to side—clearly for Sam's sake.

"Your attention, please." Ms. Hana's voice rang out sharp and cold through the microphone. "Each year, we invite a guest speaker who upholds the values of Camp Foster. This year, we had an unfortunate last-minute cancelation. However, another guest has generously offered to fill the vacancy. He is best known for his hit internet series, *Wild&Free*, in which he demonstrates lifesaving survival skills, unparalleled ingenuity, expertise, and raw talent in all things wild and free."

She extended a hand to Mr. Lobing, who stood off to the side. "Please help me welcome Guy Lobing!"

Mr. Lobing took to the stage and immediately launched into a story about getting a fire going in the rain. But Ronnie couldn't focus on the talk. Her mind kept wandering back to witch-hunting dokkaebi. Their faces shifted from kind and friendly to warped and deadly and everything in between, making them completely undetectable. Ronnie had no idea how to spot one.

But there was someone who might.

Ronnie leaned in to whisper to Jack. "So, I heard Gigi say you can spot a dokkaebi by using a mirror because they don't have reflections." Sure, it was a complete lie, but given the rumors Gigi had started about Min-Young, this seemed not only possible but fair.

"That's so stupid," he hissed. "Why does everyone think all supernatural creatures are the same?"

"Anyway, so I can correct her next time, how do you spot a dokkaebi?" She tried to sound ninety percent indifferent and only about ten percent invested in the answer—just enough to get Jack to respond, but not enough to raise suspicion.

But she must have overdone the indifferent part because Jack shook his head and said only, "I don't think people can," before turning his attention back to the speaker.

Someone in the audience asked Mr. Lobing about hunting wild game, and Jack's eyes lit up the way they did when he found out a house in their neighborhood was supposedly haunted.

"Jack," Ronnie whispered, poking him in the knee.

He shifted his knee out of her reach.

"Jack." She tugged at the sleeve of his shirt.

He swatted her hand away. Hard.

"Ow!"

"Ronnie!" Olivia hissed through her teeth. "Ms. Hana is staring right at us. Do not drag me down with you."

Ronnie turned to Olivia, who promptly poked Ronnie's cheek with a finger, guiding her to face forward. "Stare straight ahead."

And Ronnie did. For about ten seconds. Then she turned back to Jack. "Why can't you spot a dokkaebi?"

He sighed before answering, speaking fast so as not to miss too much of Mr. Lobing's story. "They look like normal people and can be detected only while using their magic, but people can't pick up on it anyway. That's why their greatest enemies are those who can see through their Persuasions and expose them for what they really are."

He was talking about witches. He was talking about *her*.

There was a pinch on the back of her arm.

"Ow!" she whisper-shouted at Olivia, rubbing at the spot. Ronnie dragged her eyes back to the front. Her gaze collided with Ms. Hana's frigid glare. Even after she ducked her head, the ice of Ms. Hana's stare lingered between Ronnie's eyes.

Keeping her head down, she poked Jack to get his attention. But when she opened her mouth to get more information, Olivia's hand clamped over it. Ronnie stuck out her tongue.

"Ew!" Olivia shrieked, snatching her hand away.

Mr. Lobing fell silent. Everyone turned to stare, including Ms. Hana. Olivia's eyes nearly popped out of her head, and she slapped her hand over her own mouth. Ronnie could tell the exact moment when Olivia realized it was the same hand Ronnie had licked. Olivia's eyes went from bright with shock to dim with disgust.

She dropped her hand and ducked her head until Mr. Lobing resumed his talk, drawing everyone's attention away. Ronnie's shoulders shook with silent laughter.

"That's what you get," Ronnie whispered to Olivia.

Olivia reached over and wiped her palm furiously on Ronnie's shorts.

Ronnie ducked down again to hide her laughter and spotted a Sinbi issue, "Goblin in the Woods," inside Jack's open backpack on the floor at his feet. On the cover was a forest. Sunlight filtering in through the trees shone down upon a man with a perfectly normal smile on his unremarkable human face. He looked nothing like a dokkaebi. There were no signs. No warnings. And that somehow felt inexplicably *sinister*.

Grabbing the issue, Ronnie flipped through the pages until she came across a frame with the dokkaebi digging out a small metal box from the forest floor. Inside was something long and slim, like a pen. But upon closer inspection, she saw it was a whistle.

She flipped ahead to see if someone would come along and destroy it. But this wasn't a dokkaebi villain story or martyr tale. It was a dokkaebi hero myth, and the whistle was his touchstone that served to make him stronger.

The microphone screeched. Ronnie startled, her eyes jumping up to the front.

"Remember," Mr. Lobing said, "there's nothing this world can throw your way that you can't overcome with the will to survive."

The words fell flat for Ronnie. She was dealing with creatures not of this world.

TWENTY

PROOF

T he next day was the beginning of the second week of camp, and a campfire was scheduled to mark the occasion. Ronnie waited until she and Olivia were nearly at the Pit to announce a last-minute run back to the cabin to grab more mosquito repellent. She insisted on going alone to use the potion and recite the unispell in private.

When she climbed up to her bunk, she found a letter from her dad on top of her sleeping bag.

> Dear Ronnie,
>
> Hey, kid! It was such a wonderful surprise to receive a postcard from you! I miss you so much! As you requested, I'm including a drawing of the character etched into your dohl ring. I hope this helps. You'll have to tell me the entire story of why you wanted this when I get you back. Has it been two weeks yet?
>
>

Her dad's drawing was identical to the hanja she'd seen in the gallery. Ronnie felt a strange mixture of satisfaction that she'd been right and confusion as to why. But for now, she continued reading her dad's message:

> I miss you, but I'm over the moon to hear you're enjoying camp! I must admit I had my doubts after dropping you off. But now I can forget all those unpleasant concerns, just as you shouldn't worry about troublesome things like the rhyming. Have fun and make good memories, Ronnie!
>
> I love you,
>
> Dad

Ronnie reread the message two more times, hoping to find some comfort in his words. All she found was the same pattern of her dad pushing a problem out of his mind— and trying to push it out of hers as well. But even if she gained control of the rhyming, she could never stop being a witch. It was as much a part of her as her blood. Her lungs squeezed at the nagging thought that while *she* couldn't walk away from this problem, her dad certainly could.

Ronnie arrived at the campfire to a raucous repeat-after-me activity.

"I said a BOOM chicka-boom!" the counselors called out.

"I said a BOOM chicka-boom!" the group echoed.

"I said a boom CHICKA-boom!"

"I said a boom CHICKA-boom!"

"I said a boom chicka-rocka, chicka-rocka, chicka-boom!"

Ronnie slid into an empty seat on the log bench in the far back of the group, unnoticed as the voices grew louder and louder with each line. She wanted to stay as far away from the campfire as possible since smoke repelled insects, and for once, she wanted to attract them. She'd been wearing the mosquito repellent potion and reciting her unispell for nearly two days now, and it seemed to be working. Ready to put it to the ultimate test, she had worn a short-sleeved shirt and shorts to allow maximum exposure for hungry mosquitoes. So far, so good.

"One more time, puppy style!" The counselors curled their hands under their chins like paws. "I said a WOOF chicken bones!"

Ronnie didn't echo that one since chicken bones weren't safe to give to dogs. She didn't even have a dog, and she knew that.

"Mrow!"

The commotion nearly drowned out the discordant meow of a cat. Ronnie tracked it to the shadows along the edge of the clearing. There, two gold eyes were trained on her.

"I said a woof CHICKEN bones!"

"Boo?" Ronnie called out in a loud whisper. The meow came again. This time, she heard the urgency in his tone. After a quick glance around at the distracted counselors, she slipped away.

"I said a WOOF digging-holes-into-the-ground-to-bury BONES!"

The light of the campfire didn't extend far, and with just a few steps she was enveloped in darkness. She couldn't turn on her flashlight—that would attract attention—so she waited for her eyes to adjust as she scanned the area for Boo.

Once again, it was the glow of his eyes a few steps away that caught her attention first. She could just barely make out his form but noticed something bunched up under his front paws.

"What's that?" She moved closer and squatted down to stroke his fur. He let out a soft purr and nudged her hand with his head. Even up close, it was too dark to tell what he had bundled in his paws, but it looked like it could be a shirt or some sort of fabric. But when she reached out to touch it, Boo let out a menacing hiss and tucked the item deeper beneath his belly.

Ronnie snatched back her hand. "If you didn't want to show me what you have, why'd you call me here?"

Boo blinked at her nice and slow as if to tell her to not make any sudden movements. Then, keeping his eyes on her, he grabbed a bit of the bundle in his mouth. Ronnie stayed still as a stone as Boo paced back toward the campfire, unrolling a long train of fabric in his wake.

Boo stepped into the light, and Ronnie saw it at last. Between the cat's teeth was one end of a long red silk scarf.

The blood drained from Ronnie's face as she tottered back and tripped, falling on her bottom. One hand pressed into the soft earth while the other wrapped protectively around her throat.

"Wh-why do you have that, Boo?" Ronnie rasped, her entire body shaking. It was no wonder he wouldn't let her touch it. "Where did you get it from?"

A low growl emitted from Boo's throat as his eyes flashed at the campfire. Ronnie followed his gaze to a cluster of kids, Sam among them. On the ground between his feet was his backpack, unzipped halfway. Ronnie drew in a sharp breath. What was Sam doing with a scarf of silence?

The dokkaebi must have Persuaded Sam into helping him. Sam had hated her from the moment they'd met, but he wouldn't want her dead. She was fifty percent sure of this. Shuddering, she recalled how he had followed her into the forest the other day. She didn't want to imagine what he might have done had Boo not shown up.

"You're a very good cat, Boo," she whispered. "Now, can you bury it or something? Really far away and really deep. Somewhere no one will be able to find it."

Boo mewed and darted off into the trees, the scarf of silence trailing behind him.

When Ronnie slipped back into her seat, the counselors had moved on to a skit involving oversized diapers, princess tiaras, and a party-sized bag of Hot Cheetos. The warm glow of the fire made it easy for Ronnie to push away what she'd seen in the dark. And the sweet smell of roasted marshmallows and melted chocolate on graham crackers made her second-guess whether it was Sam that Boo had been looking at. Maybe she was jumping to conclusions.

He was just a kid, eating s'mores and laughing at the counselors' jokes like everyone else. Well, not at that exact moment. Just then he was bent over, digging furiously through his backpack. He was frantic as he rummaged through it three times over before giving up, his shoulders slumping. Then he zipped his bag up, slowly raised his head, and met Ronnie's eyes across the fire.

Even from a distance and under the dark of night, one eye glinted green. And even with the heat of the blazing campfire hot against her cheeks, Ronnie shivered from the chill of his frosty glare. She told herself it was just a Persuasion and nothing more.

TWENTY-ONE

KAYAK RACE

The next day, under the heat of the afternoon sun, Ronnie buckled on a life vest and lowered herself into the front seat of a double kayak for the first round of the race.

"This is going to be epic!" Jack shifted in his seat behind her, making the kayak wobble.

Ronnie grabbed the sides of the kayak and braced herself until it steadied. "Since when are you so into this stuff?"

"I've always liked kayaking."

This was true. They lived near Alki Beach, and Jack and his dad were out on the water a lot.

"I mean all this summer camp stuff. Like treasure hunts and water balloon toss and risking your life to cross ridiculously dangerous bridges just for the challenge of it?"

He shrugged. "We're at camp. It's what you do. And it's fun. You'd know if you weren't always so checked out."

"I'm not checked out!" Ronnie pushed her paddle into the water. "Maybe if Sam wasn't always in my face . . ."

Jack dipped his paddle into the water. Together, they

heaved the kayak into motion. "Would it kill you to make friends?"

Ronnie was tempted to say yes—at least when it came to Sam. "I made friends," she said instead with a disgruntled huff.

Working in harmony, they gently guided the kayak to the starting line alongside five other teams. Behind them on the shore, nearly all the remaining campers had come out to watch.

The whistle shrilled and the race began. Ronnie's thoughts faded into the background as she focused on building up a steadily increasing rhythm for Jack to mimic behind her. A quick glance at the competition gave her a boost of confidence, helping get her head in the race. One team knocked paddles every few rotations. Another couldn't quite find their rhythm. A third moved everywhere but straight. That left two teams to beat, and Ronnie and Jack were already ahead.

The shouts and cheers along the shore spurred Ronnie on, pushing her to paddle harder. Soon her arms were aching, but she told herself *just a little more*. It might not have been true at first, but she and Jack were making good progress.

But then another kayak pulled up next to them.

"Keep your eyes on the finish!" Jack shouted from behind. She could hear in his voice that he was getting tired.

Ronnie's arms were burning, and a cramp had formed in her side. She remembered now why she never went kayaking with her dad again after that one time. But as much as she wanted to stop paddling and let Jack and her momentum take them over the finish line, Jack's accusations kept ringing in her ears.

She might not care for camp, but Jack was her best friend. And she hadn't come to camp just to get her dad to back off about moving or finding her a stepmom. Ronnie knew that if she wasn't careful, Jack would make new friends who did things like go to summer camp and win kayak races with him. Then he'd forget all about her.

Ronnie pushed harder. The race had started off with them in the lead, but they were now in that annoyingly uncertain fifty-percent-chance-of-winning territory.

"Cut through water like a fin, paddle faster for the win!" In the heat of the moment, the rhyme slipped past her lips as effortlessly as exhaling. The *tingle, tingle, crackle, fizz* that followed gave her a jolt of energy.

Suddenly she was paddling harder, propelled by an electrifying second wind. And it wasn't just her, but also Jack who was driving them forward with renewed energy. Surging ahead of the other kayak, they gained a comfortable lead and were quickly approaching the finish-line rope.

But they didn't slow. Ronnie *couldn't* slow. Even after the kayak skated over the rope, her arms continued rowing. It was like picking up too much speed and momentum while running down a hill. If she didn't stop the kayak soon, they'd crash into the shoreline and all the kids standing on it.

Burying his paddle in the water, Jack shouted at Ronnie to stop. His paddle slowed them down, but her arms kept rotating over and over, pushing them closer and closer to the shore. Ronnie squeezed her eyes shut and tensed every muscle in her body.

Only a few feet from the shoreline, she regained control. She plunged her paddle deep into the water, digging into the sand and rocks. The kayak made a sharp fishtail turn before coming to a stop.

Ronnie twisted around to meet Jack's eyes. His expression was downright gleeful, and he wore a wide grin to match hers. They'd won! Jack whooped, grabbed his paddle, and started rowing back out into the lake.

"Where are we going?" Ronnie called out, laughing with relief as much as exuberance. Pulling her paddle from the water, she set it across her lap. She wasn't ready to row again so soon.

Jack took them back over the rope before climbing to his feet. He pumped his fist in the air in victory, making the kayak sway a little. And then a lot. With a yelp, Ronnie dropped the paddle and gripped the edge of the kayak. Squealing, she yelled at Jack to sit down before the kayak flipped over . . . and then it did just that.

The second Ronnie came back up to the surface, Jack started splashing water in her face. He beamed like he'd just won the Olympics and his too-perfect boy-band hair was a mess, sticking to her forehead in sopping clumps. It reminded Ronnie of last summer at the pool. And the summer before that. And the summer before *that*. Like nothing had changed—not really.

Smiling even as lake water shot up her nose and into her mouth, Ronnie splashed back. Soon she and Jack were both screaming and laughing, trying to make their splashes bigger than the last as they backed away from one another.

The other kayak teams caught up and jumped into the water. Then suddenly the kids on the sidelines started running in, too. It got loud and crowded with dozens of kids splashing and shoving one another. Counselors' cries went ignored. Ronnie didn't know where to look.

Next thing she knew, Jack got pulled into a massive group water fight while she got bumped and jostled out into the periphery, which was far enough away from the shoreline that she couldn't touch her toes to the lake bottom. Ronnie was a good swimmer, but she didn't want to drift farther out.

But before she could push her way into the horde, a tug on her right ankle brought her to a halt. She glanced down, but it was too dark to make anything out below her torso. She tried kicking the thing off, but whatever it was moved down and wrapped itself around her shoe, making her foot feel like it was encased in stone—one heavy enough to drag her down. If it wasn't for the life vest—

There was a click, followed by the zip of a strap pulling through a plastic buckle. The vest was yanked away with the force of a determined hand. Without the vest, the weight on her foot yanked her under. She didn't even have time to scream.

Ronnie reached up, but her fingers didn't break the surface. She was too deep. And she was trapped. She had to free her foot from her shoe—*fast*.

Crouching down, she found the ends of her laces and tugged them loose. But as she was wriggling her heel free, a strong current pushed her sideways, knocking her hands away.

A flash of familiar red silk crossed her vision, rippling in the water like an eel. Like an eel that wanted to wrap around her neck and squeeze. Terror sent Ronnie's arms and legs into motion, but they were slowed by the water. Like in her nightmares, she thrashed in slow motion. A scream bubbled up her throat, and in her panic, she released the last bit of air she had been holding on to.

Ronnie's lungs constricted, and her chest tightened painfully. She was running out of oxygen. Out of strength. Out of time. And the dokkaebi was there with his red scarf to silence her.

Lungs burning, Ronnie twisted from side to side looking for help. But all she could see in the water were ripples cast by kicking legs and splashing hands. The muffled sounds of joyful squealing and shouts carried down to her, but no one noticed that she was trapped underwater.

No one would question a submerged red scarf. And no one would think to help her because she had never asked for it. She had pushed Olivia away every time she tried to help Ronnie with anything, which happened a lot because Olivia was constantly trying to be a good friend. Ronnie kept telling herself it was because she already had Jack, her *best* friend, but she had even kept everything from him. None of her friends knew about the danger she faced. To them, a red scarf was just a red scarf.

Her struggling slowed as her limbs grew heavy.

The sounds above quieted, and her vision dimmed.

A ripple of water moved toward her, streaked bright with red. *The scarf.* A hand strained behind it, willing it forward. Then a familiar face with two hazel eyes. One speckled with green. Both determined and furious.

It was the last thing Ronnie saw before her vision went dark.

"Ronnie!"

Ronnie opened her eyes right in Ms. Hana's face, inches from her own. She was different. Younger. And there was something unexpectedly gentle in her eyes.

"Are you hurt?" Ms. Hana cooed.

A warm feeling filled Ronnie's chest and eased her sobs. It was only then that she realized she had been crying for some time. She reached out, and Ms. Hana lifted her into her arms.

"Seek the injury and the pain. Restore and soothe. Health regain." A younger Ms. Akemi cradled Ronnie's pudgy little hand in her own and rubbed a cool salve on an angry red cut. It felt better immediately.

Sitting high up on her dad's shoulders, Ronnie peered down at a younger Ms. Pavani. Her dark brows were knitted together—she was worried, maybe scared. But she smiled when she caught Ronnie looking.

"I thought it would help, but it didn't." Her dad's voice sounded strange—angry and tired. Reaching up to Ronnie, he pulled her down and handed her off to Ms. Pavani.

"Theodore," Ms. Pavani said gently. "She wouldn't want—"

"But she's not here, is she? It's just me and Ronnie now. What about what we want?" Her dad faded away.

Ms. Pavani bounced Ronnie on her hip. "How about a snack and story?" Her voice was strange, too—cheerful but unhappy.

🌲🌲

"Ronnie!"

Someone called her name, but the voice was too far away.

TWENTY-TWO
SECRETS

The lake was on fire. Bright and blazing, it engulfed everything in sight, including Ronnie.

But the fire was strangely cold against her cheeks, along her arms, and down her legs. Everywhere but in her chest. There, the fire scorched hot, coating her lungs and stealing her breath. There was only one way to get rid of it.

Ronnie coughed violently, heaving and spitting up scalding liquid.

Several voices called out her name. She opened her eyes to a sea of faces that blurred together. All but one. Her eyes focused on Sam's face—crystal clear as the memory of his green-speckled eye underwater. *Sam had controlled the scarf. He had tried to silence her. Sam was a dokkaebi.* It all made sense—his hatred of her, his peculiar behavior, the scarf in his backpack.

Pushing herself up on her hands, Ronnie tried to scrabble away, but her arms and legs sagged like cooked noodles.

Two strong hands pressed down on her shoulders, holding her steady. *"Easy."* It took her a moment to recognize the guest speaker, Mr. Lobing from *Wild&Free*. He was crouched before her, his presence calm and controlled like in his videos. His eyes were the blue-green of the ocean, identical to the stone backing of the compass hanging from his neck.

She tried to talk, but her chest and throat burned. Mr. Lobing wrapped a blanket around her shoulders and tucked it in firmly. "You're going to be fine." He flashed his internet-famous smile.

Ronnie drew in a deep breath. It stung, but the air steadied her. She held it in her lungs for a second before releasing it slowly. She had escaped Sam's attempt to silence her, and he wouldn't try to do it again in front of the entire camp. She was safe. For now.

"I'm going to send you to the nurse," Mr. Lobing continued. "You'll need to get checked out, and they'll probably want to keep an eye on you for a bit. Do you need transport?"

Ronnie pushed herself up to sitting and tested out her legs, bending and straightening. She shook her head. "I think I'm okay," she said, her voice hoarse. "I can walk myself."

"Okay, but I'll escort you." Mr. Lobing nodded at her as though escorting her had been Ronnie's idea and he was simply in agreement.

Olivia moved into her line of sight, her face scrunched up with worry. "I'll go, too."

Jack stepped forward with Sam at his side. "Yeah, we'll all go." He gestured at himself and Sam. The sight of Sam's green-speckled eyes sent a jolt of fear straight to Ronnie's heart.

"No!" She bolted up, her back straight as a rod. "Just Olivia!" Ronnie's voice came out shrill. She cleared her throat and tried to stuff down her panic. "It's a girl thing," she added at the sight of Jack's hurt expression. That worked like a charm, and he stepped back with an encouraging nod.

But it wasn't a girl thing. It was a dokkaebi thing. There was just no way Ronnie could explain it all right then and there.

Mr. Lobing helped her to her feet. After making sure the blanket remained snug around her, he handed her off to Olivia and dispersed the crowd of onlookers. Olivia placed an arm around Ronnie to support her, and together they crossed the field and headed toward the manor.

"Hey, Ronnie," Olivia said when they were alone. "What was that about? What girl thing?"

Ronnie tugged the blanket closer. "I said that because I had to get away from Sam. I just . . . get this weird feeling around him, I guess." What could she say? That Sam was a dokkaebi who was threatening her with a scarf? "I think you're wrong about his crush. He's had it out for me since we first met."

Olivia's brows pinched together, her brown eyes soft with concern. "Ronnie, did he do something? You know you can tell me, right?"

Hope surged through Ronnie, making her feel light despite the weight of the wet blanket around her shoulders. Maybe she could tell Olivia. Then she wouldn't feel so alone. But Olivia would want to help. And if Olivia got involved, she could get hurt.

What happened today made the danger all too real. Sam wasn't just some kid. He was a *dokkaebi*—an ancient,

mythical monster who manifested in the form of a harmless, trustworthy middle schooler. He wouldn't just shut her
up, he would *kill* her. And if he was willing to do that for
a witch-dokkaebi rivalry that didn't involve him, there was
no telling what he'd do to someone who found out his true
identity, especially a nonwitch like Olivia who had no way
to protect herself.

When Ronnie didn't say anything, Olivia continued. "It's
just that . . . he was the one who saved you."

"Saved me?" Ronnie thought back to what she'd seen.
Sam was there with the red scarf, and he was definitely not
trying to *save* her. She shook her head, the word *dokkaebi*
perched on the tip of her tongue.

"Even though Sam and I were right at the shoreline, it
was hard to see much." A shadow fell over Olivia's face at
the memory. "I saw you and Jack fall in. Then someone suggested we all jump in, and one by one, kids started pulling
other kids into the water. There were a few kids really egg-
ing everyone else on, and soon *everyone* was jumping in.
It was total chaos. I don't know how Sam saw you were in
trouble, but I don't even want to think about what would've
happened if he hadn't."

"If he hadn't, then Jack would have been the one to pull
me out."

Olivia shook her head, a grimace on her face. "Ronnie . . ."

"There's a bunch of stuff you wouldn't understand,"
Ronnie added.

Olivia bristled. "Stuff only Jack would get?"

"Well . . ." Ronnie wasn't sure how to answer that. Jack

knew more than Olivia did about dokkaebi, but he had no idea that Sam *was* one. Or that Ronnie was a witch.

"You kept saying you'd tell me what you've been up to," Olivia said, her tone clipped. "But maybe that's also something only Jack would get."

Ronnie's mouth opened and closed as the look on Olivia's face changed from hurt to angry. The urge to confess everything was long gone now. This wasn't about Ronnie not trusting Olivia to catch her like in the trust fall. This would be Ronnie asking Olivia to catch her while she was on fire in the middle of the woods in summer.

Ronnie was on her own. She *had* to be.

Olivia grabbed the door handle and tugged it open. "We're here. I hope you feel better." As soon as Ronnie stepped through the door, Olivia stormed off in the opposite direction.

Olivia would never believe her. She hadn't been in the water. She hadn't seen what Ronnie had. She didn't know all that Ronnie knew.

And it was better that way.

TWENTY-THREE

WITCHES

Ronnie had taken two steps into the manor when Ms. Pavani, Ms. Akemi, and Ms. Hana descended upon her.

"Ronnie!" Ms. Pavani's eyes were almost as big and round as the glasses that framed them. "We got word of what happened at the lake."

Ms. Akemi fussed with the blanket, tucking it around Ronnie's shoulders. Her curls were askew around her face, like she'd been running her hands through them. "Are you cold? Hot? Is it hard to breathe? Does your chest hurt?"

Ronnie couldn't remember the first question. But it didn't matter because Ms. Hana began ushering them into the library. "We're taking you to the library for some privacy because there are a couple of children with poison ivy in the nurse's office at the moment. Not to worry, though, we've got a cot set up and we'll close the library for the time being."

Once they were inside, Ms. Hana helped Ronnie into the alcove and handed her a pair of shorts and a shirt with the Camp Foster logo on it. Then she pushed Ms. Akemi and

Ms. Pavani back to the main library to give Ronnie some privacy.

Slowly, Ronnie peeled off the soaked layers, put on the clean clothes, and sat down on the cot that had been wedged into the small space. The alcove was warm, but the sight of a jar of dried red flowers and a book with a red cover made her shake. Images of a slithering red scarf with green-speckled eyes flashed before her eyes, and a rush of cold slammed over her body repeatedly.

Ronnie gasped at the sensation of water filling her lungs. She coughed again and again, but try as she might, she couldn't expel the water lodged in her chest. And no matter how violently she shook, she couldn't free herself from the invisible grip holding her in place as the scarf drew closer.

The pounding of footfalls was followed by distant voices, the sound run through with panic. But all she saw was red.

"Ronnie!"

"Fetch her another blanket."

"Get her on oxygen."

"Would you just let me cast!"

There was a pause. When the voice came again, it was calm and steady. "Seek the injury and the pain. Restore and soothe. Health regain."

A tingle vibrated from the soft pad of a thumb as it smeared a cool gel across Ronnie's forehead, down the bridge of her nose, and along the base of her throat. Almost instantly, the shaking stopped, the chill disappeared, her vision cleared, and her breathing eased.

Ronnie blinked up at Ms. Akemi, Ms. Pavani, and Ms.

Hana. They had surrounded the bed and were peering down at her with foreheads lined with worry.

Ronnie bolted up, nearly head butting the women. "You healed me with a spell!"

Ms. Akemi clapped a hand over her mouth and made a poor attempt at hiding her smile. Ms. Pavani's eyes grew wide behind her lenses, and she turned to Ms. Hana, who kept a straight face, waiting for Ronnie to continue.

"You're all witches," Ronnie said. Memories from long ago came rushing back. Running around the manor with free rein over every room on both levels. Eating family-style dinners together. Sleeping in the bedrooms upstairs for days or weeks at a time. Ms. Hana holding her, Ms. Pavani telling her stories, and Ms. Akemi soothing her injuries. "I remember."

Ms. Hana held a hand up to Ms. Akemi and Ms. Pavani. She addressed Ronnie. "What do you remember?"

"Everything," she whispered. "I used to call you all auntie, or eemo . . . I—I used to speak Korean—especially when I came here to visit . . . which was a lot, right?" Korean words came to her mind with the same ease as English.

배고파요 Baegopayo. *I'm hungry.*

화장실 Hwajangshil. *Bathroom.*

감사합니다 Gamsahabnida. *Thank you.*

고양이 Goyangi. *Cat.*

부적 Boojuk. *Talisman.*

마법 Mabeob. *Magic.*

She knew these words—like *really* knew them—and the familiarity brought tears to her eyes. Rediscovering this part of herself felt like coming home. She hadn't realized how homesick she'd been.

"What else do you remember?" Ms. Hana pressed, her face expressionless.

"You all cast spells. And I believed in magic." Ronnie laughed a little at the thought of her younger self readily believing in the one percents.

Ms. Hana's cold, hard expression crumbled, and she let out a sob. She brought her hands to Ronnie's face and cupped her cheeks. "Ronnie, you're a witch!"

"Oh, thank the stars," Ms. Akemi sang out, her soft brown eyes glistening with tears.

Ronnie's head spun with a million questions. They tumbled over one another fighting to be released first. Drawing in a deep breath, she asked, "Why did I forget? And why am I remembering now?"

There was just enough room for the three witches to squeeze past the cot and plop down onto the cushioned bench along the bay window. They exchanged nervous glances with one another before Ms. Hana spoke. "When you were five years old, you and your father were Persuaded to forget about the supernatural world. That included us and Rhee Estates. The reason you're able to remember now is because your witch blood has been activated."

But there was something else Ronnie wasn't remembering, something she was missing. It was just out of reach in her mind. "My mom died in a car accident when I was five, but I barely remember anything about it. Why would I forget that?"

"Ronnie," Ms. Pavani said, ignoring Ms. Hana's warning look. "Do you recall your mother's name?"

"Elizabeth," Ronnie answered with a confidence she lacked about anything and everything else in that moment.

Ms. Pavani pushed up her glasses. "That was actually her middle name—though she sometimes preferred it. Do you recall her first name? Or her last name?"

Ronnie opened her mouth to respond, but nothing came out. "I—I can't remember. I guess no one really asks me that. Is that weird?"

"Not at all." Ms. Akemi wet her lips. "Most people don't ask too many questions about the dead—it makes them uncomfortable. And you've never asked because you've been Persuaded not to."

"Elizabeth—your mother—was like a sister to us, Ronnie," Ms. Hana said softly. "We were a family, which makes you family. That's why we've kept track of you all this time. That's why we brought you to this camp."

"Wait." Ronnie shook her head. "You brought me here?"

Ms. Hana nodded to Ms. Pavani, who took over. "When you turned twelve and we caught wind of your rhyming, we had to intervene. You see, witch-hunting dokkaebi pick up on witch magic unless it is done in a protected space, such as this manor. So, we mailed you and Jack an invitation—"

"Which I infused with a spell to compel," Ms. Akemi cut in with a smirk. "Then all that was left was for us to determine with utmost confidence that you are, in fact, a witch. We watched you as closely as we could for signs, but it was hard to be sure. Not to mention we were frequently distracted by the very real duties of running a summer camp! So, we asked Samuel to keep an eye on you, and though he wasn't keen on the idea, he has been so helpful to us."

All the air in Ronnie's lungs whooshed out at once. "No—he's a dokkaebi! He tried to silence me in the lake!"

Ms. Pavani fixed her bright amber eyes on Ronnie. "There *was* a dokkaebi at the lake today, that's for certain. From what the counselors have related of the incident, the children rushed from the shore in a sort of frenzy, unresponsive to instructions and warnings. And yet they were perfectly synchronized in starting a rather distracting water fight far from where Ronnie had been found by Samuel." She looked to the other witches. "All evidence points to Persuasion."

"Sam was the one who found me because he was the one who created the distraction so he could attack me with a scarf," Ronnie insisted.

Ms. Hana chuckled, and Ms. Akemi pressed a soft hand to Ronnie's forehead. "Oh dear, you're warm and exhausted. I can't imagine the stress you've been under."

Ronnie palmed her forehead in frustration. It was obviously going to be Sam's word against hers. But Ms. Akemi was right. Ronnie was exhausted. Too exhausted to convince them that the boy they asked to protect her was trying to silence her. Not when she still had so many questions. "How have you all survived for so long, all together, out in the open like sitting ducks?"

The women shared yet another look among them.

"Dokkaebi don't make a habit of silencing every witch they come across." Ms. Pavani cleared her throat. "For the most part, dokkaebi and witches leave one another alone. But the Rhee family has a long history of dokkaebi banishment."

Something—a thought—tickled Ronnie's brain. "So, you're saying you aren't being hunted by dokkaebi right now?"

The witches shook their heads. They watched Ronnie, waiting for her to understand something that she didn't.

"But I'm being hunted," Ronnie said numbly. "And I was being hunted even before I knew anything about dokkaebi. Even before I knew I was a witch."

Ronnie met each of the witches' eyes in turn, wishing one of them would just tell her whatever it was they weren't saying. She turned away and ran her eyes over the rows of cookbooks. Her gaze caught on a shimmering black decorative stone placed on a stack of books on a high shelf. The top of the stone was cut flat with an engraving of the hanja that matched the one on her baby ring. The one Ms. Pavani had said stood for the name Rhee.

Ronnie's entire body tingled. "Are there any pictures of me from when I visited the manor?"

Ms. Hana smiled—a real one that was happy and warm and a little bit teary-eyed. Stepping onto a stool, she reached up and pulled out a pale green book from beneath the stone. She placed the cookbook, *The Ultimate Book for the Diabetic Cook*, on Ronnie's lap. Ronnie swallowed hard. She could sense that what came next would be momentous.

She whispered the spell around a lump in her throat.

192

"Reveal the spells within this book. For witch eyes only, let me look."

With trembling hands, she opened the cover to the first page to find a handwritten note that read: *Veronica Ji-Young Miller, ages 3 to 5 years.* This wasn't a grimoire; it was a photo album. *Her* photo album.

"I have a middle name. *Ji-Young.*" She said her middle name aloud again, captivated by the sound of it. She didn't worry about having an American accent. She didn't care. After all, it was *her* name.

Ronnie flipped past the first several pages, which contained every variation possible of a close-up of her toddler face. Impatient to find what she was looking for, she passed over the first three-quarters of the album to a random page near the end.

Four-year-old Ronnie, dressed in a peach-and-tan-patterned jumper, stared up from a colorful plot in the gardens. She was holding hands with a young Korean woman with long, straight dark brown hair. Her mono-lidded eyes were an unexpected pale brown—the same color as the freckles scattered over her high cheekbones and across the bridge of her dainty nose.

Ronnie clapped a hand over her mouth. It was a human version of Min-Young.

TWENTY-FOUR
PERSUASION

Everything clicked into place with a series of flashbacks: *Ronnie digging her small fingers into Min-Young's thick and silky hair and delighting in how it never tangled like her own.*

Min-Young's monolids forming double lids when her face bloated the morning after eating salty ramyeon before bed.

Ronnie imitating the way Min-Young smeared sunscreen on her cheeks and nose as she warned against catching too much sun.

Min-Young naming the plants and flowers in the gardens . . . a picnic under the pergola covered in lavender wisteria . . . follow the leader along the pathways that wove around the different plots.

Ronnie released a soft gasp.

Min-Young was her mom.

Ronnie scrambled off the cot. "I have to go see her. I have to tell her!"

The witches were immediately upon her, pressing her gently back down onto the mattress.

"Ronnie, you must not," Ms. Akemi said, her wide eyes imploring.

"She'll want to know! I've been helping her get her memories back—she's been wanting them! She wants to remember!" Ronnie's chest felt as though it might burst. She could give Min-Young everything she wanted. And she could have her mom back.

The nurse patted Ronnie's knee. "Of course she does. For a gwishin, forgetting is painful. But, Ronnie dear, if she is confronted by a memory she isn't ready for, she could regress. The shock of it can cause more harm, and she could reject it . . . and you."

Ronnie deflated, her entire body drooping like a wet blanket. For a moment, she had thought the impossible was possible: She was going to reunite with her *mom*. But she understood now from the looks on the witches' faces that remembering could not be forced. The fresh ache beneath her ribs made it easier for her to understand why her dad often chose to forget.

Ms. Hana folded and unfolded her hands on her lap. "It has already happened once. When Min-Young was first silenced. We tried to talk to her, to ask her what she would like to do about you and your father. She didn't take it well. She rejected us all and has kept her distance from us since. She has been completely lost to us these past seven years."

"So, you haven't even been trying?" Ronnie looked to the witches—the ones she once called aunties—and her anger rose. "You just let us all go our separate ways? You abandoned us!"

Ms. Hana's face went ashen. "We didn't have much of a choice, I'm afraid. Though we had to be discreet and keep our distance, we have been watching you all your life, Ronnie. Allowing you and your father to live in peace was the only way to keep you both safe."

"That and to prevent Theodore from going insane," Ms. Pavani said, earning one of Ms. Hana's trademark glares. "What? It's true! What happened to Geneva, my very human neighbor, when they forced a Remembering on her after she was Persuaded? That's right—she went mad!"

Ms. Akemi nudged Ms. Pavani. "She deserved it. She never picked up after her dog's waste. Piles of poop everywhere you stepped!"

"Sisters!" Ms. Hana snapped. Her face was practically purple. Ms. Akemi and Ms. Pavani both covered their mouths, but it was impossible to tell whether it was to stop from saying more or from laughing.

The fight in Ronnie left as quickly as it had come. "What happened to my dad?"

Ms. Hana drew in a deep breath, and her face started to return to its normal color. "Your father tracked down the dokkaebi that silenced your mother and challenged him to a wrestling match in an attempt to banish him."

"Dad lost?" Ronnie whispered, afraid to hear the answer.

"Actually . . ." Ms. Akemi trailed off and looked to Ms. Hana, who heaved a great sigh.

"He won," Ms. Hana said with a nod. "But Theodore found that banishing the dokkaebi didn't ease his grief over losing your mother. And so he asked Ambrose—Samuel's father—to Persuade him and you to forget the loss and pain."

Ronnie felt as if the floor beneath her had fallen away. "Ambrose is Sam's dad?"

"Yes," Ms. Akemi said with an affectionate smile. "Those two are so much alike."

"So it must have been Ambrose who silenced my mom and then Persuaded me and Dad! That's the only explanation. Dad wouldn't want to forget Mom." She looked at the witches, frantic for them to see what was happening for what it was. Witches couldn't be Persuaded, so how could they not get it?

Ms. Hana grabbed Ronnie's hand and pressed it between both of hers. "Ronnie, Ambrose was already more human than dokkaebi at that point. He only complied because Theodore begged him to and Ambrose felt he owed it to your mother to do whatever he could to help."

Ronnie shook her head furiously. That couldn't be right. "Why would my dad ask Ambrose for anything?"

Ms. Pavani cleared her throat. "The three of us"—she nodded at Ms. Hana and Ms. Akemi—"reconnected with Lia after Sam was born. As for Min-Young . . . well, she could be quite stubborn." Her affectionate smile softened the criticism. "She made herself scarce, running off into her beloved woods whenever Lia, Ambrose, and Sam visited. But she never asked Teddy to go with her, and it's no surprise that he and Ambrose got along. I suppose deep inside, Min-Young knew Ambrose wasn't a danger to witches, but it's not an easy thing to reconcile the fact that he was a dokkaebi like the ones who had murdered generations of her family, including her own mother."

Ronnie squeezed her hands into fists. She wouldn't fall for these lies, even if the witches had. She owed it to Min-Young and herself to find out the truth. "How do you know for sure Ambrose wasn't the one who silenced Min-Young?"

"Because it's all recorded in a Remembering. We've seen it many times in order to try to identify the dokkaebi."

"I want to see it."

"I'm not sure that's appropriate," Ms. Pavani said haltingly. "In any case, it went missing a few years ago."

Ronnie dropped her gaze to the photo in her lap. Min-Young—her *mom*—smiled at her, alive and happy. Anger and frustration tightened her throat like a scarf around her neck. Her eyes snapped back to Ms. Hana. "If my dad banished the dokkaebi, then who's after me?" Before Ms. Hana had the chance to respond, Ronnie remembered what she'd read about banishments. "No one ever found his touchstone. His spirit regenerated."

Or so that was Ambrose's story.

"Can a dokkaebi transfer his spirit to another human form?" Ronnie asked as casually as possible, as though the question stemmed from mere curiosity. But Ms. Pavani gave her a perceptive look over the top of her glasses, a small smile on her lips.

"You are asking if Ambrose could have transferred his dokkaebi spirit to Samuel?"

Ronnie shrugged. "In theory, could he?"

"I suppose anything is possible," Ms. Pavani answered. "Except for the idea that Samuel is trying to silence anyone. That is out of the question."

"In fact," Ms. Akemi added, "Ambrose and Lia have devoted their lives to finding this dokkaebi's touchstone in order to destroy it and stop him for good."

Ms. Hana nodded. "They travel all around the world on weeks-long trips. The hunt is arduous given the fact that the touchstone can be anything from a jeweled crown to an antique glass figurine."

Like a glass fish ornament. Or a strange, useless pen.

The ocean roared between Ronnie's ears. No matter how much the witches denied it, it was possible that Sam was the new human form of the dokkaebi her dad had banished—whether that was Ambrose or not. And if the witches didn't believe her about Sam, she was on her own against him. Now she absolutely *had* to get his essence for the repellent. Thinking about the repellent made her realize that she wasn't completely alone. Min-Young would believe her.

"I won't tell Min-Young about me," Ronnie said to the witches as she worked to hide her panic. "But I have to tell her what happened at the lake."

Ms. Hana's frown returned. "Now is not the time to go traipsing through the woods. Not only is a dokkaebi actively and quite unabashedly hunting you, but all eyes are on you right now. You nearly drowned."

Ms. Akemi wrung her hands. "We'll have to call Teddy and let him know."

"No! If you tell him I almost drowned, he'll make me go back home! Then he'll definitely get married to Emilee-with-two-Es or Shayna-with-a-Y who'll ship me off to boarding school in Switzerland!"

"Come now," Ms. Pavani clucked.

Tears swelled in Ronnie's eyes. "You don't know my dad. Or at least you don't know what he's like since the Persuasion. If there's a problem he can't fix, he'll get rid of it. He'll get rid of *me*. It's like he's Persuading himself to forget anything bad. If I'm too much trouble, he'll want to forget me just like he forgot Mom."

Ms. Akemi's mouth fell open, and she rushed over to wrap her arms around Ronnie. "Oh, my dear, that would never ever happen. I know your father, and he would never allow it."

"Persuasions are imprecise," Ms. Hana said in a strained voice. "The trauma of one can have long-lasting impact like you've seen in your father. He has learned that pain *can* be forgotten, but he must still *choose* to forget. And he would never choose to forget *you*, Ronnie."

Her dad had chosen to forget the bad memories, but in doing so, he created gaps in his past. Was this why he was so focused on creating new memories? Maybe his ideas of a mother figure, a Korean community, and a new home were just his attempts to fill the holes he'd made by forgetting her mom, the witches, and the manor. Maybe deep down, he felt their absence.

Ms. Akemi reached out to smooth down Ronnie's hair before turning to the other witches. "We don't have to call Teddy, do we, sisters?"

"Akemi!" Ms. Hana cried.

"We know she's in perfect health! We've made sure of that!"

Ms. Pavani nodded vigorously. "And she's much safer

here than at home. It's why we brought her here in the first place!"

Ms. Hana threw her hands up. "Fine! It's true you're safest here, Ronnie, so there's no need to worry your father. But you'll call him and tell him you're all right. You don't need to go into details, but I'll feel better knowing we at least partially followed protocol."

Ronnie perked up at the idea of speaking to her dad. All this talk about him made her realize just how much she missed him.

"For now, surround yourself with friends," Ms. Pavani said. "That and the spelled river stone perimeters set up around the campgrounds are the best protections."

Ronnie chewed on the inside of her cheek nervously. "Are the stones here strong enough to keep dokkaebi out?"

Ms. Akemi pursed her lips. "No, only their magic. And only if the stones form a circuit with no more than a yard between adjacent single stones. Stacking them yields even greater strength and reach, so a stack of two stones can tolerate a distance of three yards. A stack of three, six yards. And so on. But can you see the problem with these larger distances between stones, Ronnie?"

Ronnie recalled how often she had knocked over stone stacks by accident. "It's harder to keep the higher stacks standing."

Ms. Akemi nodded. "And the larger the perimeter, the harder it is to measure and maintain it."

Ms. Hana put up a finger. "So keep yourself and your unispells within the manor grounds or a spelled stone perimeter. Outside of those protections, dokkaebi will pick up on unispells like sharks to the scent of blood."

🌲🌲🌲

That evening, Ronnie used the phone in the manor to call her dad's cell phone.

"Hello?" His voice sounded worried. He must have recognized the phone number.

"Dad? It's Ronnie."

"Is everything okay? Why are you calling from camp?" Yup. He was worried.

"Everything's fine, Dad," Ronnie reassured him. "Ms. Hana—the camp director—wanted me to call you because I fell into the lake while kayaking. Even though I'm fine, she said it's protocol."

"Were you wearing your life jacket?"

"Of course." *Until the dokkaebi magically removed it.*

"Oh good. Well then, are you having fun?"

Ronnie could hear his relief through the phone. "Yeah, so much fun. But . . . I was wondering . . . why did you send me to camp?"

"Send you? That makes it sound like I shipped you off to boot camp!" His tone softened. "Are you sure you're having a good time, Ronnie?"

"Yeah, it's just . . . I thought maybe you were trying to get rid of me because I kept doing that weird rhyming thing."

"Ronnie, I would *never* want to get rid of you. I just found the camp very compelling. I thought it'd be really good for you. But I hope you know I completely regret sending you because I miss you so much."

Maybe it really had been Ms. Akemi's spell that made her dad want to send her to camp. Relief unfurled beneath her ribs and spread warmth through her entire body. It was like drinking a hot chocolate on a snowy day. "I miss you, too, Dad."

"In fact," he continued, "I'm never letting you go anywhere ever again until you're thirty."

"Even if I keep rhyming uncontrollably and scare away another Kristie?"

He laughed. "Even if you scare away all the Kristies in the world. It's you and me, kid, no matter what. You could never scare *me* away."

Ronnie bit down on her lip. She really, really wanted to believe this. "Yeah?"

"Yeah. Even if you got bitten by a radioactive vampire and turned into a dokkaebi. Isn't that what you and Jack are always on about?"

Mentioning dokkaebi should have made Ronnie tense, but the way her dad butchered so many fantasies and so much lore in a single sentence put her at ease. "Wow, Dad. Wow. Don't ever let Jack hear you say that."

"Point is, even then, I'd never let you go. I'd keep you with me and let you feast on my brain."

"Da-ad," Ronnie groaned.

"No, really," he pressed on. "That's how much I love you,

Ronnie. Even if you grow thick, coarse hair over every inch of your body, start howling at the moon, and eat everything in sight—"

"You're bringing in werewolves now?"

"No—teenagers." He cracked up at his own dad joke.

Ronnie laughed, too. Not because the joke was funny—it was terrible—but because her dad hadn't been trying to get rid of her. He didn't want to forget her, no matter what.

TWENTY-FIVE

THE SILENCING

Ms. Hana was right about one thing: All eyes were on Ronnie. Well, Ronnie and Gigi, who had somehow managed to make Ronnie's near drowning all about herself. When Ronnie rejoined camp the next morning, Gigi—clad in purple sweats—had everyone convinced Ronnie's "accident" was just another attack of the camp ghost.

As annoying as it was, Ronnie had to admit there were some perks. Gigi took away a lot of the attention Ronnie didn't care to have. And pretending to be freaked out by the curse of the camp ghost was a great excuse whenever Ronnie acted strangely, like jumping at anything red or staring off into the distance in the hope of seeing Min-Young.

It even helped her get back into Olivia's good graces. Olivia felt so sorry for Ronnie she accepted the apology Ronnie had agonized over all night. That also meant Olivia had been extra supportive, which made it nearly impossible to study grimoires. At least Ronnie had been able to spend most of her time at the manor yesterday going through cookbooks. That and painting spelled river stones. The witches insisted upon Ronnie carrying around no fewer than four stones in her backpack—a to-go insta-dokkaebi magic barrier. Painting them served two purposes: one, it was less weird to be caught with decorated stones in your backpack, and two, they'd be easier to identify.

"Ronnie?" Olivia asked, peering into Ronnie's face.

Ronnie dragged her gaze down from the treetops. They were back at the ropes course, and this time, they faced the high course. Ronnie took one look at the bridges she was expected to cross to reach a zip line and immediately backed away.

"Wait, where are you going? Are you okay?" Olivia called out to her.

Ronnie shook her head over and over. "No way. Nope. Not gonna happen."

"Whoa!" Willa planted her hands on Ronnie's shoulders, preventing them from colliding with each other. "What's up, Ronnie?"

"You cannot seriously expect me to cross that nonbridge and then zip-line my way down to certain death."

Willa laughed as though Ronnie had made a joke. "The zip line is totally safe. We test it before every camp."

Olivia ran up to Ronnie and tugged on her arm. "Let's go!"

Ronnie dug her heels into the wood chips. "Do you know the number of injuries and fatalities that occurred on these structures?"

Willa laughed again, stopping abruptly when she realized Ronnie was waiting for an actual answer. "Uh, zero? It's been used safely millions of times."

Olivia gave two thumbs-up. "See—one hundred percent safe!"

"Actually," Ronnie said, crossing her arms, "it's been reported that for every million people using zip lines, over eleven are injured. Not exactly one hundred percent. So, if the camp hasn't had any accidents here, then we might be due for one soon."

Willa mirrored Ronnie and crossed her arms. "So maybe I was exaggerating about this course being used millions of times. It's probably more in the hundreds. Satisfied?"

Not even a little. But before Ronnie could respond, a commotion broke out.

"He's bleeding!" someone shrieked.

Willa jogged over to a group of kids surrounding someone on the ground before Ronnie could say, "I told you so."

Olivia moved over to a low tire swing and stepped up onto it for a better view of the action.

"See anything?" Ronnie asked.

Olivia gasped. "It's Sam!"

Ronnie bit her tongue, reminding herself that if she didn't have something nice to say, then say nothing at all.

"He's holding his face—his nose! Oh, I think it's just a bloody nose."

One of the counselors waved his hands over his head at the gathered crowd. "Okay, nothing to see here! Back to your courses!"

The crowd dispersed, and Jack came running up to Ronnie.

"What happened?" Ronnie asked as he neared.

"He was hit by one of the tire swings," Jack said. "His nose opened up like a faucet. Blood everywhere."

Ronnie wrinkled her nose in disgust. Then it occurred to her that this was her chance to get Sam's essence! She carried everything in her backpack—including tissues. Digging them out, she rushed over to Sam, pushing against the urge to run in the opposite direction.

"Here." Ronnie thrust the tissues to the counselor helping Sam make his way off the course. He grabbed them from her and pressed them to Sam's nose. Within seconds, the blood seeped into the tissues, turning them crimson.

Digging into her backpack once more, she fished out a small sandwich bag and held it out. "You can toss the used ones in here." The counselor hardly looked her way as he shoved the bloodied tissues into the bag.

"I think . . . yup . . . we've got it," the counselor said as he checked Sam's nose from various angles. He patted Sam on the shoulder. "We've got to pay a visit to the nurse and get cleaned up."

Ronnie carefully pressed the zipper closure of the bag and held it between two fingers. "And I'll get this in the trash."

"Thanks for your help!" The counselor gave Ronnie a smile. Ronnie avoided Sam's gaze, but she could feel it on the side of her face.

Olivia caught up to her and shot her a sly smile. "So, what was that about? Did you have a change of heart about Sam?"

"I—uh—sort of, I guess," Ronnie lied through her teeth.

"I mean, he helped me on the lake, so . . . I guess this was the least I could do, right?"

"Oh. Em. Gee!" Olivia waggled her brows all lovey-dovey, which honestly made Ronnie queasier than the dokkaebi blood. She shook the bag in Olivia's face. "Better go toss this!"

That did the trick. Olivia leaned away and let Ronnie run off under the pretense of going to the trash bin. But she walked right past it and made her way to the cabin. Before entering, she paced the perimeter, checking that the river stone piles were present and accounted for. They were in mostly singles or stacks of two along the outside walls, within a yard of one another, and formed a complete loop. Satisfied, Ronnie kept her painted stones with her and entered the cabin. She was eager to drop the bloody bag, which had grown warm in her hand.

Grabbing a dustpan, she plopped down on the floor and dumped the tissues—careful to not make contact with any of the blood. She opened the grimoire and found the spell. But she hesitated before casting it, Ms. Hana's words echoing in her ears. *Dokkaebi pick up on unispells like sharks to the scent of blood.* But Ronnie had checked the stones herself, and she had extras in her backpack. So she rubbed down the tiny hairs that stood on end along her arms and drew in a breath. *"For essence must, break down to dust."*

There was a soft shushing sound as the soiled tissues collapsed into a heap of brown dust.

She tried not to think too hard about what the dust had come from as she mixed it into her basic repellent and smeared it onto her wrists, inner elbows, and behind the ears. She muttered her unispell: *"Dokkaebi witch hunter, don't come near. Dokkaebi magic won't work here."*

Ronnie shuddered as a *tingle, tingle, crackle, fizz* ran from the back of her neck down to her fingertips.

Now she was ready to see Min-Young.

▲▲▲

Ronnie paused before entering the clearing to take a few deep breaths. She was way more nervous now that she knew Min-Young was her mom. She poked her head in first and found Min-Young at one end of the clearing, surrounded by a small but powerful windstorm.

Min-Young's long hair stood on end, whipping viciously above her head. The red scarf swirled before her pallid face in a terrifying but graceful dance. Her white nightgown that usually hung lifelessly on her thin frame billowed out around her, puffed up with gwishin wind magic, making her appear larger than life.

Despite the wind raging all around her, Min-Young was as still as a painting with her head tipped down and her gaze fixed to the ground. Her arms floated up and out, as though she were poised to take flight.

Seeing Min-Young in this terrifying state helped Ronnie separate her mom from the gwishin. This eased some of her nerves. Like a good sixty percent of them. Or maybe fifty.

"Min-Young!" Ronnie called out through cupped hands. But Min-Young didn't hear her. Dirt and pine needles swirled up to Ronnie's knees as she drew closer. Then a small twig shot out and embedded itself in her hair. Nearly being impaled stopped her in her tracks. She wasn't risking drawing any closer.

"Min-Young!" Ronnie tried again. This time, the wind abruptly died out. Min-Young's hair fell back down over her face and shoulders. Her white nightgown deflated like a balloon. The dirt and debris settled onto the floor. Then, at last, Min-Young spun around.

"Ronnie! Thank the stars!" Min-Young looked happy, but her voice was thinner than ever before, sounding more like a faint breeze than the storm Ronnie had just witnessed. "Will you help me?" She waved Ronnie over to her and sent a tiny burst of wind to agitate a rainbow friendship bracelet pinned beneath a large stone. The bracelet bucked up and down until Ronnie shoved aside the stone and tugged it free.

It was dusty and slightly frayed, but intact and warm. A tingle radiated out to Ronnie's fingertips and up to her elbow. It was as if it wanted her attention. "Um, Min-Young?"

"Do you sense it, too?" Min-Young swooshed down, kneeling inches above the ground. She ran a pale finger over the bracelet, causing a loose thread to shiver. "This is the one. *I know it.*"

Gooseflesh pricked Ronnie's arms. Min-Young was talking about her silencing. The Remembering wasn't lost like the witches believed. It was *here.* "How did you get this?"

Min-Young grinned. "Boo, of course." Then her eyes turned as hopeful as a gwishin's eyes could. "Will you?"

Ronnie nodded, her entire body buzzing with anticipation. This was the proof she needed to implicate Ambrose and maybe even Sam. Dropping down to the ground, she tied the bracelet around her wrist and closed her eyes. *"Take me there, to when and where. A memory that's saved to share."*

When Ronnie opened her eyes, she was in Min-Young's perspective. She was aggravated and paced the clearing under the golden light of late day.

Min-Young's steps halted abruptly when a young man stepped into the clearing. Ronnie's stomach lurched. It was Ambrose. With honey-blond hair and hazel eyes, he looked like an older version of Sam.

This was it. The silencing.

This had always been part of the plan—to remember the silencing and identify the dokkaebi. But Ronnie hadn't expected to experience it directly. And she hadn't known until a couple days ago that the one being silenced was her mom.

Ambrose moved toward her in slow and measured steps, the way Ronnie would approach a frightened, aggressive animal. Though his expression was impossible to read, Ronnie felt Min-Young's defenses rise.

"I was so sure we'd see you at Samuel's first birthday," he said. "It's been four years since that party and Lia's still holding out hope you'll show up." He sighed and moved a step closer to Ronnie. She wanted to back away, but

Min-Young stood her ground. "I suppose it's just as well you didn't show. Sam shouldn't have to suffer senseless witch rivalries," he said.

Ronnie felt Min-Young's face flush. "Senseless *witch* rivalries? What is senseless is the silencing of witches for simply being born a witch. What is *senseless* is dishonoring your family and turning your back on your best friend"— her voice caught on the last word—"to marry a *dokkaebi*." The word tasted foul in her mouth.

Ambrose flinched as if she had tossed a well-aimed shard of glass at him. "Anyone worth keeping around would have stuck around," he said, his tone low and angry. "You know, to this day she speaks so highly of you. All the while you've only shown yourself to be a poor friend. Again and again, you turn your back and run away. But I'll never abandon Lia like you did."

"*She* made a choice . . . and it wasn't me." Ronnie's vision blurred with a flash of hot tears. Her heart ached. Her fists clenched. Min-Young was heartbroken and resentful. But she wasn't afraid.

"You have a choice here, too." Ambrose advanced, nearly closing the gap between Ronnie and him. Ronnie's own pulse kicked up into a gallop.

Get away from her! Ronnie screamed in her mind. But she couldn't sway a memory.

"If you would just listen," he pleaded, his anger dissolving into something else . . . like desperation? For what, Ronnie didn't know. "You can't hide forever. Veronica turned five in April, right?"

Every muscle in Min-Young's body tensed at the mention of Ronnie.

"She and our Samuel are the same age," Ambrose continued with a smile that irked Min-Young to the bone. "Lia showed me a picture of Veronica's dohl. Did you know you both chose the same venue for the first birthday celebration?"

Ambrose paused, waiting for a response. When Min-Young remained stone-faced, he continued. "Did you receive the dohl ring we sent? Lia had the surname Rhee engraved on it. Said it's your family tradition."

Tradition? Was this an underhanded threat about all the Rhee witches being silenced by dokkaebi?

Ronnie couldn't breathe, though she couldn't tell if that was how Min-Young had felt then or how Ronnie felt now. Everything—all of their senses—were blending.

Min-Young began to shake with rage. "You shouldn't be talking about Veronica," she snapped. "You shouldn't even know about her. I'll never forgive Lia for putting my child at risk."

Ambrose raked a hand through his hair. "If you would just stop pushing—"

"*Never*," Min-Young hissed.

"She'll turn twelve before you know it," he replied, his voice strained. "Then it'll be too late—"

Ronnie gasped as a silk scarf wrapped once, twice, three times around her neck.

It happened so quickly. She didn't perceive the danger until it was too late. But the pain that followed consumed all her senses until all she could see, hear, smell, taste, and feel was *agony*.

The last thing she saw was the hazel of Ambrose's eyes—one specked emerald—glowing bright against her darkening vision.

TWENTY-SIX

MIN-YOUNG REMEMBERS

Ronnie's eyes flew open, her hands at her neck. The scarf of silence was gone. She was back in her own body. She was alive.

"Well?" Min-Young's voice was windy again—a faint memory of her voice in life. She peered at Ronnie with bright inky eyes set against a lifeless complexion. "Was it my silencing? Did you see the dokkaebi?"

Ronnie told Min-Young everything. Everything but the part about Min-Young being her mom. Min-Young's body grew increasingly transparent as she listened. By the end, Ronnie could see right through her.

"She chose Ambrose," Min-Young whispered, her gaze unfocused. "Ambrose, a dokkaebi . . . who silenced me in this very clearing."

"Do you remember now?" Ronnie tried to tamp down her hope.

"I do." Min-Young drifted about as if she were being carried by the wind. "After Lia married Ambrose, we drifted apart. She left our coven, and I didn't see her for years. Then she had a baby and . . ."

Ronnie's heart kicked like a bucking animal in her chest. "And?"

"Her . . . *son* . . . was . . ." Min-Young's gaze regained focus and latched on to Ronnie's face. "He must be twelve now. Your age. Right?"

Ronnie nodded, afraid to say anything that would cause Min-Young to veer from this path of memory that was leading to the only memory that mattered. The memory that would bring her mom back to her.

Min-Young's form flickered. "Wh-what was I saying?" Her voice was so thin, her words were almost impossible to distinguish from the wind. "I'm afraid all this remembering has weakened me."

Ronnie's racing heart stuttered in her chest. "You were remembering Ambrose and Lia's son. His name is Sam and he tried to silence me a couple days ago."

Min-Young cocked her head. "The child is a dokkaebi?"

"Isn't that what happens when you have a dokkaebi for a dad?"

Min-Young wound the ends of the scarf together. "I wouldn't know. He may very well be the first-ever child of a witch and dokkaebi. Not only that, but dokkaebi usually take adult human form."

"But I know what I saw in the lake. He tried to drown me and attack me with a scarf of silence. I'm sure of it. And I know how I can banish him. For good." Reaching into the inside pocket of her backpack, she pulled out Sam's pen. "I think it's his touchstone."

The scarf slipped from Min-Young's fingers. "I'm afraid

I do not have it in me to train one child to banish another."

"Even if Sam has already been trained to silence me?" Ronnie bristled at the thought that Min-Young would care more about the life of a witch-hunting dokkaebi's kid than her own.

"We don't know for certain." Min-Young blew out a long breath, kicking up dirt from the forest floor.

Frustration bubbled up in Ronnie's throat like vomit. Why didn't anyone believe her except for Boo? "Wait! Boo hates Sam. And Sam is terrified of Boo."

Min-Young cocked her head. "Familiars do have a strong instinct, and they despise dokkaebi. The feeling is understandably mutual. But this is not sufficient evidence for banishing a child. For now, it is best we focus on protections. How is the repellent working?"

Ronnie extended her arms and legs to show off bite-free skin. "I got Sam's essence and made a repellent specific to him, too. Just in case."

Min-Young nodded. "As for the touchstone, keep it with you for leverage only. Just in case." She began hover-pacing. "I don't understand why a dokkaebi would choose to assume the form of a child."

"Maybe Ambrose thought it'd be more meaningful to keep it in the family," Ronnie said bitterly. "Like the Rhees."

"What do you mean?" Min-Young asked abruptly. "Keep it in the family?"

Ronnie slapped a hand over her mouth. She hadn't meant to say that.

Min-Young's pacing became erratic. She moved faster

and faster, plumes of dirt rising up around her. She made a pained noise and began flickering in and out.

"Min-Young?" Ronnie's voice wobbled and her eyes stung.

If she is confronted by a memory she isn't ready for, she could regress. The shock of it can cause more harm and she could reject it . . . and you.

Ronnie had ruined everything. She messed it all up and now Min-Young would forget her completely. Forever. She made no attempt to stop the tears from rolling down her face. Her mom was here, but her mind had gone. She'd left Ronnie. Again.

Turning away, Ronnie ran out of the clearing. She wanted to run all the way back home to her dad, but her tears were coming down so fast and hard that she was forced to slow to a walk.

Her tears ebbed about halfway back to the campground and the wind dried her cheeks. The breeze was warm and familiar, and wrapped all the way around her like a parent's hug. Ronnie stopped in her tracks and slowly turned around.

Min-Young stood before her, no longer flickering, but still translucent. Something fluttered between her fingers. Without a tangible grip, Min-Young held on to it by pressing wind together. She allowed the wind to die, and a torn newspaper clipping fluttered down to the ground.

Ronnie picked it up. It was a section of an obituary.

"It's mine," Min-Young said softly. "See where it says who I was survived by?"

Ronnie scanned the few sentences on the newspaper scrap. "No one. No family."

Min-Young's lips curved into a small smile. "My death was preceded by the deaths of every other Rhee witch before me. One by one, my loved ones were taken from me—and all in the same manner." She gripped her scarf with both hands as though she would tear it. But then she let it go and smoothed it as she always did. "But it was more than the scarf connecting our deaths. We all died at the hands of the same dokkaebi—one who manifested new human forms each time a Rhee partially banished him."

Ronnie looked at the tips of her sneakers, not wanting to hope again. But Min-Young reached out and placed a finger under her chin. It was wispy but warm as it guided her face up to meet Min-Young's gaze.

"And that same dokkaebi is after you, Ronnie," Min-Young said, her voice stronger now. "That obituary is wrong. I was survived by you, the last Rhee witch."

Ronnie's breath caught in her throat. "You remember," she choked out. "You remember *me*?"

Min-Young nodded. "Of course. You're my daughter. You're the reason I'm still here."

Tears filled Ronnie's eyes so quickly it was as though they had never stopped. "But you're not really. You died," she whispered, her throat swelling. "You died and then you forgot about us, and we forgot about you."

Min-Young sank down onto her knees. "I'm so sorry, Ronnie. I'm so sorry I forgot. I don't know how I could. Not when you were—and are—the most important thing in the entire world to me." Her eyes shone with tears. "When did you find out?"

"I remembered a couple days ago, after the attack at the lake." Ronnie averted her gaze. "I'm sorry I didn't tell you right away."

Min-Young sent a warm breeze to blow Ronnie's hair from her face and dry her tears. "I'm the one who's sorry. I should have been the one to tell you."

Ronnie's stomach lurched with sudden understanding. "That's right. You *are* here because of me. I think the reason Ambrose hasn't removed your scarf is because he learned about me from Lia."

Min-Young's lips parted with a small sigh. "You're right, Ronnie. He knew of your birth but didn't know if you'd become a witch. He had to wait until you turned twelve."

"So *you* were the bait after all. He knew we'd find each other."

"He was right." Min-Young gave Ronnie a wry smile. "But he was wrong to underestimate us."

Ronnie tried to smile back, but another thought caused her spirits to sink to the ground. "But what happens if we banish him completely?"

"Complete banishment would remove the dokkaebi from this world entirely—his spirit. His power. All of it."

Ronnie's chest constricted. "You'd leave too."

"Ronnie, you are the love of my life and death." Min-Young's voice rang out with renewed strength. "Now that we're together, I'm not leaving you again. Anyway, we have a lot of catching up to do."

Ronnie squirmed against the way her heart ached with hope. "It'll probably take a while. . . ."

Min-Young tapped a windy finger to Ronnie's nose. "I will be with you so long as you need me to be."

"Are you sure?" When Min-Young gave a curt nod in response, Ronnie narrowed her eyes. "*How* sure?"

"One hundred percent."

"I don't believe in one hundred percent."

"Do you believe in me, Ronnie?"

Ronnie nodded. "Ninety-nine percent."

"You know that remaining one percent?"

Ronnie nodded again. "That's for chance."

But Min-Young shook her head. "That's for *faith*. And that faith—that one percent—was what brought you to me, seven years after we parted."

Ronnie had never thought of it that way.

"Don't just *believe* in me. Have *faith* in me. Know with one hundred percent certainty I will be here." Min-Young opened her arms, and Ronnie fell into a hug that felt too warm to be shared with a gwishin, and too solid to be anything less than one hundred percent real.

TWENTY-SEVEN
REMEMBERING

From the moment Ronnie woke up the next morning, all she could think about was seeing Min-Young again. It had taken every ounce of her self-control to walk to the dining hall instead of running directly to the forest. She was about halfway to the buffet when that self-control ran out. She stopped so abruptly that Olivia collided into her back.

"Hey, what's the deal?"

Ronnie arranged her face into her most pitiable expression before spinning around. "I don't feel so good. I'm going to go to the bathroom."

Olivia's face went stony.

Wrapping her arms around her middle, Ronnie faked sick. When Olivia didn't say a word, she moaned. "It must be something I ate—"

"You didn't eat yet."

Thinking quickly, Ronnie replied, "I snuck some candy here and I had—"

"You're a terrible actor." Olivia pursed her lips, unmoved by Ronnie's performance. "Where are you trying to sneak off to again?"

Ronnie tugged on her backpack straps for something to do—anything to fill the awkward silence.

Olivia narrowed her eyes. "Are you breaking the rules?"

Ronnie looked everywhere but at Olivia. "Of course not!" Why did her voice come out so high-pitched?

Olivia sighed. "Are you at least being safe?"

Ronnie nodded emphatically. "Of course I am!" This time, her voice was too low. She cleared her throat.

"You're a really bad liar." Olivia crossed her arms. "And I'm not lying for you again, especially if you can't even tell me why. It's not fair. And if you really are my friend, then you wouldn't ask me to."

Ronnie shifted uncomfortably on her feet. She should have known better than to try to use the same trick twice. "But I really do need to use the bathroom." That part wasn't a lie; she did plan to use it. At least the sink and window that were *in* the bathroom.

"Fine. I'll go with you." Olivia lifted her brows in challenge.

Ronnie pulled her lips into a tight smile. "Sure! I guess pooping with friends is all part of the camp experience."

Olivia's eyes looked like they were about to pop out of her head. "Oh. Em. Gee. Ronnie, the number system is *so* easy!"

Ronnie winced. "Well, in that case, it's more like number three—"

"You're on your own." Olivia hastened away as if Ronnie had gone number three right then and there.

Ronnie made her way quickly to the bathroom, her

stomach clenching with guilt for deceiving Olivia. Again. But there were only three days of camp left, and Ronnie was running out of time to be with her mom.

Inside the bathroom, Ronnie climbed up onto the sink and popped her head out the window to survey her exit route. She half expected Min-Young to be there by the Welcome to Camp Foster sign. Then she recalled that the locked door had been a trap set by the dokkaebi. Ronnie shuddered. She peered out into the woods but couldn't make out anything beyond a few feet past the tree line.

Ronnie gathered her courage and forced herself to think of Min-Young, her mom. Wiggling herself through the window, she jumped down and landed easily on her feet. With everyone inside the dining hall for breakfast, her path to the forest was clear.

Or so she thought.

Ronnie was steps from the forest border when Ms. Hana stepped out from the shadows—arms crossed and a livid expression on her face.

"Veronica Miller." Ms. Hana's tone was so cold Ronnie shivered. "I thought I had made it clear you are not to be alone—even on *genuine* bathroom trips. And you are most certainly not to go looking for Min-Young in the forest."

"She knows everything," Ronnie blurted out.

"What?" Ms. Hana's entire expression changed like someone had hit her in the stomach with a tire swing. "She knows *everything*?"

Ronnie winced, nodding. "About Ambrose, too. I saw it with my own eyes. Or actually, through Min-Young's eyes."

Ms. Hana pressed a hand to her forehead. "Ronnie, we must tread carefully here. If Min-Young gets the wrong idea, the consequences could be dire. For more than one person."

Realizing she wasn't going to get anywhere with Ms. Hana, Ronnie came up with another idea. "Why don't you come with me?"

"What?" Another tire swing.

"If you came with me, I wouldn't be alone, right?" Ronnie inched forward. "And you could see Min-Young's silencing for yourself. She has the Remembering bracelet."

Ms. Hana considered this. "Well, I suppose it couldn't hurt to go say hello. I mean . . . I haven't seen her in years." She wrung her hands nervously. "What if she doesn't remember me?"

"She has to," Ronnie said. "She remembers me and Dad and everything."

Ms. Hana's lips turned up at the corners. This smile had no teeth; it was all in the eyes. "Let's go, then."

Ronnie couldn't walk fast enough. Her heart was a tornado of hope, impatience, and anticipation. But when she burst through the trees and into the clearing, her heart dropped into her stomach.

The place was a shambles. Branches, torn from their trees, were strewn about. Pine needles littered the ground, now more green than brown. The stones that had marked the perimeter were gone.

"Someone is quite messy." Ms. Hana clucked her tongue.

Ronnie craned her neck from side to side and up to the treetops. Min-Young was nowhere to be seen. Her eyes fell on something red snagged on a broken tree branch. She moved toward it in a daze, her heart beating rapidly with recognition.

"Ronnie?" Ms. Hana called after her.

It was a small scrap of fabric in a familiar shade of the brightest red. Ronnie extended a hand. The very tips of her fingers grazed it—and it *burned*. She cried out and snatched back her hand.

The tips of her middle and ring fingers had turned completely white.

"Ronnie! What happened?" Ms. Hana ran to Ronnie. Her eyes moved from Ronnie's cradled hand to the piece of red fabric. She gasped. "Is that . . . ?"

"I think it's Min-Young's," Ronnie whispered. "What if the dokkaebi got to her? What if he finally removed the scarf?"

Ms. Hana glanced around the clearing as if she were seeing it for the first time. "That would explain the mess here. It looks like there's been a struggle."

Ronnie dropped her hand. The sudden and overwhelming agony in her chest made the pain in her fingers disappear. "She's *gone*?"

"He's had seven years to come for the scarf," Ms. Hana muttered, more to herself than to Ronnie. "Seven years. Why now?"

"Is *because he's a dokkaebi* enough of a reason?"

Ms. Hana looked at Ronnie as though she only just realized she was there. Suddenly she raised an arm in front of Ronnie like a shield and swept her gaze over the clearing.

"Do you think this has something to do with me?" Ronnie spoke quietly, but the question seemed to fill the entire forest.

Ms. Hana gave her a sharp look. "Oh, I do not *think*. I *know*. This was meant to be a trap." She gestured for Ronnie to follow her out of the clearing.

Ronnie's lower lip trembled as she fought back tears. "It's my fault she's gone, isn't it?"

"Now, that's not what I said, Ronnie." Ms. Hana's head swiveled from side to side as she hastened through the woods. "But if this is a dokkaebi's handiwork, then he is closer than we thought."

Anger flashed through Ronnie and dried the tears from her eyes before they could fall. She knew exactly where the dokkaebi was. He was at camp stealing her best friend and plotting to silence her. Ronnie's steps turned to stomps as she hurried after Ms. Hana. "Maybe you should check where Sam is right now. Or his dad?"

Ms. Hana's stride faltered.

"Wait," Ronnie said, planting her feet. "What are you not telling me?"

Ms. Hana heaved a sigh. "You might as well know. Ambrose and Lia arrived last night."

"Why are—"

Ms. Hana put up a hand. "They are here at our request. We thought you needed more protection."

Ronnie's eyes bugged out. "So you sent for my mom's murderer?" She gestured wildly behind her in the direction of Min-Young's clearing. "This is obviously not a coincidence!"

Ms. Hana stared into Ronnie's eyes. "Ronnie, your mother trusted us to keep you safe. I'm asking you to trust us, too. Will you do that?"

Ronnie tore her gaze away and aimed it at the ground. If Ms. Hana could see her eyes, she'd know Ronnie was lying because Olivia was right—she was a terrible liar. "Okay," she muttered.

"Thank you, Ronnie." Seeming satisfied, Ms. Hana turned around to continue out of the clearing. When she lifted her foot, Ronnie noticed something blue, gray, and white stuck to the bottom of her shoe—a friendship bracelet with the telltale threads of ginseng root.

With a quick step, Ronnie stomped down on the bracelet, tugging it free from the shoe. Then, just as quickly, she picked it up and shoved it into her pocket. It wasn't that she didn't trust Ms. Hana or the other witches. She just didn't trust their friends.

Once they emerged from the forest, Ms. Hana rushed Ronnie to the nurse's station. Ms. Akemi wasn't there, so Ms. Hana rummaged around the cabinets and fished out a healing balm for Ronnie's burns.

"How's that?" Ms. Hana asked after murmuring a quick spell along with the application.

Ronnie nodded. "Much better." But she had forgotten all about the pain back at the clearing. All she could think about was the friendship bracelet.

"Ronnie, about Min-Young," Ms. Hana said, speaking carefully. "We can't say for sure she's gone. There are a dozen possible explanations for why the clearing looked the way it did."

"But which is most likely?"

Ms. Hana didn't say anything.

"That's what I thought." Ronnie hopped down from the exam table and slipped her backpack over her shoulders. "Can I go find my friends now?"

"I'd feel better if you stuck around the manor."

Ronnie frowned. "Is Ambrose staying here?"

Ms. Hana sighed. "All right. I suppose you're safe among the other campers." Her expression hardened. "But this time you *must* not go off on your own, Ronnie." She glared into Ronnie's eyes until she nodded and squeaked out a "yes, ma'am."

Ms. Hana insisted on walking Ronnie out the back way through the gardens. Then she watched her make her way across the entire field to the lake, which was especially noisy that day. The sound that reached her was loud and charged, like cheering—

The second kayak race!

It had been set for today after breakfast, and Ronnie had forgotten all about it. But it was clear by the stormy look on Jack's face as he marched toward her that he hadn't. Dread pooled in Ronnie's gut as she forced her feet to move forward to meet him. Sam and Olivia followed behind Jack, keeping their distance as if to avoid being burned by the rage radiating off his body like flames.

"Where were you?" he demanded as he neared. Several kids nearby turned their heads.

Ronnie winced. "I'm sorry! I lost track of time."

Sam stepped forward, looking almost as angry as Jack.

"We looked *everywhere* for you. Ms. Pavani is losing her mind right now. Because of *you*."

"Sorry," Ronnie repeated, even though she was confused as to why she was apologizing to *Sam*. "Ms. Hana found me, so I'm sure she'll tell Ms. Pavani. I wasn't feeling well, and I wanted to walk a bit to clear my head. Get some fresh air."

Olivia rolled her eyes. Irritation spiked through Ronnie.

Jack scowled. "What? Who are you, our dads?"

He was right. Only their dads ever said stuff like that. "I'm sorry I missed the race. But I'm not sure about going back out on the water after almost drowning the last time." That was a lie. It wasn't the water she was afraid of.

Olivia crossed her arms and kicked at a patch of thick, overgrown grass. "Are you sure it wasn't that you'd rather go hang out in the forest doing who-knows-what than find the last two scav hunt tokens with the rest of us?" She pressed two tokens into Ronnie's hand.

Sam shook his head in disbelief. "You've been sneaking off into the forest again?"

Jack looked from Olivia to Sam and then to Ronnie. "The forest? Again? Ronnie, what are they talking about?"

"Nothing," Ronnie hissed at Olivia. "First you tattle to Ms. Hana and now Jack? Why don't you go blab to the entire camp?"

Olivia's eyes filled with hurt, and her shoulders sagged. "I—I didn't tattle. Ms. Hana asked me where you were, and I told her you went to the bathroom. I don't know what you expected me to say to her, but I wasn't going to lie for you without even knowing what I was lying about."

Ronnie huffed. "Some *friend*."

Olivia jerked back as if Ronnie had thrown a punch. Then her eyes watered as if it had landed square in the nose.

"Hey, guys?" Sam said in a low voice. "I think everyone should calm down a little."

"Whatever," Olivia muttered, her voice trembling. She spun around and ran off toward the lake.

Ronnie whipped her head around to look at Sam and advanced toward him. "Calm down? How can I calm down after what your dad did! Yeah, I know all about it now."

"Ronnie, stop it!" Jack stepped between her and Sam. "You're taking this way too far."

Ronnie's entire body strained with outrage. *"Me?"* She jabbed a finger in Sam's direction. "He's the one trying to silence me! He's the one trying to prove something to his dokkaebi dad by *killing* me! And I'm the one going too far?"

Jack's mouth opened and closed. Then opened again. "Whose dad's a dokkaebi?"

"You've got it all wrong." Sam shook his head. "I'm trying to *help* you. So is my dad."

Ronnie stared at him for a moment, unnerved by his ability to lie so well.

Jack threw his arms into the air in exasperation. "I don't know what's gotten into you, Ronnie. If you didn't want to race, all you had to do was say so. I could've asked Sam to take your place. But you never showed, so I had to forfeit."

Ronnie gritted her teeth so hard her jaws ached. "Geez, I'm sorry, okay?"

"No, it's not okay!" Jack's face twisted with frustration. "And this isn't just about the race. You don't like anyone or anything here! You disappear all the time. I mean, why did you even come to camp?"

To run away before Dad could. To make Dad forget my problems so maybe he'd remember me again. To make sure you don't forget I'm your best friend. But her reasons for being here had changed. Her problems were so much worse now.

And that was all because of *Sam.*

Ronnie balled her hands into fists. "Well, maybe I shouldn't have come! It's not like you would have noticed. You never want to do anything I want to do anymore!"

"That's because you never want to try do anything different!" Jack roared back. "We're at camp, Ronnie. We get to try new things here, but you're too controlling to give them a chance!"

Ronnie shook her head. If only Jack knew about all the new things she's had to face since arriving at camp. "You have no idea what I've been going through."

"Because you don't tell me!" Jack gestured angrily with his hands. "It's one thing to try to edge Sam out, but it's another to do it while being a horrible friend at the same time!"

Ronnie felt as though the wind had been knocked out of her. She searched for something to say. But all the apologies, defenses, arguments, and attacks got jumbled in her head. It didn't matter anyway. Because Sam had won. He had taken Jack. Just like Ambrose had taken her mom.

♣♣♣

Ronnie had promised Ms. Hana she'd stay with the others, but she couldn't bring herself to go to the dining hall, where Jack, Olivia, and Sam would be. Plus, she needed to be alone to go into the Remembering. So as a compromise, she found Boo and took him back to her cabin. Luckily, he was willing to play along.

With Boo at her side on her bunk, Ronnie tied the bracelet around her wrist and closed her eyes. *"Take me there, to when and where. A memory that's saved to share."*

The tingles were instant. When Ronnie opened her eyes, she was stepping into Min-Young's clearing, where the forest floor was streaked with the golden light of late day. Before her was Min-Young—in the flesh and close enough to reach out and touch. Finally, Ronnie could see Min-Young up close. Not in a photograph. Not by reflection. Without the glare of the water or the shade of a baseball cap.

Her hair was thicker than Ronnie's—longer, too. It ran down her back with a glossy sheen that picked up the late-day light. Her complexion was fairer than Ronnie's, and she had more freckles. But they had the same monolidded eyes and thick, arched brows that gave away every emotion. Like right then: Min-Young was angry.

The distance closed between them, and Ronnie's head tipped down to meet Min-Young's eyes.

Tipped down?

Ronnie's stomach lurched at the realization that she was

in Ambrose's memory. She braced herself to feel his emotions clash with hers. But he wasn't bloodthirsty. He was hesitant. And he wasn't vengeful. He was *remorseful.*

This couldn't be right. Maybe her own feelings were mixing with his. Maybe the memory wasn't properly recorded because he was a dokkaebi. Or whoever spelled the Remembering must have gotten something wrong because Ronnie was ninety-nine percent positive that Ambrose had stepped into that clearing prepared to silence Min-Young.

But when Min-Young used the word *dokkaebi* as an insult, Ambrose shrank back with shame. And when he lashed out by calling her a bad friend, he was feeling defensive and hurt. There was no true fight in him no matter how hard Ronnie searched.

Min-Young shook with visible rage. "You shouldn't be talking about Veronica," she snapped. "You shouldn't even know about her. I'll never forgive Lia for putting my child at risk."

Ambrose raked a hand through his hair. He was tired of fighting, but he was desperate for her to listen. "If you would just stop pushing—"

"*Never,*" Min-Young hissed.

His heart dropped, heavy with sorrow. Sorrow that his and Min-Young's children couldn't grow up together. Sorrow that Lia had lost her best friend. Sorrow that it was all because of him.

"She'll turn twelve before you know it," he replied, his voice strained. "Then it'll be too late—"

His dokkaebi ears picked up on it first—the swoosh of

a silk scarf slicing through the air. A split second later, he saw it—a scarf of silence shooting out from the trees to his left and wrapping around Min-Young's exposed neck.

It happened so quickly; he didn't have time to block it. All he could do was watch, horrified and helpless, as Min-Young fell without a sound. It was the thud of her body hitting the forest floor that brought him back to himself. And then there was only rage. Red-hot rage.

Movement in the thick of trees where the scarf had originated caught his attention. Then a flash of blue-green—a reflection of some sort—as the person in hiding rose to their feet.

That was all Ambrose needed in order to know it was the witch-hunting dokkaebi. Fueled by grief and fury, he broke into a run and charged into the trees.

Ronnie blinked her eyes open. They were wet with tears. For Min-Young. For herself. For Ambrose, too.

The witches were right. Sam and his dad were not her enemies. But then . . . who was?

TWENTY-EIGHT
FRENEMIES

Ms. Pavani looked up as Ronnie stepped into the foyer. "Ronnie! What brings you in here?" She clucked her tongue. "And *alone* at that?"

Ronnie shot Ms. Pavani her most winning smile. "I'm not alone! I'm with you!"

Ms. Pavani arched a brow.

Ronnie dropped her gaze and poked at the hardwood floor with the toe of her shoe. "I—um—I'm looking for Sam. He wasn't at lunch, so I thought he might be here."

"Hold on one second." Ms. Pavani began typing on her cell phone. "I'll text Lia. I believe she and Ambrose are with Sam upstairs."

Ronnie's breath hitched. She clearly had not thought this through. She figured it would be easiest to get the apology and confession over with right away—like ripping off a very big, superglue-level-sticky Band-Aid. She didn't think she'd have to do it in front of Lia and Ambrose.

Tossing a glance over her shoulder, Ronnie shuffled back a few steps. "Actually, maybe I'll catch up with him later."

Ms. Pavani glanced up from her phone. "Sam's on his way down."

"Just Sam, right?" Ronnie's voice squeaked. Ms. Pavani nodded, and Ronnie breathed a sigh of relief. "I'll wait in the library."

"I'll send him in."

Inside the library, Ronnie dropped her backpack and sank into a leather chair. Lia and Ambrose were *here*. They were here in a way Min-Young never would be—in the flesh. She didn't know how to feel about that. All she knew was that her tummy was a frenzy of butterflies.

The door swung open. Sam strode in and took the seat across from Ronnie. "You wanted to see me?" He didn't look or sound mad, but he didn't seem happy, either.

Ronnie chewed on the inside of her cheek. She should have planned out what to say.

"I hope you're not here to yell at me some more." Sam scratched behind his ear. "Or banish me?"

Ronnie winced. "No yelling. Or banishing." She reached down into the side pocket of her backpack, her fingers hovering just above the pen. She couldn't bring herself to pull it out and hand it to Sam. He might not silence her, but he could get angry. He could tell Jack and Olivia what she'd done, and if they didn't already hate her, stealing could very well seal the deal.

Sam looked at her, patiently waiting, open to hearing her out even after she accused him and his dad of some truly horrendous things. She had to get it over with. Rip off the Band-Aid.

Ronnie drew out the pen and held it out. "I wanted to give this back to you."

Sam's eyes grew round. "*You* had it?" He accepted the

pen with two hands, like it really was as precious as life itself.

"I didn't steal it or anything," Ronnie said quickly. "I found it on the ground, and I was going to give it back to you, but . . ."

"But?"

"But then I thought you were trying to silence me, so I kept it for protection?" She shrugged her shoulders and flashed him a toothy grin.

Sam rolled the pen around in his hand. "Well, I guess that's fair. You *are* being hunted. But you should know it's not an active touchstone. It was my dad's, but he's human enough that this is now just a pen that doesn't even write."

Ronnie's grin fell, and she heaved a sigh. "I'm really sorry I accused you and your dad of trying to kill me."

Sam dropped his eyes, his face shadowed in shame. "My dad's not a witch hunter; he never was. But he was connected with a group of hunters. He doesn't remember much about those days, or even about being a dokkaebi. The stuff he remembers—like some of the magic—he works hard to hold on to because he's needed it. To protect you."

"Me?" Ronnie glanced around like someone else in the library needed protecting.

Sam looked up, his eyes bleary. "Mom and Dad blame themselves for your mom's silencing, and they've vowed to protect you. They're away a lot, either chasing after some clue about the dokkaebi's touchstone or hunting other known witch-hunting dokkaebi. My mom says that for every witch hunter they banish, that's one less dokkaebi that could be after you."

"The hunted became the hunter," Ronnie said, nodding.

"Eat or be eaten." Sam's lip curled up into a half smile. "That's why the witches brought you here, to keep you safe while they figured out if you're a witch or not."

Ronnie knew Sam knew she was a witch, but it was different hearing him say it out loud. Different and *better*. Letting go of the secret to just one other person made her feel light and free, like lying flat on your back in the grass after surviving the ropes course. She never would have guessed that the first person to know her secret would be Sam.

"So your parents knew about me? The whole time?"

"It's been like this all my life. They're so obsessed with hunting down witch-hunting dokkaebi that they spend way more time protecting you than being with me." Sam's voice grew quiet, and his shoulders hung forward. He looked and sounded the way Ronnie felt whenever she gave up without trying. "They kept such close track of you that I swear they know more about you than they know about me, their only child."

"I'm sorry," Ronnie said quietly, her eyes fixed on her lap. She thought back to how angry she'd felt when Min-Young didn't immediately want to banish Sam. At the time, she thought her mom caring about the life of another kid meant her mom cared less about Ronnie. Now Ronnie's cheeks grew warm with shame. "I guess I can see why you hate me. I hated you, too, when I thought your dad had taken my mom away."

Sam sighed. "I don't hate you, Ronnie. I just wish my parents would see me, like *really* see me. And even though the supernatural world is their entire life, they don't want me to have any part in it."

Ronnie looked back up and peered at Sam curiously. "So, you *want* to be a part of it? Like, you want to be a dokkaebi? Or a witch?"

He glanced around before leaning forward to whisper, "I'm pretty sure I'm both."

"What? *Both?*"

"Shhh!" He gestured wildly at her. "My parents don't suspect a thing."

"Why not just tell them?" Ronnie whispered. "I mean, your mom's a witch and your dad is—or was—a dokkaebi. It's got to be easier than telling my dad. He's a gastroenterologist."

Sam laughed bitterly. "You don't get it. My dad is terrified that being a dokkaebi means I'd somehow be less human. Mom doesn't want me to be a witch, either. She was a total wreck the year before I turned twelve." He rolled his eyes and threw himself back into the seat cushions. "If you could have seen how happy she was when I didn't start spouting rhymes . . ."

Ronnie cocked her head. "But if you haven't started rhyming uncontrollably, then how do you know you're a witch? Or a dokkaebi?"

Sam hesitated. "Remember the squids in the pool?"

She nodded. Of course she remembered. She was still annoyed that she lost to him.

"That squid came to *me*, and not the other way around."

Ronnie pointed at him gleefully. "You cheated! No wonder you won! I knew it!"

Sam stared at her in disbelief.

Ronnie shook her head and lowered her hand. "But that's not the point. I get it—you have telekinesis. Go on." She waved at him to continue.

"And at the lake, when you almost drowned . . . ? I could see and hear you struggling under the water all the way from the shore."

"Dokkaebi super hearing and sight." Ronnie quickly added, "Thanks, by the way, for saving my life." Her cheeks warmed, and she busied herself moving her backpack a quarter of an inch to the right.

"You're welcome." Sam cleared his throat. "Anyway, that's been happening from time to time—moving things with my mind and having super senses. But I can't control when it happens."

"And the witch part?"

Sam wrinkled his nose. "That one's not as clear, but whenever I hear someone else cast a spell, I feel this tingle right before the magic hits. I thought it was my dokkaebi sense picking up on them for . . . well, witch-hunting purposes." The tips of his ears turned bright red. "But then, when I tried to cast those same spells, I felt that same tingle."

"Did the spells ever work?"

Sam shook his head. "So far, no."

Ronnie thought for a moment. "When I first started rhyming, I felt the tingles, too, even when the rhymes weren't magical. And now that I've cast actual spells, I notice the tingles are stronger. So maybe you're a late bloomer? I mean, you're dealing with two supernatural forces, so it makes sense it'd be complicated."

Sam smiled a real smile for the first time since they started talking.

"So, you *want* to be these things?" Ronnie asked to be sure. "A witch *and* a dokkaebi?"

He blinked his eyes wide at her. "Who *wouldn't*?"

Me, Ronnie thought. Or at least she hadn't wanted to be. Now she knew that being a witch meant she was part of something—a family—and she couldn't argue with Sam.

"So, you want to meet them?" Sam asked. "My parents, I mean."

Ronnie tensed. "Your parents?"

Sam rubbed at a spot behind his ears. "Unless you're scared of my dad."

"No!" She shook her head vigorously. "It's just . . . my mom put a curse on him. I'm not sure he'd want to see me."

Sam grinned. "That love curse would only have worked if Dad had wanted to silence Mom at some point, and they both swear they were already in love long before that. But Mom still jokes that she's grateful for the curse because it keeps Dad in line." He shrugged his shoulders, like he was embarrassed, but Ronnie could tell he was proud of his parents. "Trust me, they want to meet you. They were tracking your dokkaebi when they heard about what happened at the lake and rushed over."

If Sam had asked Ronnie even a day ago, she would have run away screaming. But now Lia and Ambrose were just two more people who had been a part of her life all this time without her knowing it.

Ronnie followed Sam into the gardens to the pergola, where his parents were waiting. They rose to their feet at

Ronnie and Sam's approach. Ambrose looked pretty much the same as he had in the Remembering—like a taller, older, tired version of Sam. Lia was about the same height as Sam, but that was where the similarities ended. Her chin-length hair was dark brown—the same color as her eyes. She was Southeast Asian, with features that Sam didn't have. But when she smiled, her cheeks dimpled and her eyes winked into little rainbows, which was what Sam's did when he grinned.

"Ronnie," Lia breathed. Her arms twitched, like she wanted to reach out but had stopped herself. "You look so much like Min-Young."

Ronnie stood a little taller. "I do?"

Lia's face lit up, her warm eyes glistening. "You sound *just* like her, too! How can this be?" She pressed her fingers to her mouth.

Ronnie's heart swelled. Somehow, talking to Lia felt sort of like being with Min-Young. Only Lia was alive, and in that moment, Ronnie needed someone solid to lean on. She ran into Lia's arms. Soon they both had tears streaming down their faces.

"You have no idea how hard it's been to keep my distance these past seven years," Lia said, her voice thick with emotion. "But it has been so wonderful to watch you grow up into the person you are today. Teddy has been a good father."

Ronnie's chest ached at the mention of her dad. She missed him, now more than ever. "Yeah. He's the best."

"How I wish you had your mom as well." Ambrose hung back, but his voice was gentle and warm—not at all like a sinister witch hunter's voice should sound. It was hard to believe this was the person who had once caused chills to skitter up her spine. "I'm so sorry she's not the one standing here before you, Veronica."

Ronnie didn't know what to say, because it would be a lie to deny it and rude to agree. She simply nodded, her nose tingling with the threat of tears she felt at the thought of never seeing Min-Young again.

Lia pushed back the hair falling over Ronnie's face. "What's the matter?"

"I think Min-Young is gone," Ronnie whispered. She told Lia and Ambrose what she had seen in the clearing. They shared a look before turning back to Ronnie.

"I think it's fair to say the dokkaebi is close, and you're in a great deal of danger," Lia said.

"But what about Min-Young?" Ronnie asked, desperate for some answers. "If there's a chance she's still here, is she in danger, too?"

"We can't know what exactly has happened to Min-Young." Lia looked to Ambrose, who stepped forward.

"The scarf of silence is her tether to this world," Ambrose said. "Typically, it is in the best interest of both the gwishin and the dokkaebi to sever that tether. The fact that it has been seven years is . . . unprecedented." He hesitated and scratched behind his ears the way Sam did. "As for Min-Young being in danger? The only thing that can hurt a gwishin is being a gwishin."

Min-Young's anguished moans came rushing back to Ronnie's mind. "She was suffering, wasn't she?" Ronnie tugged anxiously on the friendship bracelet she had kept on her wrist. "This whole time?" She searched Ambrose's eyes for the truth. "I heard her crying when she thought no one was around. I've seen her flicker, and her voice would get all whispery sometimes—especially when she used her gwishin wind magic."

"Being a gwishin is painful for the soul," Lia said gently. "It's like being tired and never being able to sleep. Or feeling thirsty regardless of how much water you drink."

Ronnie's eyes bulged. "That sounds terrible!"

"Yes," Lia agreed. "I imagine it would be. But not as terrible as leaving unfinished business behind forever. Seven years might seem like a lot, but it's a blink of an eye in comparison to all of eternity."

"So it's better she's gone," Ronnie said, mostly to herself. But her words were hollow. "At least she's not in any more pain."

It was Ronnie in pain now. Pain that made her stomach and chest squeeze. Pain that made her entire body ache. Min-Young might have taken care of her unfinished business, but now Ronnie had unfinished business of her own. Only there was no way for her to finish it now. Because you can't tether yourself to someone who's already gone.

TWENTY-NINE

STILL HERE

Leaving Sam to catch up with his parents, Ronnie returned to the dining hall, determined to make things right with Olivia and Jack. If she, a witch, could be friends with Sam, the son of a witch-hunting dokkaebi, then she could make up with her friends. After all, unlike Min-Young, Olivia and Jack were still here.

Ronnie loaded a tray with a grilled cheese sandwich and a cup of tomato soup. She squared her shoulders. She would walk right up to them and fix everything. She'd apologize and finally tell them about Min-Young and being a witch. They'd understand that Ronnie had been going through so much and see that the secrets had been for *their* protection. Then they'd make up and everything would go back to normal.

But something about seeing Olivia with the other girls from Sparrow's Nest stopped Ronnie cold. Olivia was talking animatedly, and the others were hanging on her every word. If they had been sitting at their usual table, Olivia would probably have been bored out of her mind while Ronnie and Jack engaged in their usual back-and-forth, or frustrated while arguing with Jack without help from Ronnie, or hurt when Ronnie kept secrets.

Then, when she saw Jack grinning from ear to ear with Benji as they bent over a Sinbi comic, she realized this would be harder than she thought. Not only had she been a terrible *camp* friend, she'd been a terrible *friend* friend. And if she was being honest, she wasn't ready to turn that around just yet. She couldn't geek out over imaginary monsters with Jack when there was a real one out there trying to silence her. Not when the real one was responsible for Ronnie losing her mom. Twice.

Ronnie took her tray outside, but the cheerful crowd made her feel painfully out of place and lonely. So she kept walking right past the carefree smiles and excited laughter until she found herself back in the gardens. Sam and his parents were gone, and she was alone. Almost immediately the tension running tight across her shoulders loosened and the weight on her chest lifted. She was by herself. But being in the gardens alone felt better than feeling lonely among friends.

She walked a path to the very edge, where an arched trellis created an entryway into the hedge wall facing the forest tree line. There, at the easternmost side of the gardens, the forest wasn't so far away. Plopping down onto the paved walkway, Ronnie nibbled on her sandwich as she watched the trees for glimpses of a white nightgown.

She and her mom had only just reunited, but already, her mom was gone without so much as a good-bye. Hot tears welled in her eyes.

A streak of red flashed in the forest.

Ronnie hastily rubbed the tears from her eyes and squinted into the trees. There it was again: red. It was closer this time.

"Min-Young?" It came out as a whisper. She tried again, louder. "Min-Young!"

A red scarf shot out of the forest and headed straight for Ronnie. One second it was just past the tree line, and the next it was halfway to her—low to the ground, level with her neck.

Dropping her tray with a clatter, Ronnie backed away on her hands and feet. She opened her mouth to scream, but the sound was caught in the back of her throat. There was no time for that, anyway. There wasn't even time to run.

Abandoning her attempt to scurry away, Ronnie wrapped her hands protectively around her neck. All the muscles in her body coiled in anticipation of the pain Min-Young had warned her about—the pain Ronnie had gotten a taste of in Min-Young's Remembering. But as the scarf slid under the trellis to enter the gardens, it lost all rigidity and forward motion. It poured down like a waterfall and pooled onto the ground. In her terror, Ronnie had forgotten all about the extra protections that had been set up around the manor.

A light breeze blew past, ruffling the scarf slightly before it went limp again. The spelled river stones had stripped the scarf of its dokkaebi magic. It was just a scarf now—inanimate red silk. Still, she couldn't convince herself it was harmless. And she couldn't just sit there on the ground waiting for the scarf to prove her right.

Magic tickled the back of her throat. She didn't know if it would work on a scarf, but it was worth a try.

"For essence must break down to dust."

Ronnie jumped as she felt the tingles skating down her arms and legs.

She flinched at the crackle and fizz.

And then the scarf disintegrated into a pile of pink ash.

Ronnie still couldn't get her legs to move or her heart to slow. Her eyes darted among the remains and the forest, her nerves stabbing like needle points at the slightest shiver of a leaf. Then a breeze blew by, scattering the ash and revealing a folded piece of white paper.

The breeze flipped the paper over and kicked it toward Ronnie. Momentarily forgetting her fear, Ronnie darted forward and caught it in her grasp. When she opened the first fold, some pink dust that had gotten trapped in the crease trickled into the palm of her hand. Her stomach lurched. The dust couldn't hurt her, but it reminded her that whoever had sent that scarf still could. She looked back up in time to catch sight of a tall, shadowed figure slip behind the broad trunk of a tree.

"Get up, get up," she muttered to herself, her breaths coming out fast. Launching herself off the ground, she spun on her heel and pushed herself through the nearest entrance. With her back pressed against the door, Ronnie tried to catch her breath and slow her hammering heart. Squeezing her eyes shut, she repeated to herself that she was safe here in the library. She was safe within these walls. She was safe from dokkaebi magic. *She was safe.*

Unless . . . the dokkaebi himself walked in. There was nothing keeping the dokkaebi or the scarf out, only their magic. And since no one knew who the dokkaebi was, he could easily stride right in and wrap the scarf of silence around Ronnie's neck with his bare hands.

She had to find the witches. *Now.*

Ronnie drew in a deep, steadying breath. And another. But when she forced her legs to start moving toward the door leading to the foyer, it began inching open—slow and silent. Whoever was on the other side meant to sneak in undetected.

Cold fear pricked at the base of her spine. Changing direction, she darted into the cookbook alcove and curled up in the far corner, her back to the wall and the approaching intruder. Ronnie hugged her knees to her chest, wrapping herself up into a tight ball and wishing to vanish.

The sound of footsteps started and stopped, started and stopped, as though someone was checking every nook and cranny of the small library. Whoever had entered knew Ronnie was hiding, and it wouldn't be long before they found her.

Huddled in the corner, Ronnie wondered if the past Rhee witches had felt this alone when they were silenced despite being surrounded by the magic of their ancestors. Min-Young had been with Ambrose, but she might as well have been alone the way she pushed him away. Still, she had him. Even if she didn't know it then.

Ronnie had no one. She had run away from her dad to this camp to try to fix her problems by herself. She had pushed away Olivia because she didn't want to get close to someone who would leave anyway. She had even pushed away Jack—her best friend. Instead of trying to control him or their friendship, she should have just tried to be a good friend.

And she couldn't forget about Sam. If she had given him a chance, things wouldn't have gotten so complicated. Maybe she wouldn't be alone with a dokkaebi closing in. Her tears fell silently onto her knees, but her labored breathing felt too loud, like a blaring beacon calling out her exact location.

Ronnie broke out into a cold sweat as the footfalls came faster and with more certainty. The intruder was so close now. Her stomach clenched painfully. The hairs along her arms stood on end. Her whole body shook like the camp welcome banner in the wind. Ronnie pressed her forehead into her raised knees and squeezed her eyes shut. She would be joining her mom soon.

The library door opened with a bang.

"Ronnie? Are you in here?" It was Ms. Pavani, her voice sharp with panic.

Ronnie's head shot up, but she couldn't get her voice to work. Nearby, footsteps padded away. A moment later, the back door opened and closed with a soft click.

The dokkaebi had left.

"I'm here!" Ronnie called out, her words broken up with sobs. "I'm still here."

THIRTY
MR. GOBLIN

After hearing what had happened, the witches insisted that Ronnie spend the night in the nurse's station under the protection of their watchful eyes and Rhee Manor's ancient ancestral spells. Lia and Ms. Akemi set her up in a cot tucked behind privacy curtains at the far end of the room.

"You must be exhausted from everything you've been through," Lia said with a sympathetic smile. She tucked a blanket tight around Ronnie's shoulders. "Are you comfortable? Warm enough?"

Ronnie nodded and stifled a yawn. It was barely dinnertime, but she was exhausted after going over and over the details of the scarf attack.

"Okay, then we'll leave you to get some rest."

"What about dinner?" Ms. Pavani protested as Lia pushed her out of the room.

Ms. Hana paused at the doorway. "We'll bring up some dinner shortly. You try and get some rest, if you can."

Ronnie nodded and shot her a grateful smile.

Before the door closed, Ms. Akemi stuck her head back

in. "You don't worry about a thing. We'll be watching the room all night!"

The door closed at last, and Ronnie's limbs and eyelids grew heavy with sleep. She welcomed it, wanting to forget about everything for a few hours. But with sleep came endless nightmares about red scarves at every turn. They swirled out of a bonfire like smoke, reached up from the lake floor like water plants, and spilled endlessly out of Olivia's mini backpacks like a horrifying magic trick. Each time, Ronnie woke with a start, exhausted, only to fall back to sleep to a fresh new horror.

She was being chased by a scarf the size of a parachute. It slithered after her, forcing her through the high ropes course. She ran over a tightrope, lunged across the tire swings, leaped across log steps, and crossed a zigzag bridge. But when she came to the final challenge, the bungee free-fall drop, she stopped. Behind her was the massive scarf that was intent on mummifying her alive. Before her was a jump to her crushing death.

She was trapped, and she couldn't choose which way she wanted to die. All she could do was turn her back to the drop and thrust her hands out before her, knowing it would not stop the scarf of silence. She squeezed her eyes shut, bracing for its scalding touch. But when it licked at her wrist, it didn't burn. Though it did scratch a little.

Ronnie opened her eyes to see light filtering in through the linen privacy curtain. The curtain ruffled slightly with a gentle breeze that was seeping in from a wide, narrow window just below the ceiling. She had made it to morning. Something scraped at her wrist again, and she looked down. Boo was pawing at her.

"Boy, am I glad to see you, Boo." She reached out to scratch the cat behind the ears, but he twitched them, flicking her fingers away. Then he deposited something into her lap and gave it a swat with the back of his paw. It was a tiny collar.

Ronnie sat up and laughed. "I never took you for a cat that would wear one of these." She picked up the braided collar and showed it to him. He backed away with an irritated hiss.

"Well, *I'm* not going to wear it!"

Boo nudged her again, right at the wrist.

"You want me to wear it like a bracelet?"

He replied with an impatient mew, and Ronnie gave the collar a closer look. There among the fibers, she found an inconsistent thread woven through. It was ginseng root.

Ronnie met Boo's golden eyes. "You want to show me something, don't you?"

Boo rubbed his side against Ronnie's hand.

"Okay." She slipped the collar over her wrist and closed her eyes. "Take me there, to when and where. A memory that's saved to share."

Tingle, tingle, crackle, fizz.

When the light beyond her eyelids shifted, Ronnie opened her eyes.

It was morning, and she was on the bench under the pergola in the gardens. But everything was enormous! Or rather, she was *small*. She couldn't control her form enough to look down, but she was certain that if she did, she'd see paws instead of hands and feet. And though she couldn't reach up to check, she could feel the collar around her neck.

Suddenly her eyes zoomed in on movement at the edge of the gardens. In one swift motion, she leaped down from the bench and dashed after the scarf, her movements quick and agile.

Soon she was beyond the gardens and at the very spot where the scarf had shot out from earlier that day. *This is a Remembering*, she told herself. *This is just a Remembering.* But it didn't feel like just a memory. Like how Min-Young's Rememberings always felt like they were happening to *her* and in real time, the danger of the scarf did, too, in that moment. But Ronnie didn't have a choice as Boo darted into the forest.

After a series of leaps and turns, Ronnie found herself at Min-Young's clearing. It was exactly as it had been when she'd last seen it. Once again, her eyes were drawn to the scarf remnant in the trees. Her stomach lurched. No matter how many times she reminded herself that a Remembering couldn't hurt her, she couldn't bear to be near that red silk. Her fingertips tingled and pricked. She hoped Boo didn't have plans to attack it.

I was just here. Why did you bring me back?

As if in answer, Boo growled, and Ronnie felt the ferocity of the sound deep in her throat. She picked up a familiar scent, though she couldn't place it. It grew stronger as he stalked across the clearing, his gold eyes discerning the slightest motion among the trees.

There was a stirring.

A flash of light.

With a snarl, Ronnie felt Boo lurch into the trees at full speed. The woods were thick here, but Boo's lithe movements escaped every brambly brush, raised root, and broken branch. Through the cat's eyes, Ronnie saw a man crouched low to the ground deep within the shadows. She couldn't make out many details yet, but Boo knew who this was—he had smelled him before.

Claws out, Boo launched himself straight at the man and landed on his shoulder. With a startled cry, the man jumped to his feet. He tried to dislodge Boo, but the cat's claws had snagged onto his sweatshirt. One hand tightened around a fistful of Boo's scruff and pulled. Boo retracted his claws from the man's sweatshirt and reared back. Then, with a venomous hiss, he swiped at the man's face. The resulting roar of pain sounded less like a man's and more like a monster's. The pure satisfaction coursing through Boo felt like Ronnie's own.

In the midst of the struggle, Ronnie tried to get a good look at the man, but Boo's cat vision was unclear. But as the man thrashed about in pain, there was something familiar about the way he moved. Then he passed through a streak of light, revealing a flash of blue-green eyes and a glint of the identical color emanating from a large charm around his neck.

Blue-green wasn't an eye color Ronnie saw a lot of. It

also wasn't common to wear a charm around your neck, particularly one that was the same blue-green.

Ronnie was suddenly seized by a memory of the day she nearly drowned in the lake. She had panicked at seeing Sam because she was certain he was trying to silence her. That was when Mr. Lobing had appeared with his soothing words and a warm blanket. Ronnie had been struck by his eyes. They were *blue-green*. The same color as the compass he wore around his neck.

Ronnie finally understood what Boo was trying to tell her. *This* was what he was trying to show her. She screamed the answer in her mind—in Boo's—but she could hardly hear it over the thunderous beating of her heart. Boo continued to struggle with Mr. Lobing, using his sharp claws to hold on to anything within reach, be it clothing or exposed skin.

With a howl, Mr. Lobing tore Boo's claws from his chest and neck and hurled him into the trees. For a moment, Ronnie was airborne, trees passing by in a blur. There was a sudden jolt of impact, the sensation of the collar snapping off, and then . . . nothing.

Ronnie's eyes shot open. "Boo! Are you okay?" She began lifting his paws and tenderly patting his back and sides. He flicked his tail at her in annoyance and darted out of reach.

"You're right." She ran a finger over the ginseng root threaded into Boo's collar. "There's no time to waste. I need to tell the witches."

Suddenly Boo's ears pressed back.

The hairs on the back of Ronnie's neck stood on end. "What is it, Boo?" she whispered. But the cat had already leaped from a counter to the top of a cabinet and out the window he had come in from.

The privacy curtains enclosed Ronnie, but she turned to face the direction of the door. Distant voices from within the manor grew closer until she heard the door open and two sets of footsteps cross the threshold. The blood in Ronnie's veins turned to ice when she recognized the two speakers. They were Ms. Akemi and Mr. Lobing.

THIRTY-ONE

A FINAL CLUE

The door clicked closed. Ronnie didn't dare move a muscle.

". . . climbing a tree—you know, to stay limber for my internet show—and fell down no less than twenty feet." Mr. Lobing's voice sent a chill running down Ronnie's spine.

A gasp, then Ms. Akemi's voice. "You must have hit every branch on the way down! I thought by the look of you that you'd been attacked by a cat." Ms. Akemi clucked her tongue. "Narrowly missed taking out one of those famous blue-green eyes, didn't you?"

Mr. Lobing chuckled, and Ronnie wondered if his laughter had always sounded so evil. She shuddered, and the subtle movement triggered a soft creak in the mattress. Ronnie froze, but the laughter stopped abruptly.

"Say, is someone else here?" To anyone but Ronnie, his voice might have sounded light. Curious. But Ronnie heard the sly and hungry predator just beneath the surface.

She shouldn't be there. Mr. Lobing could easily manage to wrap a scarf around her neck before Ms. Akemi even knew what was going on. And after he silenced her, he'd go

260

after Ms. Akemi. Maybe he'd silence all the witches while he was at it.

But there was no exit other than the one he'd come through.

"Ah yes," Ms. Akemi replied, dropping her voice before continuing. "One of our campers wasn't feeling well. She's probably still asleep."

There was nowhere to hide. Even so, Ronnie silently pulled the blanket up to her eyes with trembling hands.

"Is that so? You should probably check on her before you begin with me." Ronnie could swear she heard a sinister smile in his words.

Don't do it. Don't do it. Don't do it.

"You're probably right," Ms. Akemi whispered. "I'll just peek in." The squeak of her rubber-soled shoes moved closer.

Ronnie bit back a scream. She wished she could disappear.

Then she remembered that she could. She just had to hold her breath. And to do that, she had to stop panicking. Closing her eyes, she drew in slow, even breaths.

Inhale. Exhale.

There was a crinkling of paper as if Mr. Lobing was shifting his position. Probably preparing to attack.

Inhale—

Out of sight, but I'm still here, hold my breath and disappear. Ronnie mouthed the spell with the next exhale. Then, realizing the blanket would show the outline of her body, she eased it down into a rumpled heap at her feet. She sucked in one last breath right before the privacy curtain was pulled back and Ms. Akemi popped her head in.

"She's not here." She frowned. "I didn't even notice her leaving this morning."

The spell had worked! Ms. Akemi turned away, and Ronnie prepared to release her breath. But instead of closing the curtain, the nurse tugged it all the way open.

Ronnie's eyes locked on to Mr. Lobing's. His gaze slid over Ronnie's, but her heart still pounded like a water trampoline. His eyes were far more terrifying than Min-Young's ever could be.

"Well, then." Ms. Akemi held out a cotton pad, drawing his attention to her. "Let's get you cleaned up."

Mr. Lobing swiveled in his seat to face Ms. Akemi, and Ronnie watched his profile in silent panic. She was starting to get light-headed. She needed to take a breath soon or she'd pass out, and that would only make it easier for Mr. Lobing to silence her. Her lungs began to burn like they had in the lake, and she had no choice.

"Close your eyes for me," Ms. Akemi murmured, holding a cotton swab over a cut that had grazed Mr. Lobing's eye.

Ronnie seized the opportunity and released her breath. She knew the spell had broken when Ms. Akemi did a double take. Ronnie gave a tiny shake of her head as she raced through the spell once more.

"Is everything all right?" Mr. Lobing opened his eyes and peered up at Ms. Akemi.

Ronnie drew in a fresh lungful of air and blinked out of sight just as Mr. Lobing followed Ms. Akemi's gaze to where Ronnie had been visible not a moment ago.

Ms. Akemi shook her head and nudged Mr. Lobing's face back to her. "I just remembered I haven't fed the cat in a couple days. I haven't seen him, and I wonder where he's gone."

Mr. Lobing's face paled, and he cleared his throat. "I'm a dog person myself. But I find that missing pets—or people, even—are never truly gone. More often than not, you find them in the very place you left them." His eyes flicked over to Ronnie, and she was sure he was speaking to her now. "Their temporary absence serves to remind us that anything can be lost if we're not careful."

It took everything Ronnie had to stay still, to hold her breath in, to not look away. Mr. Lobing couldn't see her, and his gaze was slightly off, aimed at Ronnie's right ear rather than her face. But he knew she was there and that she was hiding. The shock of that fact cost her a good thirty seconds of air, leaving her about twenty seconds left—max.

"And sometimes a cat is just being a cat," Ms. Akemi said in a slow and easy manner that made Ronnie want to scream almost as much as she wanted to breathe. The nurse raked her eyes over Mr. Lobing's injuries and nodded to herself before grinning. "Everything is as good as we're going to get it for now. Try to keep the affected areas clean and dry—which means no more climbing trees for the time being."

Mr. Lobing made no move to leave. "I think it would be best for me to stay and lie down for a bit."

Ms. Akemi's gaze flickered over to Ronnie so quickly she couldn't be sure she hadn't hallucinated it. But then the nurse grabbed Mr. Lobing's arm and practically dragged him off the exam table and toward the door. Gone was her breezy manner. "No, no, no," she sang out. "Time to put on your brave face now! The children look up to you, Mr. Lobing, and it'd be such a shame for them to see their hero knocked out by a few scratches."

Ronnie's lungs screamed for release and fresh oxygen. She wouldn't last much longer.

"It's not that—" Mr. Lobing's head began to pivot toward Ronnie, but Ms. Akemi pulled open the door, nearly knocking it into him. He startled and snapped his head back to the nurse. Ronnie's stomach began contracting. Her limbs shook.

"Adult patients aren't so different from the children." Ms. Akemi chuckled, but it was tight and forced. "Being taken care of by a nurse reminds them of their mothers. They realize how much they miss her and get a little homesick."

"I only meant—" Mr. Lobing sputtered but allowed Ms. Akemi to guide him out the door.

Ronnie's vision darkened, like she was in a narrowing tunnel.

"No need to be embarrassed—I take it as a compliment." Ms. Akemi's voice grew distant. "Take care, now!"

Ronnie opened her mouth, and her breaths came rushing out and in, one right on top of the other, her chest and shoulders heaving.

Ms. Akemi closed the door, turned the lock, and spun around to face Ronnie. She held a finger to her lips, but her eyes were wide and full of questions.

Ronnie couldn't speak if she tried. She was too busy sucking in air and growing nauseous.

Ms. Akemi pressed an ear to the door, listening for sounds in the hallway. Satisfied, she ran over to Ronnie, snatching a container off the counter on her way. As Ronnie continued to heave for air, Ms. Akemi rubbed a salve onto the base of Ronnie's neck. Her breathing eased, and the burning in her lungs cooled.

"Now, tell me everything."

🌲🌲🌲

Ms. Akemi listened silently as Ronnie explained what she had seen in Boo's memory and pieced together from earlier clues.

Ms. Akemi shook her head over and over as she patted Ronnie's hand. "You must have been so scared, and yet you were still able to cast an invisibility spell. You really are your mother's daughter, Ronnie."

Ronnie wanted to smile, but another wave of nausea washed over her. She moaned and gingerly turned over onto her side.

"Oh dear," Ms. Akemi murmured. "Holding your breath too long can get you queasy. Let's get some of this salve onto your pressure points for nausea." She grabbed Ronnie's hands and rubbed the salve onto the insides of her wrists and between the thumb and index finger.

"Why don't you keep this with you to use as needed." Ms. Akemi pressed the small jar in Ronnie's hand. "I'll call for Lia and Ambrose to meet you in the library while I go fetch Hana and Pavani. They'll all need to hear everything you just told me."

While she was waiting in the library for everyone to

arrive, another bout of nausea washed over Ronnie. Taking a seat in a leather chair, she applied the salve in the same spots Ms. Akemi had targeted earlier. When she pushed the jar into her shorts pocket for safekeeping, something beneath it grazed her fingertips. It was a piece of paper— the one left behind by the incinerated scarf of silence. She had forgotten all about it until now. It read: *Come alone if you ever want to see her again.*

The room seemed to tilt. Ronnie used her free hand to grip the armrest. Min-Young was still here.

THIRTY-TWO
PLAN A

The door to the library swept open.

"Ronnie!" Sam grinned at her from the door, then called back over his shoulder, "Mom! Dad! She's in here!"

Lia and Ambrose stepped inside, followed closely by Ms. Pavani, Ms. Hana, and Ms. Akemi. They spoke at once—to one another and to Ronnie—asking if she was all right and demanding to know what had happened. No one took notice of the piece of paper she hastily stuffed into her pocket.

She knew what the witches would say if she told them. They'd say Min-Young was gone, and the clue was a trap. Maybe they were right. But it was possible Min-Young had run from him because she wanted to stay, wasn't it? Her chest fluttered with hope.

But the answer to that question would have to wait.

She pulled her mouth up into a smile. "I'm okay. Really."

"Yes, she is perfectly fine," Ms. Akemi confirmed. "I checked her out myself. In fact, she is more than fine." She shot Ronnie a proud smile. "She has discovered the identity of her dokkaebi."

Ronnie drew in a deep breath and launched into her story for the second time, sparing no detail.

Finished, she fell back into the aged leather chair. The stuffing exhaled slowly, and she sank into it like an embrace. Sam gaped at her from his seat, his pen frozen midspin in his hand.

At some point, Ms. Hana had risen to her feet and was now pacing around the seats, her hands clasped behind her back as she muttered, "I can't believe it. Guy Lobing!" over and over.

Ambrose leaned forward, elbows on his knees and brow furrowed. "You said you've been rhyming since your birthday in April? And you cast your first effective unispell on the fourth day of camp?"

Ronnie nodded. "A Remembering spell."

Ms. Pavani tapped at her lip. "But I received the call from Guy Lobing on the morning of the third day of camp. He arrived later that same day."

Ronnie sat up. "That's when I got locked inside the bathroom! I was going to climb out of the bathroom window, but Min-Young stopped me. She told me it had been a trap."

Ambrose's lips pulled into a thin, hard line. "It's likely you had been casting unispells even before arriving to camp. A unispell does not have to be intentional for a dokkaebi to sense it."

"That's right!" Sam pointed his pen at Ronnie. "You cast a unispell at breakfast on the second day of camp. It might not have been on purpose, but I felt when you cast it."

Ronnie winced, waiting for him to realize what he had just revealed to his parents.

Lia's lips pinched to one side. "What do you mean, you *felt* it?"

"Um, well . . ." Sam rubbed the back of his neck. He looked to Ronnie.

"I cast a spell on Jack!" Ronnie blurted out loudly. "To be nicer to Olivia." She nodded a few too many times as she squirmed under Lia's discerning gaze. Ronnie wasn't sure how long Sam could go on hiding that he was a witch from his mom, who was an actual full-fledged witch, but Ronnie knew what it was like to not be ready to claim an identity. And Sam was not ready.

When Lia's eyes drifted over to Sam, Ronnie began to ramble, hoping to draw Lia's attention. "They were fighting a lot, and the rhyme just slipped out. But it sort of backfired because he tried to be nice to her thinking she didn't change her outfit for ropes course, but it sounded like he was being rude because she *had* changed and he couldn't tell the difference between pajamas and athleisure, and it made everything worse. But now that they're both mad at me they don't seem to be fighting so much, so I guess I didn't need a magic spell to make them get along after all." Ronnie sucked in a huge breath.

For a moment, no one said a word. Her face flamed and she wanted to burrow into the chair and hide inside it forever, but at least she had successfully taken the attention off Sam.

Ms. Hana cleared her throat. "The timeline matches up, then. And I have no doubt he has been waiting for you as long as Min-Young has."

Ambrose leaned back in his seat. "Now that we know it's

Guy Lobing, we need to come up with a plan to catch him while keeping you safe."

The witches shared a look, and Lia turned to Ronnie. "You should stay here in the manor—indoors and out of sight."

Ronnie was more than happy never to see Mr. Lobing ever again. But staying inside the manor meant never seeing Min-Young again, either.

"It'd be suspicious to keep her in hiding," Ms. Pavani said. "And he'd be a lot harder to corner if he suspects that we discovered his true identity."

Ronnie sank down low in her seat. She knew she should tell the witches that Mr. Lobing already knew that *she* knew. She *should* show them the note. But they'd just make her stay hidden away in the manor while they banished Mr. Lobing—and her mom along with him. So she didn't say a word.

Ambrose placed a hand on Lia's arm. "He might run."

Lia's lips thinned into a hard line. "If he runs, we'll go after him. We know his identity now. I hope no one here is suggesting using Ronnie as a lure."

Ms. Hana slowed. "Well, maybe not *directly*."

"Hana!"

"Now hear me out!" Ms. Hana turned out her palms at Lia. "Ronnie's safe as long as she keeps with a group."

Ms. Akemi tipped her head from side to side. "True. And if Lobing goes on believing he has a chance at silencing her, we would have a major advantage here."

Lia opened her mouth to argue, but Ronnie jumped in. "Isn't that why you brought me here in the first place? To keep me safe by surrounding me with a bunch of people literally all the time? If we don't stop him while I'm here at camp, then he'll attack me at home."

Lia sighed in defeat. "These are all good points." She pinned Ronnie with a piercing stare. "As long as you stay with your friends. *At. All. Times.*"

Ronnie startled at a sudden thought. "What about you?" She looked at each of the witches in turn. "What if he goes after you to get to me?" Like he did with her mom.

"Ah," Ms. Pavani said gently. "Like you, Ronnie, we are safest around others. Should he attack one of us in the presence of humans, his identity would be revealed, and human awareness weakens a dokkaebi. Silencing one of us would guarantee his banishment by any one of the rest of us before he could even hope to reach you. Guy Lobing may thrive on thrills and attention, but he's not reckless."

Ronnie eased back into her seat at Ms. Pavani's reassurance. She didn't miss the way Sam seemed to relax a little, too. He spun the pen between his fingers so that they skated across from pinkie to pointer and back again. "It might be a good idea to let Jack and Olivia know what's going on. It'd be easier to protect Ronnie if they understood."

Lia shook her head. "No way. We are not going to involve any other children in this mess."

"But they aren't Mr. Lobing's targets, and if they know about him, they'll have a better chance at evading his Persuasions," Sam insisted.

Ms. Pavani raised her brows. "Samuel has a point."

Ronnie squirmed in her seat at the thought of telling Jack that her mom was a gwishin and Olivia that she was a witch. It'd be a lot for them to take in, but it would be Ronnie's chance to explain it all. Maybe they'd accept her anyway. Maybe they'd want to help her.

Ronnie's heart sank. They *would* want to help. If they knew about her plan to sneak away to see her mom one last time, Jack would insist on going with her, and Olivia would definitely tell the witches. She'd do it because it would be the "right" thing to do.

The paper in her pocket crinkled, like a reminder. The note had made it clear that no one else could know about Min-Young, and Ronnie wouldn't risk losing her mom again.

"No, I can't tell them," Ronnie said, thinking fast. "Jack wouldn't believe me anyway after I accused Sam of hunting me. Even if he did believe me, he'd hate me for keeping these secrets. He'd never talk to me again. And Olivia doesn't need to have her world turned upside down like this. She never asked for any of it. She won't want to be a part of it." Ronnie had made all of this up. So why did the words sting in the back of her throat? Why did her eyes burn hot with tears?

"It's settled, then," Ambrose said with a pat on Lia's knee. "Ronnie will simply stick close to Sam and the other campers."

Ms. Akemi rummaged through a bag and pulled out a small lidded jar. "Some repellent with Lobing's essence can't hurt." She handed it to Ronnie. "Do you have a unispell?"

Ronnie nodded. "How did you get his essence?"

"It was reckless of him, actually," Ms. Akemi said, her dark eyes sparkling. "Got quite a bit of blood from cleaning up those cuts. I even got some sloughed-off skin!"

Ronnie recoiled as the other witches leaned forward, their eyes bright and eager.

Ms. Hana shot Ms. Akemi a hard look. "Tell me you didn't use it all up to make the repellent?"

"Certainly not!" Ms. Akemi scoffed. "There's plenty of bloody skin for the trap."

"Wonderful! In the meantime, we can set my plan into motion."

Ambrose looked up at Ms. Hana. "You already have a plan?"

Ms. Hana lifted her chin. "Of course I do. I wasn't made camp director for nothing."

"Well, actually," Ms. Pavani said, "I'm pretty sure the four of us have an equal partnership, and it was you who insisted upon the role of director."

Ms. Akemi raised a finger hesitantly. "Financially speaking, Pavani's right. Which should denote equal executive power, though it does seem like you dictate nearly all—"

"Yes, yes. We all play our roles here," Ms. Hana cut in. "In any case, I have a plan, as per usual."

"We're all ears, Hana," Lia said with an eager nod and a suppressed grin. She looked like she was barely holding back laughter.

Ms. Hana launched into her plan. Tonight, during the campfire, the witches would set up a magical stone circle trap at the lake while Ronnie remained safely hidden within the manor with Ambrose. He and Lia couldn't decide which of them would stay, but in the end, it was more important to Lia to face the dokkaebi that had silenced her best friend.

Once the campfire was under way, Mr. Lobing would

be lured to the lake by Ronnie's mosquito unispell, which would be cast by the witches. They would be spread out and hidden from view until he entered the stone circle. Once he was trapped within it, the witches would surround him and combine their magic to banish Mr. Lobing.

A cold sensation washed over Ronnie, but she couldn't decide whether it was relief or fear or some other emotion altogether. Lia must have noticed, because she moved over to sit on the armrest of Ronnie's seat.

"Don't worry about a thing." Lia wrapped an arm around her. "You just focus on staying safe."

Ronnie looked down at her hands. She wanted to be safe, and she definitely didn't want to be silenced. But if Min-Young was still here, today could be Ronnie's last chance to see her. When the witches banished Mr. Lobing, Min-Young's tether to the forest—and this world—would be broken. Then her mom would truly be gone.

"Of course." Ronnie shifted in her seat. The crinkling of paper in her pocket was conspicuously loud to her ears, but no one else picked up on the sound. Or the lie.

THIRTY-THREE
PLAN B

With the plan in place, everyone got up to leave. Ms. Hana had to return to camp director duties while Ms. Akemi and Ms. Pavani gathered supplies and sorted out spells and potions. Lia and Ambrose set out to prepare the stones for the magic circle trap and cast extra protections on the manor, all while remaining out of sight. The less Mr. Lobing was aware of, the better.

As for Ronnie and Sam, they had both the easiest and hardest part to play: acting like everything was normal. They were supposed to go back to camp as if a coven of witches and a converted dokkaebi weren't actually planning to trap and banish Mr. Lobing, a witch-hunting dokkaebi who wanted to silence Ronnie.

"You ready?" Sam asked.

"Yeah." Ronnie's voice cracked, and she cleared her throat. "Of course. Let's do this."

Sam offered her a reassuring smile. "We stick together the entire time, like my mom said." He could probably see the anxiety all over her face. At least he would mistake it for the stress of being hunted by a dokkaebi and not her plan to sneak away.

Yes, she was plenty anxious. But she couldn't help smiling at the way Sam scanned their surroundings the whole way back to the campgrounds and how he insisted on walking her all the way to her cabin.

A few days ago, she was on her own without a single ally. But now she had a coven of witches, a dokkaebi, and a half witch, half dokkaebi on her side. She couldn't tell them her plan to look for Min-Young, because they'd stop her. But that didn't mean she had to do it all alone—at least not entirely. She just needed a head start.

"You'll stay inside the cabin until it's time to walk over to the dining hall, right?" Sam asked when they reached the front door of Sparrow's Nest. It was free hour before lunch, and they had agreed it was best for Ronnie to hang out at Sparrow's Nest, where there would be less chance of running into Mr. Lobing. But the idea of listening to camp gossip when her mom was in danger sounded like torture. Ronnie had other plans . . . which hopefully did not involve torture. She had to see her mom one last time.

Ronnie rolled her eyes to hide her jitters. "You sound like your mom."

"Good! Because she'll banish me if anything happens to you."

Ronnie's chest tightened at the mention of banishment. She forced out a small laugh, but it sounded like she was wheezing instead. "Don't worry. I won't even pee without a bathroom buddy."

Sam scratched at the back of his head. "That was more than I needed to know. But I'm glad we're on the same page."

Ronnie slipped into the cabin. Half her cabinmates were lounging around on the bunk beds or gathered in small huddles on the floor.

Olivia and Gigi were in one corner of the cabin doing what looked like ballet positions. Ronnie had hoped to find Olivia alone so she could apologize, but Gigi was not a part of that plan. Ronnie already had one monster on her back and didn't need another. She picked up her pace, moving quickly past the girls, hoping to climb up to her bunk unnoticed.

But Gigi and Olivia glanced up at Ronnie's approach. Olivia quickly looked away without a word. Gigi, on the other hand, held Ronnie's gaze as she spoke—louder than necessary. "We should head out now if we want to try summoning the camp ghost."

Ronnie thought Gigi was actually talking to her for a moment until Olivia grabbed a sequined mini backpack off their bedpost in preparation to head out.

A moment ago, Ronnie couldn't get away fast enough. Now, only three steps from the bunk, she couldn't move. "You're going to try to summon the gwishin with Gigi?" she asked Olivia quietly.

Olivia's eyes flickered briefly over to Ronnie. "Gigi thought we could try asking the gwishin to end the curse."

"I figured if anyone could sway the ghost, it'd be me." Gigi stood up smiling and flipped her hair out from under her own mini-backpack straps. Ronnie scowled at the tiny purple bag. When did Gigi start using those? "And who knows, maybe she'll agree to haunt my enemies." Gigi held Ronnie's gaze long enough to get her point across.

"*Who knows?* I do! She's not gonna show for you!" Ronnie blurted out. "You haven't even met her. Believe me, I know better." She clamped her mouth shut. She'd thought she had finally gotten control over the unispells. Apparently, she was wrong. At least Ronnie's outburst had wiped the smug smile off Gigi's face. Instead she wore a face-melting glower aimed directly at Ronnie.

"Listen, Rhyming Ronnie," Gigi hissed, "just because you're Korean doesn't mean you can claim the camp ghost. I mean, your name is *Veronica*. You probably don't even *count* as Korean."

Heat hotter than a blazing bonfire burned in Ronnie's chest. She wanted to defend herself and say that she had a Korean name, Ji-Young. She wanted to say all the things Min-Young had told her about how being Korean isn't about superficial things like names . . . but she couldn't remember the specific way her mom had said it. And Ronnie didn't trust herself to speak. Not with unispells still tickling her tongue. So she just stood there, biting down on her lip with her hands balled into fists at her sides.

Olivia turned to Gigi, her arms crossed. "What does her name have anything to do with it?"

Ronnie's mouth dropped open. Gigi looked momentarily stunned before shaking it off with a stiff laugh. "Come on; Veronica isn't a Korean name."

"Well, Gigi is a French name, so does that make you French?"

Gigi huffed. "That's not what I meant! I'm just saying Ronnie doesn't get to be the expert on the ghost just because she's Korean."

"Well, I'm saying she does," Olivia retorted. "Because we're talking about a gwishin here, which is a *Korean* thing. And you're the one who brought up the fact that your cousin's stepmom is Korean like it mattered when it was about you."

Olivia walked out of the cabin, leaving Ronnie and Gigi staring after her. Ronnie had been a terrible friend, but Olivia still stuck up for her.

"I don't know what her problem is," Gigi grumbled. "That's obviously not what I meant." She looked to Ronnie for agreement, but when Ronnie scooted away, she stormed off, shouting, "Ugh! Whatever!"

As soon as Gigi left the cabin, Ronnie climbed up to her bunk. She felt more hopeful than she had in days. Olivia still had her back. Which was perfect, because she really needed all of them—Sam, Jack, and Olivia—if her plan was going to work.

She had about forty minutes before lunch to prepare three scavenger hunt clues of her own. These clues were her safety net, should she need them. Ronnie couldn't tell anyone where she was going if she wanted to see her mom again. But once she did find her mom, all bets were off.

All she had to do was buy herself enough time to get to Min-Young before anyone came looking for her. It would take Sam at least a few minutes into lunchtime before he realized she was missing. She was counting on him to check with Olivia and Jack even though he knew they were still mad at her. They'd look for her in the cabin, see her backpack on her bunk, and spot the first clue.

After finding the first clue, they would be distracted for

at least another fifteen minutes finding and deciphering the next two clues. At that point they'd seek out help from the witches. From there, things could go one of two ways. Everything could go as planned without a hitch, and she'd be back before the witches came looking for her in the forest. *Or* things could go terribly wrong and the witches would find her in desperate need of help.

Since Ronnie was determined to do this no matter what, she pushed away the tempting percentage calculations. Using a hair tie, she secured the first clue to one of her painted river stones and placed it on top of her backpack. The clue read:

Don't worry, I'm fine. I just need some time. You'll get all the answers by reading these rhymes.

I'm the guest of honor at a house made of stone. The invitation said I must go there alone. But I could use some help, more specifically three. One old friend, one new, and one ex-enemy. The not-a-backpack reveals where I've gone. And see for yourself Issue #51.

She secured the second clue to the jar of repellent and snuck it into Olivia's denim mini backpack, which was slung over their bunk post. That clue was longer because Ronnie snuck in an apology. It read:

First things first: The camp isn't cursed. But my life IS in danger, and the bad guy's no stranger. To ward off Persuasions, the tricks, and the lies, remember to never look into his eyes! As for the stones—do keep them near, and dab on the balm behind both your ears. Then please tell the witches, they'll know what to do. The Rhee Manor sign contains the next clue.

I know that I've been a really bad friend, but the three of you had my back even then. I'm sorry I lied, for the secrets I've kept. For the help that you offered, and I didn't accept. I'm glad that we're friends though I didn't show it. I could use your help now more than you know it. Have Sam fill you in on where I keep going and guess why I went without anyone knowing.

Ronnie hid the last clue—a rough map leading to the clearing—behind the stone Rhee Manor sign, just out of sight. Then she darted into the forest and disappeared into the shadows.

THIRTY-FOUR

THE GHOST,
THE WITCH,
AND THE GOBLIN

As Ronnie raced through the forest, she began second-guessing her decision to leave clues for her friends. What if they didn't understand them? What if they never even found them? She was counting on her friends to notice she was missing . . . and care.

The moment she began feeling sorry for herself, guilt bloomed in her gut. What if they *did* get the clues and got hurt trying to help her? What if Ms. Pavani was wrong and the witches got hurt, too? There was no telling how far Mr. Lobing would go to silence Ronnie.

But every worry vanished the moment she arrived at the clearing and found Min-Young hover-pacing, as usual. It was just like Mr. Lobing had said at the nurse's station. She hadn't left. She was right here.

"Min-Young?" Ronnie called out hesitantly.

Min-Young whirled around. When she saw Ronnie, the corners of her lips dropped into a deep frown. "Ronnie! What are you doing here?" Her voice was cold and edged with anger. More than that, it was as strong as Ronnie had ever heard it. Min-Young wasn't weak or injured. She wasn't gone. She was here and she was perfectly fine. But she wasn't happy to see Ronnie—that much was clear.

"I came looking for you yesterday, but you were gone," Ronnie said stiffly. "And the clearing was a mess, so I thought the dokkaebi came for you. I thought you left."

Min-Young sighed, sending a breeze over Ronnie's face. "He did come, but I managed to escape with most of my scarf." She ran a hand down the scarf, and only then did Ronnie notice the tear at one end. "I had to hide from him to protect the scarf and preserve my strength. I had to hide from *you* to protect you from him. But now you're here."

Ronnie's cheeks burned. Min-Young didn't want to see her. "I—I'll just go, then." She looked away before Min-Young could see the tears that had sprung to her eyes.

"It's too late!" Min-Young grabbed at her scarf. It twitched and tugged as if it were being pinched by invisible fingers.

Ronnie's blood ran cold. "Is that—"

"There!" Min-Young pointed to a particularly dense section of trees and bramble at the edge of the clearing. The fern grew tall and wild, and spindly branches of trees stretched out in all directions. "You must hide there. Stick close to the sturdier branches and wider trunks."

The pain of Min-Young's rejection vanished when Ronnie noticed the alarm in her tone. Ronnie bolted to the identified hiding spot, but Min-Young shook her head, dissatisfied. "No, no. Place yourself within the tangled growths so the branches and shrubbery cover you on all sides."

"It's a pitiful attempt, Min-Young," a familiar voice called out, knocking the air from Ronnie's lungs. Mr. Lobing stood at the other end of the clearing, a scarf of silence hovering at his side like a well-trained serpent. Bloody gashes cut across the left side of his face and along his arms. *Nice work, Boo,* Ronnie thought with great satisfaction.

Mr. Lobing took a few casual steps toward them. "We both know how this will end. There are only so many times you or that stupid cat can interfere. What life is he on now? Seven? Eight? Nine, is it?" His face stretched into a malicious grin. It tugged the wounds on his face, and his smile turned into a snarl. He clucked his tongue. "So much trouble for one little witch."

Min-Young glared at him. "She's just a child. She poses no threat to you."

"Yet," he growled. "She poses no threat to me *yet*. She is a witch, after all, and the fewer witches in the world, the better—especially a Rhee witch. I see that I was right to keep you around, Min-Young. What better way to trap the last Rhee witch than by using her gwishin mother as bait? But your services are no longer required." Suddenly his eyes glinted, and the scarf charged at Ronnie. It moved unbelievably fast—a blur of vivid red, like a long streak of blood shooting out from a powerful hose.

Ronnie screamed and ducked down behind the bramble.

Min-Young jumped in front of Ronnie, but the scarf passed right through her, colliding with the branches above Ronnie's head. Her muscles coiled, ready to evade its next strike, but the scarf was entangled in branches.

"Ronnie, take cover," Min-Young said, aiming her wind

at the scarf. Meanwhile, Ronnie crawled to a nearby tree and pressed her back to its broad trunk.

"Repeat this spell after me," Min-Young called out to Ronnie. *Weave in and out, stay nice and snug. No leaving now by pull or tug.*

Ronnie repeated the spell, and the scarf wove itself around the branches in an intricate pattern. Then, pulling tight, it knotted itself into place. But her relief was cut short at the sight of Min-Young flickering like candlelight in the wind, her scarf twitching toward Mr. Lobing's outreached hand.

"Min-Young," Ronnie cried out. "Your scarf!"

Min-Young reached out to smooth her scarf back down. But it bucked out of her grasp. If Mr. Lobing got hold of it, he'd sever Min-Young's tether. She'd be gone.

"No," Ronnie breathed.

"Don't worry," Min-Young said with a smile that looked more like a grimace. "He has less control over my scarf than the one who is after you." She spun around several rotations. When she was finished, the scarf hung down, once again a placid red river. "His telekinesis works by way of magic infused into things of this world. My scarf is neither of this world nor the next, so his power over it is weak and inconsistent."

"Clever gwishin," Mr. Lobing said with an easy chuckle. "But how much more wind do you have in you before you flicker out?"

"Don't you worry about me, dokkaebi," Min-Young shot back. "There's plenty more where that came from."

"Well, if you insist on keeping yours, I'll just"—he grunted—"grab the other"—effort twisted his mouth—"back!"

His eyes flashed, and the scarf he'd sent for Ronnie strained, struggling against its own knots around the creaking branches. Then it gave a final jerk, and the branches holding it in place shattered, sending the entire tangle of scarf and splintered wood flying into Mr. Lobing's waiting hands.

He caught it with a grin.

Min-Young turned to Ronnie, her haunting face fierce with anger. "Do what you can to create a barrier—anything that could catch and entangle the scarf." She spun around and aimed sharp bursts of wind to throw Mr. Lobing's telekinesis off balance.

Ronnie gathered every stick within arm's reach and added them to a pile. Then she reached into her witch instinct for a spell. *"Raise up a shield like stone and steel."*

The *tingle, tingle, crackle, fizz* burst forth, and the meager sticks arranged themselves into a barrier that reached above Ronnie's head. It didn't look like much, but when she tested it with a few tugs, it held steady. And while the scarf could still pass over the top, the barrier limited visibility and access.

Min-Young looked back over her shoulder, and her eyes flashed with satisfaction. "Perfect. Do you have the repellent?"

Ronnie nodded. "I have it on, but I left the rest of it behind."

"Any stones?"

"No . . . I left those behind, too." Ronnie wanted to kick herself. She could have snuck some in her pockets or carried them in her hands.

A scarf slammed into the barrier, making Ronnie jump. Though the sticks shuddered and creaked, they held together. On the other side, Mr. Lobing angled himself for a better view of Ronnie past the barrier.

"That's all right. We'll make do with what we have." Min-Young sent bursts of wind into the ends of the scarf that poked through the gaps in the barrier like reaching arms. "Repeat the repellent spell to refresh it. It won't be enough to stop him, but it will slow him down. And the longer we hold him off, the weaker he grows."

It was a shaky plan, but Ronnie muttered the spell and found comfort in the sensation of magic. It felt like a promise.

Min-Young gasped. "Ronnie, move!"

A scarf jumped over the barrier. Ronnie dropped to the ground and rolled herself away just as the scarf whipped past where she'd been standing seconds ago. It swerved around the tree and headed right back for her. She scampered back on her hands and feet, but it moved too fast.

When the scarf was nearly upon her, she raised her hands to shield herself, and it ricocheted. The repellent had worked!

A few feet away, the scarf hung limp in the air like a dazed animal—but only for a moment. Shaking itself off, it stretched taut and shot forward once more. Slicing through the air like a sharp crimson blade, it went straight for Ronnie's neck.

This time, it didn't spring back. This time, it made contact. And this time, it *burned*.

THIRTY-FIVE

STICKS
AND STONES

Ronnie released an agonized scream. She writhed on the ground, hearing nothing but her own strangled breaths and saw only red—from the scarf, from the pain. Her hands, protecting the front and sides of her neck, burned as she tried to push the scarf away. But it was useless because it had coiled itself around the back of her neck. It was like wrestling a snake—*on fire.*

Scarlet, blazing heat consumed Ronnie until a shock of cold cut through her senses. The feeling wrapped around the back of her raw and blistered neck. It covered her smarting fingers. And only then did the pain ease enough for Ronnie to unclench and breathe.

Slowly, her sight returned to her. Min-Young flickered above Ronnie as ice-cold air soothed her neck. It still hurt worse than anything she could have ever imagined, but it wasn't the blinding pain from before. Gingerly, she rose to her feet.

Min-Young had once again pressed the scarf into branches with her wind, but she was fading fast, and her scarf quivered as though its ends were caught in the blades of a fan. Mr. Lobing was drawing closer, his gaze sharp and gleaming. Ronnie recited the spell to entangle the scarf so Min-Young could let it go, but she continued to flicker.

"Defending with wind is not enough," Min-Young muttered. "Ronnie, I have to get closer and attack to weaken him, but that will mean I won't be able to protect you. So once I have him, you must run."

"No!" Ronnie shook her head violently over and over even though each twist caused a lancing pain in her neck. "If you get closer, he'll get your scarf!"

"Ronnie, you have to trust me," Min-Young said, her voice surprisingly strong and steady given how weak and faded her form had become. "It's the only way." She pressed a warm, airy hand to Ronnie's cheek, stopping her head shaking and holding her gaze. But in the corner of Ronnie's eye, the scarf flapped beneath Min-Young's chin like a streak of blood leaving the body, reminding her of what was at stake.

Fear brought tears to her eyes. "Please don't leave me," Ronnie choked out.

Min-Young's soft smile flickered in and out. "Have *faith* in me."

Know with one hundred percent certainty I will be here.

Ronnie tried to smile for her mom, but the loud crack of a shattering twig turned it into a grimace.

Min-Young glanced over her shoulder at Mr. Lobing, who was advancing. Her eyes cut back to Ronnie. "Run out of this forest as fast as you can. Do you understand?"

Ronnie was still nodding when Min-Young lurched toward Mr. Lobing. She encircled him with her wind, pushing him back to the edge of the clearing. His back hit a tree trunk, and she began circling faster and faster until she became Mr. Lobing's personal tornado. He tried to catch her scarf with his telekinesis, but she was moving too fast. Stumbling, he reached up to his throat, struggling for breath.

Min-Young picked up even more speed, building up enough wind power to ruffle the leaves of the surrounding trees. Mr. Lobing dropped to his knees, and the scarf tangled in the branches went slack. Hope rushed through Ronnie. Min-Young would save her. She would use her wind magic to send Mr. Lobing far, far away, and they'd both be safe.

She didn't have to run away like she and her dad and Min-Young had been doing all along. No. She *wouldn't* run away. Not this time.

But then, all at once, the wind died out and the scarf that was tangled in the twigs fluttered back to life. With a growl, Mr. Lobing caught Min-Young's scarf with his telekinesis and launched it—with Min-Young attached—across the clearing right past Ronnie. She flinched when Min-Young hit the trees nearby, but instead of crashing into them, she flew right through them. Or rather, they passed right through her. Min-Young's form continued deeper into the trees until she disappeared from view completely.

Ronnie was alone with a witch-hunting dokkaebi.

He loped toward her, his blue-green eyes gleaming with menace.

She backed away, chanting, *"Dokkaebi witch hunter, don't come near. Dokkaebi magic won't work here. Dokkaebi witch hunter, don't come near. Dokkaebi magic won't work here."*

He flashed a wolfish smile and made a gesture as if

swatting at a pesky fly. "That won't work, little witch. Because I won't be needing magic to silence you. I'll do it with my bare hands."

He stepped up to the barricade, his eyes dancing with laughter.

At her.

At her weak magic.

At her inevitable silence.

With a single flash of blue-green eyes, the barrier came crumbling down like it was nothing more than a pile of sticks. Her magic wasn't strong enough.

Reaching over the remains of the barrier, Mr. Lobing grabbed the scarf and wrapped it once around his hand. With a swift tug, the scarf came free. Wrapping the loose end around his other hand, he snapped the length of the scarf taut.

Ronnie's stomach dropped. She had nothing to protect herself from his human abilities. Not even stones to throw. That was it! Thinking quickly, she squeezed her hands into fists and muttered a unispell. *"Skin and bone strong as stone."* A tingle running up from her fingertips all the way to her shoulders was chased by a thick and heavy feeling of turning into concrete.

She reared back just as Mr. Lobing lunged. With a cry, she swung her arms out in front of her. One stone fist landed on Mr. Lobing's arm, and the other entangled itself with the scarf. Her hardened hands were strong, but they weren't immune to the heat of the scarf. Her eyes burst open at the pain. Screaming, she pushed it away with all her might, stumbling back as Mr. Lobing pressed forward. Even with her magicked arms, he was bigger and stronger than her. Soon all that separated the scarf from her neck were her burning hands, which were quickly losing their strength.

A sharp snarl sliced through Ronnie's screams, followed by Mr. Lobing's cry of pain. The scarf went slack.

"Quickly," came Min-Young's weak voice, "pull it through a tangle of roots at your feet and spell it tight."

Trembling from the pain in her scalded hands, Ronnie did as she was told. She muttered her spell and glanced up into the clearing.

At the center, Mr. Lobing was flailing his arms. Boo had latched on to his face with his claws.

"Boo!" Ronnie cried out. Boo didn't respond. He was too busy tearing into Mr. Lobing like the man was a scratch post. He bolted from one shoulder to the other, from the top of Mr. Lobing's head to around his neck, dragging his claws as he went.

But at last, Mr. Lobing got a grip on Boo's tail and wrenched him off his body. Then, with dokkaebi force, he sent Boo sailing across the clearing and into the trees.

Ronnie held her breath waiting for the inevitable thud of Boo slamming into a tree, but seconds passed, and all was quiet. Until Sam strode out, Boo safe in his arms.

Ronnie's mouth fell open. And when Olivia and Jack followed at Sam's heels, Ronnie nearly toppled over. Her heart swelled at the sight of her friends. She regarded each of them in turn, their identical expressions grim but determined.

Mr. Lobing's face was a mess of bloody slashes from

Boo's claws, but he smiled at Ronnie's friends like they were all simply running into each other in the courtyard. "What's this?"

"Surround Ronnie," Sam instructed the others as they drew near. "We've got to shield her from the scarf."

Jumping into motion, they pushed Ronnie behind them, forming a human fence around her. Boo leaped down from Sam's arms and wove in and out of Min-Young's dangling feet. She was so faded now that she looked like nothing more than a trick of the light.

"You guys came," Ronnie said in a daze as they closed in around her. "You guys came!" Her friends had come for her.

Olivia nodded at Ronnie over her shoulder. "We got your clues, and Sam told us the rest."

Ronnie suddenly remembered how much danger she was in . . . and how much danger *they* were in now because of her. "Oh no, no, no. You guys can't be here! You have to leave. You have to run!" She looked frantically at each of them.

"No way," Jack cut in. "We're not leaving you to do this on your own."

"You were supposed to tell the witches!" Ronnie turned to Sam.

"We couldn't find them, so I left them a note. One of the witches will find it and come help us." Sam looked worried, but he set his jaw. "Jack's right. We weren't going to leave you to fight him alone, Ronnie."

"But—"

"There's no time to argue," Olivia said firmly. She turned toward Min-Young, but her eyes passed right over the gwishin and she addressed the cat. "Boo, can you track down the witches and send them here?" With a meow, Boo darted off. Then Olivia grabbed Ronnie's hand and pressed a jar into her palm. It was the repellent.

Without a moment to lose, Ronnie twisted off the lid and smeared the potion onto her friends' temples and behind their ears. She repeated the spell over and over again, hoping the forest would hear her and strengthen the spell with its tree magic. They could use all the help they could get.

"Mr. Lobing," Jack called out. "We know what you are—we all do. You're a dokkaebi."

Mr. Lobing drew back and winced, as if he had been hit with a sudden and sharp pain. He flickered, as Min-Young had, and the scarf of silence slipped from his fingers onto the ground.

Collecting himself, he straightened his shirt and flashed his internet-famous smile. But the bleeding cuts across his face gave it a sinister look, whether that was his intention or not. "Come now, kids. There are no such things as dokkaebi. I'm Guy Lobing, the star of *Wild&Free*." His eyes glimmered green as he attempted to Persuade Olivia and Jack, but Ronnie had already smeared plenty of repellent on their temples and behind their ears.

"That won't work on me again," Olivia snapped. Boo, pacing circles around their feet, snarled his agreement.

Ronnie looked to Olivia. "Wait. What do you mean *again*?"

Olivia kept her glare on Mr. Lobing. "Remember when I gave you that note?"

Ronnie thought about it for a minute. "When we were in

line for the egg-spoon relay race. You came back from the bathroom with a note you found for me. I thought it was from Min-Young."

"It was Lobing," Sam cut in, his voice low and angry.

Ronnie's face paled. "So if Sam hadn't come after me . . ." She had fallen right into the dokkaebi's trap.

"I hadn't planned on killing any children that day—only little witchlings," Mr. Lobing said, his voice laced with regret. "But plans change."

His eyes sparked with a menacing glare, but this time, he aimed the scarf low to the ground for the space between Olivia's and Jack's legs. With the grace and dexterity of the ballerina she was, Olivia caught it around her calf and wound it tight. She grinned triumphantly at Ronnie a second before Mr. Lobing tugged at the scarf, causing her to trip to the ground. Free from Olivia's leg, the scarf rushed back to its owner.

"Olivia!" Ronnie stepped toward her but stopped when Min-Young swooped down directly in Ronnie's line of sight and shook her head. Her voice was gone, but the meaning of her look was clear. *Ronnie* was the target. Olivia was a distraction. Ronnie inched back behind Jack and Sam.

Olivia scrambled up to her feet. Without a single glance at the dirt smudged on her clothes, she began to chant. *"Dokkaebi witch hunter, don't come near. Dokkaebi magic won't work here."* Her voice was strong and confident, like she was one hundred percent certain the magic would work for her. And perhaps it did, at least in some way, because Mr. Lobing flickered again.

"Stop it," he snapped through bared teeth.

Jack joined in. *"Dokkaebi witch hunter, don't come near. Dokkaebi magic won't work here."*

"I said, stop it!" A scarf shot out like an arrow straight into Jack's chest. He fell and hit the ground with a grunt. Mr. Lobing summoned the scarf back to his outstretched hand.

"Jack!" Ronnie cried out.

Jack remained still for a heart-stopping moment before sucking in a large breath. The wind had been knocked out of him, but aside from a possible bruising, he was okay.

"Dokkaebi witch hunter, don't come near." Jack's voice was shaky, but his eyes remained locked on Mr. Lobing. *"Dokkaebi magic won't work here!"*

Mr. Lobing stumbled back, his shoulders heaving with strained breaths, until he hit the tree behind him. The scarf slipped from his grip and landed in a red pool at his feet. He was fading, and the moss-covered trunk at his back was becoming visible through his shirt and jeans.

His head swiveled from side to side, searching. He was about to make a run for it. But before he could take a step, four witches stepped into the clearing clad in long black capes secured around their necks. They spread themselves out around the perimeter, surrounding Mr. Lobing. Then they slowly walked in a circle, dropping a stone every other step, chanting, *"Magic ancient, strong and patient, crafted over generations. Join one to all, raise up your wall; none may cross this incantation."*

"No!" Mr. Lobing shouted, his eyes darting from one witch to the next.

It was too late—they had trapped him.

From her place along the invisible barrier, Lia scanned the clearing until she found Min-Young, whose form was starting to fill back in and regain strength. Olivia and Jack followed Lia's gaze, and their mouths dropped open, finally noticing the gwishin among them. They gaped at her semi-transparent form, her translucent skin emphasizing the deep purple shadows beneath her eyes and in the hollows of her sunken cheeks.

"It's about time, sisters," Min-Young said, skeletal hands on her hips and a surprisingly soft smile spreading across her undeniably chilling face. She met Lia's gaze. "And Ambrose?"

Lia held Min-Young's gaze with such warmth, it was evident that she saw her friend there and not the gwishin. "Someone had to stay behind, and he knew better than to try to keep me from you."

Min-Young pressed a hand to her heart, her dark eyes glistening like a midnight sky. "Thank you for coming."

"And thank *you*, Min-Young, for bringing everyone to *me*," came Mr. Lobing's voice. Like Min-Young, he was solid once more. "You really have been so helpful."

Ms. Akemi cocked her head at him. "Do you truly believe you stand a chance against five witches and a gwishin?"

Mr. Lobing cocked his head, pretending to think. "*Five?* The girl has no training; she's no challenge to me. And a gwishin is even less so. But you better believe I came prepared for every single one of you." With a flourish, he raised both hands in the air. The scarf at his feet jumped up to meet three additional scarves that darted out from the trees behind him.

Ronnie's friends tightened their circle around her, and Min-Young hovered in front of them.

"Think hard about your next move," Ms. Hana warned.

"Believe me, Director," Mr. Lobing said with a sneer. "I have been thinking about this move for the past seven years."

The scarves shot out, and Ronnie braced herself for the onslaught. But instead of aiming for her, the scarves darted in four different directions—one each to Lia, Ms. Hana, Ms. Akemi, and Ms. Pavani.

Sam cried out, reaching out to Lia. The scarf slowed but didn't stop until it was wrapped around her midsection and a tree, pinning her in place. The other witches were in the same predicament, the width of the scarves covering them from waist to sternum. Their capes tore away, exposing their necks to silencing.

THIRTY-SIX

THE FISHERMAN

S am stood rigid, frozen in shock.

"Sam!" Ronnie shouted. "Your mom!"

When he didn't move, she shoved him. He stumbled before shaking off his stupor. Then he took off running across the clearing, his hands pushed out in front of him, reaching for the scarf with his telekinesis. Jack and Olivia immediately adjusted their positions to sandwich Ronnie between them—Jack covering Ronnie in front and Olivia behind.

"We've got to help the witches," Olivia said at Ronnie's back, her voice shaking. "How do we help them?"

Ronnie looked down at her hands—red and raw from burns. "You guys should go to the witches. The scarf won't burn you."

"No way, Ronnie," Jack called back over his shoulder. His voice was so firm it edged on angry.

"Jack's right," Olivia said. "The moment we step away from you is when Lobing will send a scarf around *your* neck. You're the one he's after."

Tears of frustration sprang to Ronnie's eyes. "Then what do we do? Just sit back and watch the witches all be silenced? I can't do that. Not when they're all here because of me."

"Oh no." Olivia pointed to the witches, a hand clamped over her mouth.

The scarves were climbing. Little by little, they inched up toward the witches' necks as they squirmed and muttered ineffective spells. Even without direct skin contact, the scarves were weakening the witches' magic. With their arms trapped beneath, they tugged at the bottom hem of the scarves, burning their fingers in the process. Ronnie's palms grew hot with the memory of the excruciating pain.

Meanwhile, Min-Young swooped from one witch to the next, but the best she could do was offer a cool breeze for the inevitable burns.

Ms. Pavani was the first one to scream. The scarf had reached the skin around her collarbone that peeked out from her shirt. Soon it would be at her throat. At Lia's bidding, Sam bolted to Ms. Pavani. *Lia didn't know that Sam was part witch.* Ronnie bit down on her lip, bracing herself for Sam to cry out in pain as well.

Without any hesitation, he reached out and tugged at the scarf where it touched Ms. Pavani's skin. He didn't even flinch as he pushed the scarf down with his bare hands. Either he wasn't developed enough as a witch to be affected by it or his dokkaebi side made him immune to its deadly powers.

Ms. Pavani's screams quieted. She slumped against the tree at her back. But then another scream pierced the night. This time it was Ms. Hana. As Sam rushed to her, Ms. Akemi cried out in agony. Then it was Lia, then Ms. Pavani, then Ms. Hana, then Ms. Akemi again. And each time, the scarf got closer and closer to wrapping around their necks.

Ronnie's stomach tightened into a hard knot. "This is all because of me. This is all my fault."

"No, it isn't." Olivia gripped Ronnie's elbows. "This is all because of *him*—a murderer."

"Olivia's right," Jack agreed. "Don't give up the fight. Your backpack's got those stones in it. Sam said they can be used to make a barrier."

"You brought it!" Ronnie glanced down, noticing it was her backpack on Jack's back.

"Of course. You never go anywhere without it. Thought you could use it."

Her excitement was short-lived when she remembered she only had four river stones and the only stone magic she knew was how to keep out dokkaebi magic. "These aren't enough stones, and I don't know any better spells."

"Can't we just put them around you, at least?" Olivia asked, flinching at the witches' cries. "Or one witch at a time?"

"We could try," Ronnie said. "But Lobing would know what we're up to and he could just send an unspelled stone to knock mine out of the way. They're most helpful when they're hidden. But maybe there's something we can do."

Ronnie shoved her hand into the depth of the backpack but kept her eyes on Mr. Lobing. He twisted at the waist, his outstretched arms aimed at two writhing witches at a time. Just as Ronnie's fingertips brushed against the cool, smooth surface of a river stone, Sam cried out.

Ronnie's fingers wrapped around the stone, and her gaze

shot up. Sam had thrust his hand out toward Mr. Lobing. A broken branch the size of his arm shot up from the ground and careened toward the dokkaebi. But with a raised hand and a small gesture Mr. Lobing sent the branch crashing into a tree.

He lowered his hand, and the glint of blue-green light from the compass around his neck caught Ronnie's eye. It winked at her as if it were sharing a secret. Suddenly she knew what she had to do.

Ronnie pulled out two stones and held one in each hand, thinking quickly about how to tell Jack and Olivia the plan without being overheard by Mr. Lobing with his dokkaebi hearing.

"Hey, guys, remember the romantic fisherman in Alaska?"

"Yeah, I love that story." Even in that moment, Olivia somehow managed to swoon a little. "But maybe this isn't the best time to retell it?"

In front of her, Jack stilled. Ronnie could practically hear his mind whirring at her mention of the old dokkaebi tale.

"Are you saying you want to go fishing?" he asked, a small smile in his voice.

Ronnie grinned. "I'm saying I'm going for the ultimate catch."

Olivia shook her head in confusion. "Fishing? But what does that have to do with—" Her eyes widened with understanding. "The glass fish."

Ronnie gave a brisk nod and passed a stone to each of her friends. "Did you know," she continued conversationally, as if her four witch aunties weren't fighting for their lives, like she wasn't about to risk her own, "the fastest and most humane way to kill a fish is to hit it on the head with something heavy and hard . . . like a stone?"

"Ugh," Olivia groaned. "Poor fish."

"Not if you strike fast," Jack offered. His hand squeezed the stone so hard his knuckles turned white. But then he nearly dropped it. "Wait. You gotta catch the fish first. And to do that, you need bait." The look in his eyes made clear he knew what Ronnie was about to suggest.

"You know it has to be me," Ronnie said, trying to keep her voice steady and confident.

"Ronnie, no!" Olivia cried out.

Jack narrowed his eyes at her. "Yeah, why does it have to be you?"

"You guys have to trust me."

"Ronnie, I swear, if you're trying to martyr yourself—" Jack started.

"No way. Don't you know me better than that?" She scoffed. "I don't do anything with less than a fifty percent guarantee."

"True," he agreed, but he didn't sound so sure.

"And it's not like I'm going it alone. I need your help, and this will only work if we trust each other."

"We've got your back, Ronnie!" Olivia moved into a ready stance that reminded Ronnie of the trust fall exercise. Only this time, Ronnie didn't doubt that Olivia would catch her.

"I know." Ronnie held Olivia's gaze. "I trust you."

Jack released a resigned sigh. "Okay then, what's the plan?"

"First: Jack, I'll need you to move us closer to Lobing to

draw out any more scarves he's hiding. If he has more, he'll attack us with them, and this time, I need you guys to grab them. Tie them onto yourselves—like triple-knot."

Jack's brows drew together in thought. "How will I know when we're close enough?"

"You'll know because that's when I'll make my move."

Jack nodded but shot her a warning look. "Remember. I'm going to be so mad if you die."

"I'm not going to die."

"What percent?"

"Ninety-nine," Ronnie lied. "Now let's go."

Ms. Akemi released a well-timed cry, spurring Jack into action. He stepped toward Mr. Lobing with Ronnie sandwiched between him and Olivia.

"Mr. Lobing," Ronnie called out when she was about twenty feet away. "Please. Stop. We don't *have* to fight each other."

Mr. Lobing startled, as if he had forgotten about her. "You may be correct, but I'm pretty sure I *want* to."

"This is our ancestors' war, not ours. And to be honest, I don't think it's even been about witches or dokkaebi for a long time now. I think it's been about fear. I think you're afraid."

He threw his head back and howled with laughter. Ronnie darted a glance at the witches. Their scarves had momentarily stalled.

"Fear?" Mr. Lobing said. "What do I have to fear when I'm capable of silencing four witches while fighting off a gwishin and a meddling cat—all while exposed to two humans, a witchling, and a traitorous half dokkaebi?"

"Fear of not being human enough," Ronnie answered, undeterred. "Fear of not being accepted. Fear of not being loved." She was fifteen feet away now. "I was so afraid that not being a good enough daughter, best friend, Korean, American, or even witch would mean losing people. So I pushed everyone away. But now I know I don't have to be afraid. I don't have to be alone. And neither do you."

Mr. Lobing's expression hardened. "You forget I have millions of followers because of *Wild&Free*. I am more loved than you could ever hope to be."

Ronnie cocked her head. "That's not love. Love is letting others in. It's holding on to each other through the good times and the bad."

He sneered. "You think your father would still love you if he knew you were a witch? If I'm remembering correctly, he wanted nothing more than to forget witches ever existed—including your mother."

Ten feet away, his words hit Ronnie like a punch to the gut.

Jack reached out and squeezed her elbow. "Don't let him get in your head, Ronnie."

It's you and me, kid, no matter what. You could never scare me away.

Jack was right. She never had to worry about her dad's love. Because dad jokes aside, he was always there for her. He would never leave her if he had the choice. Just like Min-Young. Ronnie smiled. "My dad would love me no matter what I was—witch, ghost, zombie, vampire . . . or dokkaebi."

Mr. Lobing flinched, and his fingers twitched at his side.

But no scarf came rushing to him. Ronnie nudged Jack and Olivia. He was out of scarves.

"And it's not just my dad who loves like this." Ronnie reached out again to give Jack's and Olivia's hands a quick squeeze. This was the part where they had to hang back and trust her. "Plenty of people will love us for who we really are." She stepped forward alone until she was five feet away. "Don't you want to be accepted without Persuasion? Don't you want to live a life without constantly hunting? Agree to a truce and we can all walk out of here. I'm the last Rhee witch. We can end this."

Mr. Lobing smirked. "And if I say no to your little truce?"

Ronnie squared her shoulders. "Then I'll wrestle you. No scarves. Just fair and square."

His laughter boomed through the clearing, drowning out the cries of the witches. Among the voices was Min-Young's, the wind carrying her warnings close to Ronnie's ear. Ronnie ignored them all.

Before she lost her nerve, she hurtled forward, throwing herself at Mr. Lobing. Though she had the element of surprise on her side, he still caught her easily by the shoulders and spun her around. Securing an arm across her collarbone, he pinned her in place against him, his compass pushing painfully into the back of her head.

She was trapped.

"Ronnie!" Olivia cried out. She lunged for Ronnie, but Jack pulled her back by her mini backpack. He met Ronnie's eye, and she saw his message. He trusted her and would kill her if she died.

Ronnie struggled weakly. She would have only one

chance to get it right. But then, to her horror, Mr. Lobing lifted his free hand and summoned the scarf he had wrapped around Lia.

Ronnie's stomach lurched. She hadn't considered the scarves already in play.

Free from the scarf, Lia sagged with relief, but only for a second. She straightened at the sight of Mr. Lobing holding the scarf in one hand and Ronnie in the other. But again, it was only for a moment. Because a second later, the scarf was inches from Ronnie's face, and in the next, it was pressed into the side of her neck. The searing heat stole not only her breath, but every thought from her mind.

Ronnie couldn't scream. She couldn't think. All she could do was feel the pain burrowing deep into the marrow of her bones and radiating out to the tips of her fingers and toes. Weak and trembling, her legs threatened to give out beneath her.

Mr. Lobing pushed the scarf into her neck once more, and her vision darkened. The cries of the others faded in and out.

"No!" Min-Young's scream brought Ronnie back to her senses briefly, and she remembered her plan and her promise to Jack. Summoning all the strength she had left, she reached up as if to tug at the scarf. Instead, she wrapped her hand around the compass wedged between the back of her head and Mr. Lobing's chest. Holding it tight in her hand, she finally allowed her legs to give out beneath her. The leather band snapped under her deadweight.

Sensing the tug of the compass, Mr. Lobing froze. He shoved Ronnie several feet away with his telekinesis, but it was too late. The scarf remained in his hand. And the compass remained in hers.

The warm early evening air against Ronnie's tender burns might as well have been sandpaper for the way it stung. But rather than dulling her senses, the pain sharpened them. With a surge of adrenaline, she picked herself up.

Mr. Lobing released a feral growl that reverberated like thunder as he raced toward her. With the compass in hand, Ronnie raised her arm and reared back. Her arm was in forward motion when Mr. Lobing collided into her, the impact aiding the momentum of her pitch.

Ronnie opened her fist, sending the compass out before crashing hard into the ground. Registering no pain, she watched the compass arc through the air. Her friends had trusted her to do her part. Now she had to trust them to do theirs. She had to cross her arms, close her eyes, and fall back.

The compass landed inches from Jack's feet. Wasting no time, he dropped to the ground and raised a stone high above his head. But as he brought it down, the compass inched away, and the stone hit dirt. The compass tottered weakly, tugging first toward Mr. Lobing, then away, and back again, like a game of telekinetic tug-of-war.

Sam was back at Jack and Olivia's side, summoning the compass. But his telekinesis wasn't strong enough to overcome Mr. Lobing's entirely, and the compass skittered along the ground, slowly but surely making its way back to the dokkaebi.

Suddenly a strong wind picked up, low to the ground. Picking up speed and debris, it circled around the compass, creating a small tornado and cutting off all telekinetic connections. Ronnie looked for Min-Young and found her hovering next to Olivia, her face set with determination.

"Now!" Olivia yelled as she leaped forward and threw herself down between the compass and Mr. Lobing, blocking his view.

Then time slowed as several things happened in the span of about three seconds.

First, the wind died out and Jack raised his stone.

Second, the crunch of stone meeting glass and metal rang out into the clearing.

Third, Ronnie met Min-Young's gaze across the way.

And then Min-Young vanished.

THIRTY-SEVEN
I'LL BE HERE

Time caught up in a dizzying blur.

Ronnie had made her choice.

Min-Young was gone.

She disappeared the moment the compass cracked beneath the stone. But Mr. Lobing remained, flickering and fading. He dropped to his knees, holding his transparent hands before his face, watching as they continued to fade away like morning mist under a hot summer sun.

He threw his head back and roared, but his voice had lost its thunder. The hollow sound was now no more than an echo. Reaching out toward the fractured compass, he strained to summon it, but the shattered remains lay in a pitiful heap on the ground. The dokkaebi magic was gone, along with Mr. Lobing's tangible form.

With the grace of a ghost, Mr. Lobing drifted up to his feet. And with the menace of a monster, he snapped his head toward Ronnie. Face contorting with fury, he swooped toward her with the speed of the wind. A scream lodged in Ronnie's throat as he collided with her. But rather than knocking her back, the dokkaebi's form dissipated, washing over her and rising up to the sky like the smoke of a blazing bonfire, leaving nothing of Mr. Lobing behind but an old, shattered compass.

The scarves of silence pinning the witches to the trees fluttered to the ground. Without the dokkaebi, they were nothing more than strips of silk.

Olivia squealed as she ran over to Ronnie, Jack and Sam close behind. "We did it!"

Ronnie tried to smile, but she crumpled instead, tears spilling from her eyes.

"Ronnie! What's wrong?" Olivia's eyes widened at the injuries on Ronnie's neck and hands. "You're hurt! Let me call Ms. Akemi—"

Ms. Akemi was there in an instant, ushering Ronnie onto the stump to check her injuries. "Chin up. Hands out."

Unable to speak through her tears, Ronnie nodded, and immediately regretted it. A whimper escaped past her lips and Ms. Akemi's face pinched into a sympathetic wince. "This may sting a little at first, but only because of the pressure." She muttered a quick spell and rubbed the ointment over Ronnie's neck and palms. Ronnie flinched at the sudden sensation, but the pain was gone before she could cry out.

But without the distraction of physical pain, the anguish of losing her mom grew more vivid. Her tears fell faster.

A crease formed between Ms. Akemi's brows. "That should have done it."

"It did," Ronnie said between shuddering breaths.

"Then what's the matter? You should be celebrating!" Ms. Akemi's brow furrowed in confusion. "You banished your hunter!"

Ronnie looked up through tear-filled eyes. "How can I celebrate without *her*?"

Ms. Akemi nodded sagely. "You're coming down from all that adrenaline, and it's making you emotional. Ronnie, dear, just give yourself a minute. Soon as you get right, Min-Young is sure to follow. It's been a magic-heavy evening, and gwishin require more time to recuperate than you and I."

Ronnie sniffled. "Time? No, Min-Young's gone. Forever."

Ms. Akemi placed a hand over her heart. "Oh my, you think Min-Young left for good? Can't you feel her presence? Dig deep into your witch instinct. Go on, now." She prodded when Ronnie stared blankly. "It's easy to pick up on the presence of a gwishin who's laid claim to a space. And even easier to feel when they have permanently vacated it. I suppose if this is your first gwishin experience, you wouldn't know how to recognize either."

Ronnie tried to feel for Min-Young's presence, but all she could come up with was ten percent confusion, thirty percent disbelief, and sixty percent wild hope. Her lower lip trembled. "I can't feel anything."

Ms. Akemi shook her head. "Close your eyes. Trust in your witch instinct."

Ronnie closed her eyes and drew in several deep breaths. She pulled up a mental image of Min-Young, the sound of her voice, and the feeling of her wind touch. Then she felt it on her nose—a soft press of the wind. When she opened her eyes, Min-Young was hovering before her.

Ronnie jumped into Min-Young's open arms. It was like sinking into a warm cloud.

"You're still here," she said into Min-Young's chest, her heart soaring. "I thought—I thought—"

Min-Young pulled away to meet Ronnie's eyes. "You thought the dokkaebi was my tether to this world?"

Ronnie nodded.

"He was a part of it," Min-Young admitted. "But the tether goes both ways. It is both a chain and a choice. I told you I would be here so long as you needed me, and I intend to keep my promise."

Ronnie hesitated. "But . . . what if I need you forever?"

Min-Young squared her shoulders. "Then I will be here. Forever. Waiting for you."

Waiting for Ronnie. Because Ronnie didn't live at Camp Foster. In a couple of days, she would return home with her dad in West Seattle. And Min-Young would be trapped here in the forest all by herself with only her fading memories for company.

"I left you once, Ronnie," Min-Young said quietly. "I won't do it again."

This was the promise Ronnie had been desperate to hear. But along with it came the nagging reminder that being a gwishin was painful for the soul.

Ronnie hugged Min-Young again, seeking her warmth in order to chase away the chill of doubt. When they separated, Min-Young looked past Ronnie and smiled. "Akemi!"

Ronnie stepped away to allow Ms. Akemi to take her turn reuniting with Min-Young. She turned to Jack, Sam, and Olivia, who were huddled together casting furtive glances at the gwishin.

"You guys came." Ronnie's eyes flooded with fresh tears. "I hoped you would, but after the way I treated all of you, I'm not sure I deserved it." She turned to Olivia first. "I'm sorry I kept sneaking away and expecting you to cover for me when I wouldn't even tell you why. I was being selfish."

Olivia nodded and looked down at the ground. "Yeah, that really hurt. I wondered if I was doing something wrong, like I didn't know how to be a good friend because, you know, I don't really have any other ones than my sisters."

Ronnie winced. "Nope. That was me." She gave an awkward little wave. "I was the bad friend."

Olivia's head shot up, concern all over her face. "You weren't all bad, Ronnie," she said graciously. "You did give up that dresser drawer for my clothes. That meant a lot."

Ronnie opened her mouth to argue the significance of the drawer but thought better of it and let Olivia continue.

"And even though I wish you would have been honest with me, I understand why you kept those secrets, and I forgive you." Olivia smiled, her face open and bright. They came together for a hug, and Ronnie squeezed her friend until they were both laughing so hard, they had to pull apart.

Ronnie wiped away the tears that had fallen while she was laughing and turned to Jack.

"You know we're cool," he said with an easy smile and a shrug before Ronnie could say a word. Normally, that would have been enough between them. But Ronnie was tired of keeping things in for fear that letting them out would create distance. She knew now that all those uncomfortable, imperfect feelings were not the chasms she feared would separate people. They were bridges that brought the people that mattered most closer together.

"I still want to apologize," she said, peeking at him shyly through her lashes. It wasn't easy breaking away from their usual way of interacting. "I was so scared of losing our friendship that I ended up pushing you away. I'm sorry I wasn't there for you and that I didn't let you be there for me, either."

Jack ran his hands through his hair. This had to be hard for him, too, but he met Ronnie's gaze through a few wayward strands of hair. "Total self-sabotage."

Ronnie gave him a tight smile. "Yup."

"But it's not like I'm gonna hold a grudge," he said, a big grin stretching across his face. "I literally helped banish one dokkaebi, made friends with another"—he reached out and threw an arm around Sam's shoulders—"my best friend's a witch, and her mom's the gwishin haunting summer camp!" He clapped a hand on Ronnie's shoulder. "Best friend *ever.*"

Ronnie started laughing again. Olivia pulled all of them into a group hug.

When Ms. Akemi left to help the other witches cast cleaning spells around the clearing, Min-Young turned to Ronnie and her friends with a smile that could be nothing less than harrowing to anyone seeing a gwishin for the first time. To Ronnie's friends' credit, they didn't even flinch.

Min-Young narrowed her black pit eyes at Jack. "You must be Jack, Ronnie's best friend since you were preschoolers."

Jack gave a pleased nod. "Yup! And now that I know

she's a witch, I might keep her around a little longer." He expertly dodged Ronnie's fist.

Olivia stepped in between them. "I think we've had enough fighting for today. Maybe for the whole year, even."

"Olivia." Min-Young tapped a pale finger to her scarlet lips. "Are you're absolutely certain you're not a witch?"

Olivia nodded, her eyes bright.

"Well," Min-Young said thoughtfully, "witch or no, there is definitely some kind of magic in you. I can feel it."

"Really?"

"Without a doubt."

Olivia shot Ronnie a wide-eyed look and squealed.

Then Min-Young turned to Sam. She tipped her head to one side and clumped strands of her stringy raven hair fell across one hollow cheek. "You know, you look just like your father, Samuel."

Sam flushed. "Yeah, I've been told that. It's the eyes." He pointed to the one with the green specks.

Min-Young sighed with satisfaction. "It's so good to remember." She looked out at the witches, searching until her gaze landed on Lia.

"Min!" Lia ran over. The huge smile on her face chased away Ronnie's memories of her screaming in agony.

"Lia!" Min-Young reached out and cupped Lia's face in her ghostly hands. "We lost so much time . . . If only I had trusted you."

Lia shook her head. "You had your reasons, and not all is lost." She turned her head to look at Ronnie and Sam.

Min-Young looked happy—really happy—but for some reason Ronnie was overcome by a sudden mixture of guilt and grief. A weight pressed down onto her chest, making it hard to breathe. She turned to her friends. "Do you guys mind if I talk to Min-Young alone for a bit before we head back?"

Lia clasped her hands together. "How about we get a nice little fire going and burn up every single one of those scarves?"

"Definitely," Olivia agreed. As she walked away, she tossed Ronnie an encouraging smile over her shoulder.

Jack gave Ronnie a little nod before launching into a passionate discussion about dokkaebi touchstones with Sam, who humored him.

"I'm so very glad you have them in your life," Min-Young said, her voice wistful.

"Me too," Ronnie agreed. "They were there for me when I needed them most. Like you were."

Min-Young ran the back of a warm wind-hand down Ronnie's cheek. "And I always will be."

Ronnie and Min-Young shared a warm smile before Ronnie averted her eyes to ask, "How will we know . . . when I don't need you anymore?"

"Ah," Min-Young said with a nod. "I think it is every parent's hope that their children will not always *need* them but will never cease to *want* them. You will know you are ready to say good-bye when you know this difference in your heart. At which point, I would ask for you to release me."

"Is there a spell for that?"

"It's more like a ritual or ceremony." After a pause, she spoke again. "You might see it as an opportunity to say good-bye—something we weren't given the chance to do before. But more than that, releasing me would indicate the understanding and acceptance of why we must sometimes let go of those we love."

Ronnie's throat tightened, and Min-Young continued. "But I would happily spend eternity here to be with you and make up for all our lost years."

Ronnie swallowed hard and forced a smile. "Great! Can you start making up for it tomorrow?"

Min-Young's eyes crinkled with a smile. "I'll be here."

THIRTY-EIGHT

FRIENDSHIP BRACELETS

The next day after breakfast, Ronnie stopped by the library to pick up a special book. Then she made her way to the gardens, where the witches were waiting for her.

Once Ronnie was seated, Lia cleared her throat. "We asked you to meet us because we have something for you." She held up a small jewelry box. Ronnie recognized it from the gallery. It was made of dark wood, and the lid was decorated with inlaid mother-of-pearl in the shape of a flower. "Something to help you remember. Go ahead and open it."

The box was cool and heavy in her hands. When she opened it, she gasped. Inside were at least two dozen friendship bracelets. She hadn't thought anything of them when she'd first seen them. "Are these . . . ?"

"Friendship bracelets." Ms. Akemi nodded. "The *Remembering* kind."

"Some are experiences we've shared in real time with Min-Young," Ms. Hana said. "Others are memories we pulled up and recorded more recently in anticipation of finally meeting you. And still others are Min-Young's personal bracelets that we were able to find."

Ronnie eyed them hungrily. She couldn't believe there were so many bracelets, so many memories, so many experiences of her mom.

"And, Ronnie," said Ms. Pavani, "there are some that include you, from when you were a baby."

Ronnie's eyes pulled wide with panic. She didn't know what she would see. She couldn't know how she would feel. There were no percentages to calculate in order to prepare for such things.

Lia nodded. "It's a lot to take in. I would advise you to start slow when you're ready. These bracelets are everlasting hosts, so you have all the time in the world to get to know your mother as she was before."

"And your eemos, as well," Ms. Akemi added. "We don't want you to go forgetting about us after you leave this place."

Ronnie looked at her aunties fondly. "I don't think I'll need a bracelet to remember you all—or any of this. But thank you." She reached into the box and caressed the bracelets, feeling the way the rough fibers and soft threads ran over and under one another. A thin tan-and-peach bracelet sent a soft tingle through her finger. She picked it up and instinctively slipped it onto her wrist. It fit perfectly.

"Oh," Lia breathed. "That's a good one."

Ronnie's head snapped up, her heart pitter-pattering. "It is?" She bit down on her lip, wondering what she'd see. "Thank you all for everything," she whispered to the witches.

Lia bent down to wrap her arms around Ronnie. Then

three more sets of arms wrapped around her, cocooning her in their affection.

Ms. Hana released Ronnie first and then shooed at everyone else. Her eyes were glassy with tears, which she brushed roughly away with the back of her hand. "That's enough now. Get yourselves together. It's not as if the girl is leaving forever. She's only a few hours' drive away, and there's always winter camp." She frowned at Ronnie. "Well . . . isn't that right?"

Ronnie startled. "Um, yes. I want to come back if that's okay?"

Ms. Akemi's eyes had misted over, but she still managed a broad smile. "Of course it's okay! Ronnie, you're a part of our coven now."

"We don't let just anyone in, you know," Ms. Pavani added with complete seriousness.

Lia squeezed Ronnie's shoulder. "We're your family. You'll always have a place here with us."

Ronnie's throat thickened with emotion as she looked at each of her witch aunties in turn. They beamed back at her—all but Ms. Hana, who looked as if she might cry again. But she stiffened her upper lip and glanced down at her watch.

"You're going to be late for ropes course," she barked. "Off you go! Now, before you're marked tardy!"

Ronnie gingerly placed the box of friendship bracelets into her backpack while Ms. Hana practically shoved her out of the gardens.

🌲🌲🌲

At the ropes course, Ronnie's eyes drifted to the trees, her thoughts wandering to Min-Young and how she was going to say good-bye. They had only just reunited.

She was so deep in thought she paid no attention to the counselor who helped her into her harness. She didn't notice how high she had climbed until she found herself at the highest point of the high course. Before her was a net bridge. Behind was nothing but sky.

Ronnie stood level to the canopy of the forest—where she'd first seen Min-Young. Sure, she was leg-tingling high, and if she thought about it too much, she would curl up into a ball right then and there. But it was also beautiful and peaceful up there. And it made her wonder if her mom ever saw it that way. But being trapped probably stole all the beauty in it. It probably stole away any hope for peace.

Ronnie held up her wrist and ran a finger along the threads. She was afraid to dip into the memories, not knowing how she would feel. But now felt like the perfect moment.

Closing her eyes, she recited, *"Take me there, to when and where. A memory that's saved to share."*

Suddenly she was sitting up in Min-Young's bed in Rhee Manor. In her arms was a bundled newborn with a head full of soft brown hair.

With a hand that was not her own, Ronnie ran a finger lightly over the infant's cheek. Then she wiped at her own cheeks, wet with tears.

"You are such a miracle, little one." The words came from Ronnie's lips, but they weren't hers. They were her mom's. Which would make the baby in her arms . . . *Ronnie.*

"You are the love of my life," Min-Young whispered, and Ronnie's heart swelled at the wobble in her mom's voice, the catch in her breath, the intensity of her gaze.

"I love you so much, and I promise to protect you. No matter what." Her voice cracked, and Ronnie felt the way Min-Young's throat tightened. The way her eyes stung. The way her heart broke.

Baby Ronnie gurgled in response, and Ronnie wished she could remember what it felt like to be held by her living, breathing mom. But maybe it was better to have this glimpse into what her mom had felt holding her. Maybe when you're that young, it mattered more what those who held you had felt.

"You can count on our protection as well," came Ms. Hana's voice, all business as usual. She stood at the foot of the bed between Ms. Akemi and Ms. Pavani. They were smiling at the baby, and Ronnie wanted to smile back. But Min-Young's lips would not pull up.

"I know you would protect her—at the cost of your own lives, if need be," Min-Young said, and the witches nodded firmly. "But, if anything should happen to me, you three must promise to get Teddy and Veronica out of here and sever all ties to me and our coven."

Ms. Pavani moved around the bed to Min-Young's side. "What do you mean? Nothing will happen to you. You and Veronica are safe here."

Ms. Akemi moved to Min-Young's other side. "And even if something were to happen—which it won't—why would you want to remove the child from the protections of this place?" Her eyes dimmed with hurt. "And us?"

"There is no guarantee she'll be a witch. We won't know until she's twelve. And if I'm . . . *gone* . . . then I will hope she is not a witch." She drew in a deep breath and straightened before continuing. "I don't want her to live in fear of the scarf or of losing loved ones as I have. And I've lost so many."

"And if the child does turn out to be a witch?" Ms. Hana said, her face and voice guarded.

Min-Young bit down hard on the inside of her cheek until Ronnie tasted metal. "Then she will need all of you. She will need all the help she can get." Min-Young's chin trembled. "Promise me, sisters. I want her to live without having to be so careful and calculating. I want her to have a family that's not all but silenced or Persuaded away." She ran the back of her hand along baby Ronnie's face—down one cheek, then the other. "She deserves that. And so much more."

Ms. Hana heaved a sigh. "I promise."

"I promise," Ms. Akemi and Ms. Pavani echoed.

Min-Young smiled at last and nodded her appreciation. Then, tucking a finger inside baby Ronnie's little fist, she fixed her eyes on her baby's face. She studied the sweet brown eyes, the small bump of a nose, and the mini bow lips—committing every tiny feature to memory as if she feared she would one day forget. As if she knew their time was limited.

Ronnie blinked, and the ropes course returned to sharp focus. Her cheeks were wet with tears—some of them happy. She had a family of witch aunties, old and new friends, and her dad. They held on to her as tightly as she held on to them. It was what her mom had wanted for her.

But some of the tears were sad ones, too. Because deep down, she knew her time with her mom couldn't last forever. Even if Min-Young remained tethered to the forest as a gwishin, Ronnie couldn't remain with her—not always. Not even most of the time. And her mom deserved more than that. They both did.

Ronnie wiped her cheeks, and before she could lose her nerve, she stepped out onto the rope bridge. Her legs trembled and her stomach lurched with each sway and shudder of the bridge, but she didn't stop. This time, she didn't calculate percentages or probabilities. She didn't worry about her grip on the bridge or the harness's grip on her. She reminded herself that she was a witch, and she had a spell to cast.

So she put one foot in front of the other until she reached the other side. Then she trained her eyes on the treetops piercing the blue sky as she was clipped into the zip-line harness. And when it was time to release, Ronnie let go and soared.

THIRTY-NINE

RELEASE

The last ropes course of the summer wrapped up with shout-outs. Olivia, Sam, and Jack cheered the loudest when Ronnie was given a shout-out for finishing the high ropes course at the risk of almost certain death.

Then those who had won the scavenger hunt were allowed to carve their names into the large climbing wall. This ended up being every single camper because they had all shared the answers with one another. It turned out no one came to camp to do things alone.

Olivia somehow managed to carve her name in elegant script. Sam simply deepened the grooves of his carving from last year. Jack added his initials inside a carving of a compass. As for Ronnie, she also went with her initials—all of them: *VJYRM*.

While everyone else made their way to lunch, Ronnie slipped into the forest, her backpack heavy on her shoulders. When she entered the clearing, Min-Young was hovering near the stump as if waiting for her to take her seat upon it. Boo was there, too, curled up at its base. It was funny how a place could feel so familiar even after such a short time.

"Ronnie!" Min-Young's head shot up with a ready smile. She looked more solid today, and her voice was strong. "How did you sleep?" She gave the stump a pat.

The moss on the stump had filled out over the past couple of weeks and trailed down the sides of the wood. Ronnie took extra care to sit gently, not wanting to ruin any part of the clearing. She wished it would stay that way forever.

"I slept okay." She avoided Min-Young's eyes and bent down to stroke Boo's back. He flicked his tail in response.

Min-Young tipped her head. "Just okay? I always sleep so well after a good banishment." She grinned.

Ronnie bit down on the inside of her cheek. If she was going to do it, she would have to just do it. Like tearing off yet another extra-large, superglue-level-sticky Band-Aid. "I think I was a little nervous."

"About what?"

"About saying good-bye to you."

Min-Young swooped closer. "Oh, my sweet girl. I'm sure you'll find a way to visit me soon."

Ronnie looked down at her hands in her lap. "Even after I release you?"

Min-Young shook her head, a confused smile on her face. "I'm not sure what will happen when I eventually cross over. But I like to think a part of me will always be with you. And a part of you with me."

Ronnie bit her lip. "What percent?"

Min-Young paused, studying Ronnie's face. "One percent, I'd say. At least."

Ronnie slowly nodded her head. "It was enough to bring us together, right?"

"It was."

Reaching into her backpack, Ronnie pulled out a large cookbook on grilling techniques. She set it on her lap and drew in a long, shaky breath. "I found the releasing ritual in the library. I . . . I want to set you free."

Min-Young tipped her head, her brow furrowing. "But yesterday, when you thought I had left, you were so distraught."

"I wasn't ready. I hadn't had the chance to say good-bye. And I was only thinking of myself then."

A gentle breeze pushed the hair in Ronnie's face aside. "And now you are thinking only of me."

"I know you're suffering," Ronnie said quietly.

Min-Young started to protest, but Ronnie cut in. "I'm thinking about me, too. I don't think I can go back to my normal life and be happy knowing you're stuck here waiting. It'd feel like a big part of me is stuck here, too, in this forest. And it wouldn't mean more time for us. It would just mean more time for each of us to suffer separately."

Min-Young looked at Ronnie for a long, quiet moment. "So, you will save us both—again."

A lump formed in Ronnie's throat. "I think you should know that Dad is really great. He's happy. We're happy." She sucked in a shuddering breath. "It's because of him that I don't need you to stay. But I'll always want you to."

"And you should know I never wanted to leave you." Min-Young's voice wavered with emotion. "I never will."

Ronnie swiped at her eyes. She hadn't known until that moment how much she needed to hear those words. "What if you forget again, like you did when you became a gwishin?"

Min-Young cupped Ronnie's cheek with a whisper-soft hand. "Even when my mind had forgotten you, my heart had not. It's what led me to you the moment you stepped onto these grounds. It's what has tethered me to this world for the past seven years. You are the one thing I could never truly forget."

Boo rose on all four legs and arched his back. Ever so slowly, he meandered over to Min-Young's dangling feet and wove through the empty space.

Min-Young laughed. "Of course I won't forget you, either, Boojuk. How could I forget such an intelligent and faithful familiar as you?"

Seemingly satisfied, Boo jumped onto the stump and settled down against Ronnie's thigh. She stroked his soft fur, grateful for his solid warmth.

"Thank you for believing in me," Min-Young said. "For returning to me after I had to leave you so long ago." She brought her legs up into a butterfly pose and hovered level with Ronnie.

"You're welcome." Ronnie's voice came out as a whisper around the lump she couldn't swallow. "Thanks for waiting seven years for me."

"Oh, you are so worth the wait." Min-Young's voice grew softer. Her scarf fluttered in her ever-present wind.

"It's time, isn't it?" Ronnie asked, her voice thick.

"Only you know the answer to that."

Ronnie's hands trembled slightly as she opened the cookbook. *"Reveal the spells within this book. For witch eyes only, let me look."*

A singular breeze blew upon the grimoire, flipping the pages until it landed on *Release Ritual*. Ronnie nodded, jostling loose the tears lining her eyes. It was just as well since she couldn't hold them back and speak at the same time.

Somehow Ronnie kept her voice steady as she recited the spell. *"From this earth your soul set free; from this world you are released. I let you go in love and light; until the day we reunite."* Bracing herself, she lifted her head.

Min-Young flickered. When she reappeared, she'd transformed into her human appearance—the one that looked so much like Ronnie.

Min-Young reached for the scarf. But instead of running her hands over it, she lifted it up and unwound it until it was free from her neck. Or rather, *she* was free from *it*. She held on to it for one more moment before releasing it. The scarf of silence fluttered down onto the forest floor. "It cannot hurt you, but you must destroy it to complete the release."

Ronnie knew just the spell. *"For essence must, break down to dust."*

The scarf reduced to dust and scattered in the gentle breeze.

Min-Young was now transparent, no more than a shadow of the form Ronnie had seen in photographs. Ronnie hurriedly rubbed her eyes to clear her tears, but they blurred again at the sight of her mom fading. Still, she kept her eyes on the ghost of her mom until nothing remained but the afterimage in her own mind. But even that vanished when Ronnie blinked away fresh tears.

A breeze snaked around Ronnie's arms, like the gentlest of embraces, and with it came Min-Young's voice.

You are the love of my life and death.

Ronnie wrapped her arms around herself, bracing for the moment her mom left her completely. But the wind—warm and feather-soft—remained, patting Ronnie's arms, stroking her hair, and drying her tears.

Her mom would never leave her completely. Not really. Not when the wind settled. Not when Ronnie left the forest. Not when she left Camp Foster. Not even then. Her mom would be with her forever.

"Ronnie?" Sam entered the clearing.

The wind slowed, settling on her arms like morning mist.

"How'd you know I was here?" Ronnie wiped the remaining tears from her cheeks.

"You used a spell a minute ago. . . ."

"Witch-hunting, I see."

Sam's eyes bulged. "No! It's not like that! My mom sent me to check on you, I swear! Then Benji said that Gigi saw you sneaking off into the forest, so I figured—"

A giggle burst from Ronnie's lips unexpectedly. It deepened into a belly laugh that erupted into full-on hysterical laughter. Sam joined in, and the two of them were soon out of breath.

"Can you believe it? Any of it?" Ronnie asked Sam once she caught her breath. "I can't believe I *do* believe it. And I can't believe it's over."

Sam nudged her with his shoulder. "Not everything is over."

He was right. She was a witch, and that was just the beginning.

FORTY

1%

ater that night, Ronnie and Olivia made their way to the campfire and joined Jack and Sam in the line for marshmallows and sticks.

"I can't believe it's our last campfire!" Olivia wailed.

"And I can't believe you're wearing the same thing you wore to the first campfire," Jack said with horror.

Olivia's wail cut off as her gaze snapped down to her outfit. "Wait, I didn't—"

Jack shook with laughter as he moved up the line with Olivia, her arms crossed in a huff.

Sam hung back and nudged Ronnie with an elbow. "Are you okay?"

"Yeah, I think so. At least I'm getting there. How are things with your parents? Did you tell them about being part witch?"

Sam nodded. "Since my mom found out about my dokkaebi powers, I decided I might as well tell her and my dad about the witch abilities, too. They're handling it much better than I expected." He blew out an exhale of relief. "How about you? Are you going to tell your dad about what happened? About being a witch?"

Ronnie was quiet for a minute. "I'm not sure. I meant what I said to Mr. Lobing. My dad would accept me as a ghost, a witch, or a goblin. But . . . it's just been a whole lot, and I think I need a break from everything. Know what I mean?"

"Yeah, I do." He toed the dirt. "But if you ever have questions for me or my parents or want to talk about spells . . ."

Ronnie grinned. "Thanks, Sam. I'm here for you, too. Like I told Olivia, you're both stuck with me now, so I expect updates on social media, regular video chats, and daily texts—got it?"

Sam grinned too. "Got it."

"Sam's gonna visit," Jack called over his shoulder. Clearly, he'd been eavesdropping. "Beaches trump lakes!"

"We'll see about that," Sam retorted. "Because what good is a beach when it's too cold to swim?"

"Oh, come on," Olivia cut in. "Nothing beats a concrete jungle! Downtown Seattle is definitely the place to visit if you're going to be on our side. I mean, where are you going to eat or shop if you stay in West Seattle?"

"Yeah, Sam," Jack agreed in a very poor impression of Olivia. "Where are you going to shop for dresses and kitten heels?"

Olivia's mouth fell right open. She turned slowly to Ronnie, who smothered a giggle with a hand.

"How do you know what kitten heels are, Jack?" Olivia asked, her face slack with shock.

Jack's face grew redder than a scarf of silence. "What? I don't! I just heard it somewhere," he sputtered. "Probably Ronnie or—"

"Nope, not me." Ronnie shook her head. "I don't wear those."

"C'mon! I bet everyone's heard of 'em." Jack turned to Sam.

"Sorry." Sam cringed. "You know how I feel about cats."

Jack was nearly purple. "Whatever. Downtown sucks." He spun on his heel and stomped away. Ronnie, Olivia, and Sam burst out laughing.

"He actually loves downtown," Ronnie wheezed through peals of laughter.

"Yeah, downtown and kitten heels!" Olivia said between fits of giggles.

Sam ran after Jack, and Ronnie linked her arm with Olivia's. "Promise you'll come visit me and Jack in West Seattle—not just texts and video calls."

"You guys have to come downtown, too." Olivia raised a pinkie. "I'll get you tickets to our best productions."

Ronnie sealed the pinkie promise. "Does this mean we'll get to see you in action?"

Olivia nodded happily as she moved up the line. "I hope so! Being away from ballet for so long made me realize how much I love it. Without all the pressure from my family and the company, I remembered that I actually *want* to dance and perform." She grabbed a stick from Robbie and two marshmallows from Willa and immediately popped one into her mouth. "I don't know," she said around the marshmallow. "I'm going to have a talk with my parents about stepping back a little or taking more breaks. I just need to be allowed to call more shots."

"That makes sense," Ronnie agreed. "Adults mean well,

but I don't think they always know what they're doing. They could use our help—they just don't know it."

"Like your dad?" Olivia asked.

Ronnie nodded. "His memories are all messed up, so he doesn't even know he needs my help recovering them. But he does. And I need him to remember because so much of what he's forgotten is a part of who I am. Plus, I want to learn more about my mom and her Korean side—the normal human stuff. And maybe if I can help him remember my mom, then he'll remember the rest—the supernatural stuff."

"It'll work. I know it!" Olivia squared her shoulders and sent Ronnie a confident grin.

"Or if that fails, I can just near drown him in the lake with a red scarf to jog his memory," Ronnie deadpanned.

"Ronnie!" Olivia hissed under her breath as if Mr. Lobing would return from banishment.

"What? It worked for me!" Ronnie giggled, and Olivia shook her head, muttering "Too soon," even as a restrained smile dimpled her cheeks.

As Ronnie grabbed her own roasting stick and marshmallows from the counselors, thoughts of home filled her mind. It seemed so far away and long ago that she was last there.

A twinge of sadness washed over her. Was this how she would feel about this place once she was back home? Would the clearing in the forest seem like some distant memory? Would her mom become just another part of her fading past?

But as Olivia and Sam wheedled Jack into accepting

their peace offering of the longest stick and best-shaped marshmallow, Ronnie's worries blew away with the smoke of the campfire. And like the fire warming her deep down to the bones, she knew: Camp Foster, her friends, the witches, and her mom would always be a part of her. Because the past that connected them was a part of the everything that made her whole. The part made up of faith. The constant, unrelenting, in-it-for-the-long-haul one percent.

FORTY-ONE

100%

T he next day, Ronnie plopped down on her duffel bag in the parking lot to watch for her dad's SUV. But her gaze kept drifting up to the forest canopy, where the mist liked to hover in the mornings. Where the sunlight met the shade. Where she'd first seen her mom as a gwishin.

A flutter of white moved among the peaks of tall firs, and her stomach did a flip. But it was only a bird. Her mom was gone, and Ronnie had made peace with it, but she couldn't help the one percent that thought, *Maybe*.

And she couldn't help the very small—but very sharp—pang in her heart when the ninety-nine percent gave a resounding *no*.

Dragging her gaze back down, she reached out to Boo, who had curled up next to her foot, and scratched him behind the ears.

"Ronnie!" It was a voice she could pick out in a packed stadium.

She jumped to her feet as her dad ran toward her, his arms open wide.

"Dad!" Ronnie sank into his embrace. He was warm and solid and smelled like his favorite orange-mint soap.

"I missed you so much!" He pulled back to study Ronnie's face. "Just as I suspected. You neglected the sunscreen, didn't you?"

"Maybe a little," Ronnie admitted.

Her dad reached out to take her backpack, but when he had it in hand, he dropped it on the ground with an exaggerated wince. "What's in this thing? Rocks?"

Ronnie grinned. At the witches' urging, she had taken a few grimoires and a dozen or so river stones. "Yeah. I painted some. Wanna see?" Reaching inside her backpack, she pulled out a stone covered with thick evergreen trees and handed it to her dad.

"I like this one." He closed his fingers around the stone and looked back at her with a slightly surprised smile. "Hey, your freckles are back. It makes you look just like your mom."

Ronnie flushed with pleasure. "Really?"

He tipped his head and examined her for a minute. "Yes. You remind me of her more and more each day. In fact—his eyes scanned the forested landscape surrounding them—"seeing you here is bringing back some memories I'd completely forgotten about. I think we might have visited this place before."

Ronnie's heart hummed in her chest like a humming-bird. "You and me?"

He scratched his temple with his free hand, the spelled stone still enclosed in the other. "You, me . . . and your mom." He sounded surprised at his own words. "I think your mom really loved the woods."

Ronnie's chest swelled with happiness and hope that she and her dad could help each other remember. "I love them, too."

He met her eyes with a clarity of someone remembering. "I'm not surprised," he said, his voice low and soft. "You're a lot like her."

A wide smile stretched across Ronnie's face even as her nose tickled with the threat of tears. She couldn't speak past the lump in her throat, but she didn't mind. In that moment, it felt right to say nothing at all. She allowed his words to hover between them, uninterrupted, as they solidified into a clear and lasting memory.

Her dad reached down and began zipping up Ronnie's bag. He stopped to pull out a cookbook. It was *Korean Comfort Foods*. "What's this?"

"They were giving away books from their library," Ronnie said, thinking quickly. It was mostly true since the witches gave them to her. "I know you don't want to, but I'd like to try cooking Korean food."

His mouth twisted to one side. "I'm not sure. From what I hear, the art of cooking Korean cuisine is passed down in families. I wish I could offer that to you—"

"You don't have to," Ronnie interrupted to stop her dad from blaming this lack on not being "Korean enough" or something. "The cookbook has handwritten notes from a Korean cook and everything! Plus, I think I'm old enough to start making more decisions around the house. We can start with what we cook on the weekends." Ronnie held her breath as her dad absentmindedly rubbed a thumb over the river stone.

"Is that right?" His mouth untwisted, stretching out in a broad smile. He looked . . . proud. "Well, there's a new Korean grocery store downtown that I've been meaning to check out. I bet we'll find all the ingredients we need there."

The air left Ronnie's lungs with a whoosh. She wasn't sure if it was her dad who had changed or herself. Maybe it was fifty percent each. But she was ninety-nine percent positive nothing would ever be the same again. And for the first time, she was glad for it, because she knew the things that mattered most were here to stay. "I missed you so much, Dad."

He responded by throwing his arms around her for another hug—a super-tight one that lifted her off her feet and lasted an embarrassingly long time.

But Ronnie didn't mind being held on to. It was a reminder that no matter what she was or who she became, whether they were together or apart, her dad would always be there holding on. Just like her mom.

And she was one hundred percent sure about that.

ACKNOWLEDGMENTS

When I first had the idea over ten years ago to write a middle grade novel set at a summer camp in Washington State, the first person I wanted to talk with about it was my sister. Thank you, Seung, for graciously listening and encouraging this out-of-the-blue idea to write a novel. Thank you even more for reading multiple drafts, including the very first one, and believing in me as a writer despite them! I would not have started or continued writing without you. I also would not have tested a pair of scissors on my favorite shirt of all time if not for you, but that's another story for another time.

I also want to thank my Author Mentor Match mentor and friend, Shana Targosz, for so many things—for *all* the things. There will truly never be enough words to express the whole of my gratitude, but I will say that this book would never have been published without your brilliant guidance. It's so rare to meet someone who is not only incredibly talented but also unendingly generous and unfathomably kind. You never let me settle (even when I thought I wanted to) and always pushed me to be better (but in the least pushy way possible). To this day I'm wondering why in the world you believed in me so much and how I got so lucky to be able to learn from you. Shana-without-a-Y (clearly the superior spelling): Let's share a torte and tweet about it.

Speaking of genius people, Rob Land, Renée McCormick, and Nicole Magoon are three of the most talented writers I know, and three of the best critique partners a writer could ever hope for! Thank you for sticking with me all these years and sharing your vast knowledge of writing craft. Your insights have been (and continue to be) invaluable to me! Rob and Renee, not only are you both skilled writers, but you're also fantastic teachers. I mean it when I say you should start your own writing workshop. I'd be the first one to sign up!

My eternal gratitude to my MG mentee fam for the support, cheerleading, making me laugh on a nearly daily basis, and just being the most wonderful people. James Blakemore, Connie Chang, Jessica Haster, and Jennifer Kaul: We've been through so much in such a short time! Baby IM, *so* much tea, Wednesday-night Zooms, depressing literary theories, gentle anger poems, and, of course, the corpse puppet. Oh, I almost forgot that terrible whip GIF! You all make the good things even better and the not-so-good things more tolerable. You know what I'm talking about. But in case you've forgotten, Connie probably has receipts.

To the AMM family: You all are truly amazing and I am in awe of each and every one of you. Jenny Mattern, I admire your willingness to be vulnerable and I cherish our honest talks. (And a special thank-you to Lydia Mattern: Your beta read was incredibly helpful and I'm so grateful to you.) Tiara Blue, your big heart and unfailing confidence in me mean so much! Daphne Dador, thanks for being my friend even though you're way too cool for me. Ryan James Black, I will read anything you write—thanks for reading what I write as well! Karina Evans, Taleen Voskuni, Sophie Li, Stephanie Sosa, and my entire AMMazing MG cohort—thank you so much for your advice, feedback, and encouragement! It means so much to me, and I feel incredibly lucky to know all of you.

A huge thank-you to Carey Blankenship-Kramer, my querying partner and the sun-shiniest grump I've ever known. I wouldn't have survived the query trenches without you and your cheerleading, commiserating, and talent for finding the perfect GIF every time!

Before I entered the writing community, the encouragement of my non-writer friends was what truly kept me going. To my golden girls Monica Kim (who has read way too many of my unpolished drafts!), Esther Cho, Yoojin Lee, and Jessica Ma, thank you for being there for twenty-plus years and always believing in me no matter what. Jessica Winston, Jane Cho, and Jooyoung Kang: Your encouragement and excitement for my writing journey have been such a blessing—thank you with my whole heart!

To my agent, Emily Forney: You're a rock star in this industry and I will be forever grateful to you for taking a chance on me and this story. Thank you for your work in getting this book into Christine Collins's most capable hands.

Christine, I cannot express how lucky I feel to have had you as the editor for my debut book. Thank you for believing in this story and taking such good care of our Ronnie! Your keen and discerning editorial eye was exactly what this book needed. Because of you and Emily, there is one more middle grade book with characters that look like me and so many others who deserve to see themselves in stories.

Also, a gigantic thank-you to the entire team at Disney Hyperion! I'm sure I'm leaving out some names here because it truly takes a village and I haven't met all of you, but you all were integral to the making of this book and I'm so grateful to each of you, including the following folks:

Deb JJ Lee, cover artist
Kieran Viola, editorial director
Zareen Johnson, designer
Sara Liebling, managing editor
Guy Cunningham, copy chief
Jerry Gonzalez, production manager
Matt Schweitzer, marketing director
Holly Nagel, marketing
Danielle DiMartino, marketing
Dina Sherman, school and library marketing
Maddie Hughes, school and library marketing
Ann Day, publicity director
Crystal McCoy, publicity
Andrea Rosen, VP of sales
Monique Diman, sales
Vicki Korlishin, sales
Michael Freeman, sales

To the entire team: Thank you so much for sharing your incredible talent with me (and the world) and your dedication behind the scenes!

Last, but most definitely not least, I want to express all my love and gratitude to my family. To my parents for doing your very best with what you were given so that your children could strive for even more. Uncle Rick and Aunt Sinja, thank you for bringing our family to the US and keeping us together. We all owe so much to you both.

To my husband, Shay, and our kids, Zayden and Alexis: I wouldn't have persisted in the arduous pursuit of publication if not for your enthusiasm for this book and my writing long before I had an agent and a book deal. Thank you, Oppa, for keeping me fed and caffeinated all these years while I spent so much time holed away writing. Some people ask, "How do you do it all—working full-time, writing, and being a mom?" The answer is that I simply don't. None of this would have been possible without the most supportive and understanding partner. Because of you, I can dive deep into my story worlds knowing you've got everything more than handled in the real world. Zayden and Alexis, you two are the wonderful and beautiful center of my universe, and I love you more than everything.